High praise for *New York Times* bestselling author
MELODY ANNE
and her sizzling Unexpected Heroes series!

HER HOMETOWN HERO

"An engaging romance where feelings are expressed with sincerity and often plenty of spunk."

—*Single Titles*

"[Melody's] books are always enjoyable reads."

—*The Hopeless Romantics Book Blog*

WHO I AM WITH YOU

"The perfect read to give us the romance we want with characters that we like!"

—*Two Classy Chics Chat*

"This novella was the perfect quick romance that was packed with emotion, sincere characters, and sizzling hot romance."

—*Smut Book Junkie Book Reviews*

HER UNEXPECTED HERO

"An engaging story of second chances and true love that will appeal to readers. A terrific sense of place brings the small-town Montana setting to life, and tackling the main characters' pain head-on makes their eventual redemption that much more touching. The opening scenes are as surprising as they are riveting."

—*RT Book Reviews*

Also available from Melody Anne and Pocket Books

MELODY ANNE

Her Forever Hero

Pocket Books

New York   London   Toronto   Sydney   New Delhi

Pocket Books
An Imprint of Simon & Schuster, Inc.
1230 Avenue of the Americas
New York, NY 10020

This book is a work of fiction. Any references to historical events, real people, or real places are used fictitiously. Other names, characters, places, and events are products of the author's imagination, and any resemblance to actual events or places or persons, living or dead, is entirely coincidental.

First Pocket Books paperback edition March 2016

POCKET and colophon are registered trademarks of Simon & Schuster, Inc.

For information about special discounts for bulk purchases, please contact Simon & Schuster Special Sales at 1-866-506-1949 or business@simonandschuster.com.

The Simon & Schuster Speakers Bureau can bring authors to your live event. For more information or to book an event, contact the Simon & Schuster Speakers Bureau at 1-866-248-3049 or visit our website at www.simonspeakers.com.

Manufactured in the United States of America

10 9 8 7 6 5 4 3 2 1

ISBN 978-1-4767-7859-4
ISBN 978-1-4767-7862-4 (ebook)

This final book in the Unexpected Heroes series is dedicated to my amazing and absolutely perfect daughter, Phoenix. I have been so blessed to have you in my life. You inspired me to begin this career when I didn't think I could do it and you make the world a brighter place to live in because you are here. I love you with all my heart.

ACKNOWLEDGMENTS

For those who think a book is written by the person printed on the cover, they are so very, very wrong. There are many people involved in the process of writing a book. Some of those people don't even know how crucial they are to the story. As I take a walk down a country road and see a couple walking hand in hand, my mind wanders and I begin to create a story for them. Who are they? What have they gone through that leaves that secret smile on their lips as they look into each other's eyes? What would be the first words they would use to describe their partner? So thank you to my small community of Harrisburg, for all of you who inspire me, stand beside me, and make me so grateful to be a country girl. The town of Sterling is very much modeled after my hometown.

And thank you to my team at Pocket Books for your faith in me, your encouragement, your support, and your enthusiasm and love of books. There are so many people behind the scenes who I get to meet only a couple of times a year, and I appreciate you so much. And there's Lauren, who is encouraging and wonderful and makes me feel like there's nothing I can't do. And last, but most certainly not least, is Abby, my amazing, confident, funny, and encouraging editor. Thank you all so much for believing in me.

And thank you for the many who do so much for my career. Alison Parker, you have forced me to be a better writer and not to slack. Kathy D., you pimp me out all over the place and I love ya for it. And my team at InkSlinger, you do amazing!

Then there are those on my hometown team: my colleagues, my friends, and my family. Because you are one and the same. Adam, Eddie, Kathiey, Krisi, Jeff, Patsy, Breezy, Kyle, and Bethany, you work so hard, storyboard with me, help me create ideas, research things for endless hours, and do all those ridiculous things I ask, even when the text message comes at three in the morning. I love you all, and these stories wouldn't happen without you.

And then of course there's my patient husband, who will go days or even weeks with barely a glimpse of me, and my son and daughter, Johnathan and Phoenix, who I can't imagine not knowing and loving and who make the world a better place. And to my kiddos: my nieces and nephews, and the kids I've chosen as family. You make me smile and remember it's more than okay to stop and play. Because I get great ideas by doing that, too, and because I love you endlessly.

It was quite the welcome home. The railing and eaves of the porch were decorated thickly with spiderwebs, and weeds were doing their bit, too, creeping up between the now rickety boards to act almost like potted plants. Mother Nature had pulled out all the stops in her honor.

Grace picked up a dull gray stone, tossed it upward, then felt its expected weight as it landed back in the palm of her hand. She did the same thing over and over, her mind adrift and haunted.

Why was she here? Why was she tormenting herself?

Because she had nowhere else to go. Her life had been in shambles for the past ten years, ever since she'd left Sterling, Montana. She could fix up her childhood home. The spacious rooms could be cleaned, the rotten boards replaced, the cobwebs torn down. But she didn't have any desire to live in a house—never a home—with no pleasant memories within its emotionless walls.

Her happiest times in Sterling had been outside

this house, this mausoleum that had been her mother's pride and joy. No, they hadn't been the wealthiest family in town, but they'd had a lot, and Mrs. Sinclair felt true love for her possessions, especially the six-thousand-square-foot home now standing nearly empty before her daughter.

Her journey down memory lane—tiptoeing through the funeral tulips—wasn't finished yet, though. Letting the rock drop to the ground, Grace pulled out her key and walked up the rickety steps, cautiously avoiding the sticky cobwebs. She tested the door handle, only to find it locked. She hoped the key still worked.

It took several tries but, by twisting it a little this way and that, she finally managed to get the lock to free itself, and then, with the help of a strong push, the door was swinging open. Sunlight filtered in through dust-coated windows, showing years' worth of grime covering the floors, counters, and the few pieces of furniture that had been left behind.

"Somebody should call *Better Homes & Gardens*!" she said out loud to break through the gloom. It didn't work.

Her father had said he wouldn't sell the home, that someday she might want to return to it. This property had once belonged to her grandfather, and to her grandfather's grandfather before that. They had moved to Sterling in the 1800s and had made a beautiful settlement for themselves.

Her mother had wanted to tear down the original

homestead, a quaint one-room cabin with a woodstove and loft. Her father had refused and restored it instead. That was where Grace had created some of her best memories, because they had been outside the walls of her jail, the Big House. She and her best friend Sage had spent many nights sleeping in that small cabin, telling each other their hopes and dreams for the future.

Never had she thought back then that her life would turn out this way. Never had she thought she'd become a bitter, broken woman. *No.* She wasn't broken. She was too strong for that. As soon as she had time to heal, she would be back to normal. Her zest for life would return, and she would once again show the world that Grace Sinclair was a fighter.

The old piano she had spent so many hours play-ing sat forlornly in the corner of the family room. Damn! Even thinking the word *family* made Grace laugh bitterly. Her father had once tried to be a good man, but he was so focused on making the next dollar for her mother that he wasn't capable of real love, and her mother—well, her mother was the pro-verbial . . . okay, the Total Bitch of the West. Grace had tried to escape them every chance she got, once she'd learned that, on the outside, away from this house, real families existed. But her parents always managed to get their chains back around her, making sure she knew exactly the limits of her freedom.

Although her father had wanted a son—all men did, didn't they?—she ended up being his only child, so once every few years he would try to do something fatherly, such as giving her the title to the land and house he knew he'd never return to. Her parents' displays of affection always involved money. Hugs were unheard-of in her family, and real emotion was to be held inside. They had a reputation to maintain, after all.

Drawn to the piano, Grace trailed her fingers absently along its lid, smearing them with dust. She lifted the curved wooden cover of the ebony and ivory keys only to discover more filth. The instrument was out of tune, but it at least brought up good memories. She'd taken lessons her entire childhood, and although she was no master, she still enjoyed the soothing music a piano could create.

Sitting down on the bench, she hung her head. "It's time for a new start. First of all, this house needs to go—though I think I'll keep the piano," she said aloud, her eyes closed as she fought emotion. There would never be a day she could live within these walls again, never a day she could start thinking of this house as her home. She'd rather live in the tiny cabin tucked in the trees behind this monstrous monument to hypocrisy.

"I remember when you used to play for me."

Grace's shoulders tensed, and she didn't need to turn around to see who had walked in uninvited and unannounced. That voice had lived only in her dreams since the day he had so coldly walked out of her life. Camden Whitman, her first and probably only true love.

She stared at the dusty keys of the piano, unwilling to face him. "What are you doing here, Cam?"

"My dad told me you were coming back to town. Maggie Winchester said she spotted your car heading out this way."

From the sound of his voice, she could tell he was standing at a distance, probably in the entryway to the room. So he hadn't stepped inside yet. She turned slowly and looked him in the eye for the first time in many years.

"I forgot what it was like to live in a small town. There's no such thing as privacy," she said acerbically.

And then their eyes met and something shifted deep within her. Only one person had ever made her feel an unquenchable love that consumed the entire heart, and what a fool she'd been to think time and distance would make that feeling go away. Not even another lover had diminished the feeling.

Even worse was knowing that, although his features might appear composed to anyone else, she once had known his soul, and for one unguarded fraction of a second she saw surprise leap into his expression before he snapped the shutters closed and gave her a cool, nearly mocking look.

The moment was so brief that she wondered if maybe her heart was asking her to see something that really wasn't there. Maybe her traitorous emotions were just reaching for something familiar.

To ward off the pain, she allowed all-too-familiar

anger to pour through her fragile bones. How many times and in how many ways had she tried to forget this man? And in a single millisecond, all of that hard work almost came to naught when she misread something in Cam's eyes.

One look at him had slid back the bolt she'd placed on her heart. Although she'd called him a liar, a cheater, a heartbreaker, it was really she who deserved to be scolded, because she was the biggest liar of them all. She'd lied to herself for years, almost enough that she'd started believing those lies.

The velvety sound of his voice slowly brought her back from her grim thoughts. "That's certainly true. You can't do anything here without it being broadcast at full volume by morning light." His tone was light, careless. That was Cam—the life of the party, and everyone's best friend.

He was also the guy who'd decided she just wasn't good enough for him.

"It's good to see you, Grace. I've missed you."

She stared at him incredulously for a few heartbeats, before her lips curled into a smirk. The lyrics of an old Rihanna hit, "Take a Bow," flooded her mind. He certainly was good at putting on a show, but she wouldn't be fooled by him ever again.

"Well, now that you've seen me, you can go," she replied, syrupy-sweet sarcasm in her voice.

"Have you spoken to anyone since you've been back?"

"Do you listen when I speak?" she countered.

"I haven't spoken to you in nearly ten years, so I guess we'll find out." He leaned against the doorframe and smiled, the smile that had haunted her for so long.

"No. I haven't spoken to anyone because I haven't been ready to announce my return."

"Are you staying?"

"That's really none of your business," she told him.

Without taking notice of her clear dismissal, he told her, "I'm meeting a client at the offices in an hour, but I should be out of there by five. Why don't I pick you up and bring you to my dad's so you can visit with everyone? I'm sure they'll be more than thrilled to see you."

"Not gonna happen."

He stared at her quizzically for a few seconds before speaking. "Come on, Grace. You've been gone a long time. The prom queen is back, and you know your court will want to hold a ball."

He thought he was *so* amusing.

"It's funny you should mention that particular event, considering you promised to come back and take me to the dance. But your new girlfriend most certainly wouldn't have approved of that. No, you had become a college stud by that point." The bitterness in her tone gave away far more than she wanted, but she couldn't rein her feelings in. Her heart thudded like a galloping Thoroughbred at the chance to say what she'd bottled up all these years.

"That was a long time ago, Grace. I think we're both mature enough to let bygones be bygones."

"I don't forget anything, Cam."

"We were young and foolish back then, and both of us made mistakes. It doesn't mean we can't be friends now," he said, and took a step toward her.

No. That wasn't what she wanted. She needed him to retreat, not come closer.

"That's exactly what it means, Cam. I don't want to sit around having idle chitchat, I don't want to reminisce about the past, and I don't want to be friends with you."

"What happened to the girl who used to laugh and dream and always reach for the stars?" he replied.

"That girl has been dead and gone for a long time," she said, her voice firm, her manner stiff. "If she ever really existed in the first place. You can see yourself out." With that, she turned back to the lonely piano and once again sat on the hard bench. Even when she heard his steps retreating down the porch stairs, she refused to look.

Grace's shoulders sagged once she knew he was gone. Coming back hadn't been a good idea—not a good idea at all. Camden Whitman still had far too much pull over her emotions. But hell would freeze over before she ever let him know that.

1

SIX MONTHS LATER

"You know, it's customary for the best man and maid of honor to dance."

Grace was grateful for the few glasses of champagne she'd managed to down before the music and dancing had begun at Spence and Sage's wedding. Because with Cam in a tux standing before her with his hand out, she felt her insides melt.

All day she hadn't been able to tear her gaze away from him, and now she was expected to fall into his arms for a romantic song. "Could I Have This Dance" by Anne Murray began playing and a shudder passed through Grace.

She didn't get a chance to say yes or no. Suddenly she was in Cam's arms and, dammit all, it was exactly where she wanted and needed to be.

"As we swayed to the music . . . I fell in love with you . . ."

"Don't sing to me, Cam," she insisted, her emotions rocky at best.

"I happen to love this song," he told her as he dipped her backward, his arms cradling her before he lifted her back up and pulled her in tight. When his fingers slipped downward and massaged the top of her butt, moist heat flowed through her, forcing her to stifle a groan.

As he leaned forward, she had no doubt that was his hardness pressing against her boiling core. She also knew she wanted to damn the consequences and have this man again—even if it was only for a single night.

So being more bold than she'd ever been before, Grace decided to take the romance away from this situation—romance she couldn't handle, sex she could—and she reached between their bodies and lightly rubbed her fingers across his bulging pants. He went stock-still as she reached up and whispered against his ear.

"Let's get out of here, Cam."

Cam immediately looked up, ensuring that no one was paying attention to them, and then the dance stopped as he grabbed her hand and led her from the dance floor, and didn't quit moving until he found a secluded gazebo about a hundred yards away from the party.

It wasn't far enough, but at least she could get a small taste, have his lips caress hers in privacy, have something to help relieve the ache inside her before they moved on. Without a word, his hand slid down her side and then moved below the hem of her short dress and began traveling upward until his fingers brushed against her silky panties.

She groaned against his neck as she felt her body respond. It wouldn't take much to fall over the edge if he continued caressing her the way he was.

"You are so wet already," he groaned before making her whimper as he pulled away.

"Don't stop, Cam. Please," Grace begged him.

"We need to get farther away, Grace," he cried out as she reached down and grabbed his thickness through the pants. She couldn't go any farther. She needed him now.

Dropping to her knees, she undid his belt, loving the panting that was escaping his throat as he tried desperately to remain quiet, fearful of them getting caught. That was only adding to her excitement.

Finally, she undid his button and pulled the zipper down, and when she freed him of his tux pants, she was the one panting. So solid. So thick. So hot. When she swept her tongue across his head and tasted the bead of moisture there, she had to squeeze her thighs together, she was so turned on. The pressure was almost too much to bear.

She was barely able to suck him into her mouth before his fingers were grasping her hair and pulling her back.

"Enough," he growled as he dropped to the ground with her. "I need to be inside you."

Those words were music to her ears. She fell backward and spread her thighs, needing him to cradle himself between them. He didn't make her wait.

With a quick tug of his fingers, he ripped her panties away and pushed her dress out of the way before his weight rested on top of her.

"You're so beautiful, Grace. I wish I could see you better," he said before his lips began nibbling on hers while his thickness rested against her wet center.

"Please, Cam. I need you," she whispered.

He didn't keep her waiting any longer. With a hard thrust of his hips, he sank deep inside, and the pressure of being filled by him after so long without sent her spiraling out of control. Her body squeezed around him as she cried into his mouth, his lips now fully over her own.

He groaned as he moved in and out of her, letting her fully enjoy her orgasm, and then he rested between her thighs. She could almost feel the deep satisfaction oozing off him.

"Ah, baby, you always were so responsive," he said before he began moving again, building the heat right back up within her.

Tugging on the straps of her dress, Cam freed her breasts while trapping her arms at her sides. She wiggled against him, but it was to no avail. She quit struggling when his head moved down and he captured her aching nipple with his teeth while he continued pumping in and out of her moist folds.

When her second orgasm rushed through her she felt him stiffen against her as his body shook, and together they saw more stars than were in the sky above them.

Neither of them said a word as they lay there together, arms linked, bodies close. Music could be heard quietly reaching out to them, but for this moment Grace was in a haven. However, soon that peacefulness evaporated and she knew she'd made a mistake.

Without a word, she stood, rearranged her clothes, and walked away, not with regret, but with great pain to once again leave this man she couldn't seem to ever stop loving.

2

Camden Whitman raked a hand through his hair once again—he looked like a refugee from an ancient punk band—and let out a long-suffering sigh. "It doesn't matter how many times I go through this file. All arrows point straight to Grace," he snapped before leaning back in his desk chair and pushing the file away, disgusted with all of it.

"We both know she's not capable of doing this, so you have to be missing something," said his father, Martin Whitman, seated comfortably across from him. He didn't seem worried at all.

"You've looked at it, Dad. You tell me what I'm missing."

"The file turned up on *your* desk, Cam. I'm not the one who's supposed to help her," he said before pausing and throwing his son a smile. "You are."

"I would love to know who put it there. That's still a big mystery. Somehow I don't think either of her parents cares enough to want to help her. But I certainly do want to. The problem is that every time I approach her about this, we end up in a fight. She doesn't want to have anything to do with me."

"Well, then, you'll just have to make her listen," Martin said, as if there was nothing easier than getting Grace to pay attention to anything Camden had to say.

"Ugh! It's not that simple. We have history together. It's just . . . I don't know, it's complicated. When she came back to town last year, I could see she was bitter, but as time has passed, nothing I do seems to change those feelings. I can only help her if she allows it."

Camden moved to the window and looked out over the small town square. Two kids played chase in the park while their mother sat on the bench watching them. Sterling was a great place to live, to work, and to raise a family. It's why he'd come back. At one time he'd wanted to settle down with Grace, have children, and live a happy, normal life. But the world had a way of intercepting the ball even in the best of plays.

Grace and Cam had been friends from the time he moved to Sterling. She was four years younger than he was, but tougher than any boy, and their relationship began out of respect. They stayed in contact while he was away at college.

The summer he came home with his degree in

hand before going on to law school, he saw Grace in a whole new way. She was eighteen, beautiful, and going into her senior year of high school.

Their love blossomed over the summer, and when he left for grad school, he was sure their relationship could last—but he was wrong. By the end of his first year of law school, there was nothing left of them to come home to.

Now the odds seemed to be forever in their disfavor, and it appeared there was nothing Cam could do about it, nothing but annoy a woman who just might wind up in prison.

"The file landed on your desk because whoever put it there knew you wouldn't stop until you solved this case," Martin told him.

"I don't think it really matters who has the case. It looks pretty airtight—seems like she did it." Cam cringed as he said that out loud.

"Ah, but you know not everything is as it seems, son."

"I've been fighting with her for a year on this," Camden said. "It's not long before the feds get involved, as you well know."

"Okay, boy. Let's take another look at the file together and see if there's anything we can come up with."

"Might as well." Cam grabbed the file off his desk and sat down at the large conference table in his office.

His father joined him and they pulled out the three-inch-thick pile of papers.

Martin flipped through the stack and stopped. "Right here is where it all began."

"Yeah, Dad, that's the first incident I can see of the embezzling."

"Wait. We're already off to a poor start," Martin said. "Why don't you describe to me what you've figured out, start to finish?"

"C'mon, Dad. You know everything I know."

"Sometimes putting things into story form helps clarify it," Martin said. "Let me start our little fairy tale off. Five years ago, one Grace Sinclair, the accused, opened a nonprofit by the name of Youthspiration. You pick it up from there."

"This is so lame . . . okay, okay," Cam said when his father gave him a warning look. "To an outsider, an auditor—hell, to the average person—it looks like all is well in paradise. If you look closely, the donation amounts coming in and then going back out all match up perfectly."

Martin broke in. "There's nothing wrong with starting up a nonprofit."

"What are you doing here, Dad?"

"I'm playing devil's advocate, pretending I know nothing."

"This isn't a game. It's serious. What can you possibly be smiling about?"

"I'm not enjoying the fact that Grace is in trouble.

It's just a pleasure to see you so focused about work, to see you on a mission," Martin told him. "Besides, I like playing dumb," he added with a laugh.

"I don't think you can pass as dumb, not with all the years you sat as the county judge, or the fact that you have successfully run three businesses worth billions of dollars," Cam reminded him.

"Right now I'm just Joe Schmo, juror, at your service."

"All right, I'll play along. About a year ago, somebody made an anonymous tip to the IRS, telling them that they might want to dig a little deeper into this nonprofit. They dug and found nothing. So then this file pops up on my desk and, me being me, I can't help but do some of my own digging. The nonprofit looks aboveboard. But when you peel away the layers of the onion and get to the heart of it, something's rotten. All the outgoing checks are written and seem to be going to real organizations, but there are duplicates, and those are heading straight into offshore accounts. Whoever's doing this is smart, though, because the money is siphoned off in such a way as to not raise red flags and to keep the culprit highly protected."

"How so? If *you* found offshore accounts, can't the feds?"

"Yes, they can, and I don't see how they haven't yet," Cam said. "Anyway, all signs point directly to Grace."

"And what does Grace have to say about it?" Martin asked.

"She said I was out of my mind. That she never opened up this or any other nonprofit and she certainly didn't take any money."

"Her word is good enough for me," Martin piped in.

"You're Joe Schmo, juror, remember?" Cam pointed out. "They don't know Grace. Hell, Dad, *we* don't know her anymore, either. She left home for a very long time. Life has a way of changing us."

"That's BS and you know it, son. Little Gracie would never be involved in something like this."

"I don't think she would, either, but there's a bank account in her name where large dollar amounts are randomly deposited and then immediately taken out as cash. The withdrawals coordinate with the times she's in the area of that particular branch of the bank."

"What do you mean?" Martin asked.

"I mean that she goes to Billings, and then there's a withdrawal."

"So it looks pretty bad for her, huh?"

"Yeah, it looks pretty bad. And each time I've tried to discuss this with her, she puts her head in the sand, says she has nothing to do with it, that it's not her, and then we get into a fight."

"You have no other choice but to make her listen."

"Easier said than done, Dad. Our history isn't exactly a smooth road."

"This could mean the difference between her going to prison and not going."

"It gets worse," Cam said with a sigh, shutting the folder.

"How can it get worse than Gracie going to prison?"

"I think she either knows who is actually involved and she's protecting them, or she's been aware of this scheme the entire time."

"No way!" Martin exclaimed. "There's not a chance."

"I don't know for sure. But I can't contact the IRS without her hiring me as her attorney, and I'm really at an impasse until she agrees to do something about this mess."

"Have you thought of option number three?" Martin asked.

"What?" Cam asked, exasperated. He didn't have time for these games, not even with his father.

"Maybe she wasn't aware this was going on, but she has an idea of who it could be and she's in denial."

"Wouldn't she want to go after the people smearing her name?" Cam asked.

"Not if it's someone she loves and trusts, and she doesn't want to find out they've betrayed her. We tend to bury our heads in the sand when the truth is too much for us to take."

Cam didn't know how to respond to that. It was

an option he hadn't even considered. There were very few people in Grace's life who she truly loved, Cam knew that much for sure. Maybe her parents, although he couldn't see her taking the rap for them, and definitely she loved her best friend, Sage, who had just married Cam's brother Spence.

It couldn't be her parents. They were wealthy—far too wealthy to need to embezzle, especially these sums. Yes, the total amount added up to a couple of million dollars, but that was chump change to them.

And Cam refused to believe it could be Sage. She was an incredible woman, in training to become a surgeon just like Cam's brother. No. There had to be another explanation.

"I have to go, Dad." He stood up and moved toward the door.

"Where are you off to in such a hurry?" Martin asked as he quickly followed Cam from the office.

"I'm going to see Grace," he said, determination in each stride. "It's time for a showdown."

"What's the plan?" Martin asked before he got in the car.

"I'll think of one on the way." Her time of fighting him was over. Cam wasn't one to take no for an answer—not when it was something he wanted.

3

Looking around the formal dining room of a restaurant she didn't care for, Grace shuddered. She hated going to public places with her mother. She never knew how the conversation was going to go and, more importantly, she wasn't sure that she'd be able to keep her cool. So, it was much better to meet her mom in a private setting.

But today wasn't going to be that easy on her.

"Why have you summoned me, Mother?"

No polite hellos, no hugs, no sign of a bond between mother and daughter. Hell, not even a suggestion that they were polite acquaintances. It was stiff and formal, and Grace was holding herself together by a thread. She always was when she saw her mother—or, more accurately, the woman who'd given birth to her.

"My friends the Griers are planning a wedding for their only daughter, Kitty, and she was so impressed with the event you put on last summer at Molly's wedding that she has specifically asked for you to be her wedding planner."

Grace blinked at her mother. It took a few minutes for the woman's words to sink in. "Why would I want to plan that spoiled brat's wedding?"

"I don't know what in the world is wrong with you to make you say such a hateful thing!" Victoria gasped. "Kitty is a wonderful young lady with impeccable manners."

"You've obviously never gone to a college party with the unblemished Ms. Kitty," Grace said. "I once watched her get up on a table and do a striptease for a room full of frat boys. I was stupid enough to accompany her to a sorority function she was in charge of. Lesson learned."

Victoria made haste to correct her daughter. "Grace Sinclair, you mustn't say such things about a girl with such fine parents and such a spotless reputation."

"Grow up, Mother. This is the real world. Only in the elite social circles you insist on being a part of do people turn the other way when confronted with scandal. I guarantee you everyone speaks about it; they just don't mention it to your face."

"I don't know what all of this attitude is about. I already told Olivia that you were free and would love to plan her daughter's wedding. Do *not* disappoint me."

"You think you can tell me what to do? Really, Mother. You had a lot more pull before I found you all hot and heavy, panting up a storm while riding the man who raped me."

Victoria almost choked. Her eyes darted around, and her shoulders only loosened up the smallest amount when she felt assured that no one was paying attention. Before she could vent her outrage, the server interrupted to take their order.

Grace sat back and watched in irritation as her mother ordered for both of them. Normally, Grace would call her on this, but she wasn't going to get in a public fight over food. Old grudges, maybe, but not food.

When they were alone again, Victoria looked at her with so much ice in her eyes, Grace waited to be frozen. Neither said anything for a few tense moments. Grace wasn't about to break the silence.

"You worthless, ungrateful little brat. I ruined my perfect body to give birth to you, raised you with everything you could have ever asked for and then some, and you even got a generous trust fund from your grandparents. I will not sit here and have you throw the past in my face. You *will* do this wedding or I will destroy the reputation you've built in your event-planning business. There is no way I want Edwin and Olivia to guess that my daughter is a spiteful little bitch."

She said all of that without her expression altering.

"When did you become this bitter, cruel woman?" Grace asked, sitting back, not offended in the least by her mother's words. She would have to care about her mom for the words to actually hurt her.

"I became what I had to in order to survive. You're doing the same thing, precious little Grace. You think you're so much better than me. I see it in your eyes every time you look at me. But just remember that you won't be young and beautiful forever. Pretty soon, the lines will start showing up around your eyes, and then—joy of all joys—you'll discover that gravity is a real bitch. You aren't any better than I am."

"I won't need to get a hundred surgeries trying to look twenty when I'm past forty," Grace replied evenly. "I'm not vain like you. I don't care if my body ages naturally. That just means that I've lived my life."

"Whatever, Grace. It's easy to say that now while you're still young. But I won't discuss that anymore. I came here for one reason and one reason only."

"I'm not doing the party," Grace said, determined.

"You *will* do this wedding, and you'll do it because you actually care about your pitiful career," Victoria said.

Grace sat there silently for a few moments while she counted to a hundred. Her mother was likewise silent, and once their meal had been set before them, Victoria began to eat as if nothing were wrong.

Her mother was correct. Grace did care about her career. She'd begun her own event-planning business, and as much as she despised her mother, she also knew the weight the woman pulled in the circles that could afford to hire an event planner.

Grace scooted her food around on her plate, unable to take even a single bite. Is this what her life had come down to? Ultimatums and sacrifice? It seemed that every which way she turned, someone wanted something from her—something she wasn't able to give, or something that required her to give too much.

"Fine. I'll plan Kitty's wedding. But don't for one moment think this is going to bond us," Grace said, no emotion in her voice.

"Don't worry, darling. I don't want that, either. I'm done raising you. I will have Kitty call you right away."

Victoria stood and walked away, leaving her daughter to pay the bill. Grace would bet her entire trust fund that her mother had never paid a check in her life. She actually believed her presence was worth paying for.

Before Grace had a chance to get up and abandon her lunch, which was now too cold to eat, someone plopped down on the opposite side of the table. How rude.

"What are you doing in Billings? Making a bank run?"

What in the world? Grace looked across the table at Cam, not knowing what to say.

"What in the world are you talking about, Cam? And what are you doing here? Did you follow me?" Without giving him a chance to answer, she continued, "You know what? Never mind. I didn't invite you to join me, much less to have a conversation with me, so don't answer, just leave."

Cam said nothing for a few heartbeats, but she didn't understand why he looked unhappy. He was the intruder, so if anyone should be in a snit, it should be her. And she wasn't happy, either. So if a fight was what he was looking for, then a fight was what he would get.

4

"Why are you all the way over here in Billings?" Cam asked.

"What in the hell business is it of yours where I am, Cam? The last time I looked, I didn't have to check in with anyone about where I go."

"You're right," he said, immediately backing off a bit. "It's just that your case has me flustered and I've been trying to get you to see the importance of it and talk to me."

"And I've told you that it's not *my* case. If I hire an attorney on the basis of this information, then it will look like I'm guilty. Is that what you want? Do you want me to spend time behind bars?"

"That's not how the law works, Grace. They don't excuse you if you play dumb and pretend to know nothing."

"Isn't a person innocent until proven guilty?"

"In theory, yes, but unfortunately, that's not always the way it works. I've seen innocent people get framed for crimes. And I don't want that to happen to you."

"Why, Cam? We're nothing to each other anymore. I told you when I first came back to town that I didn't want to renew our relationship or our friendship. I've been saying the same thing emphatically for the past year. Let this go."

"You weren't saying that a few months ago," he reminded her.

Grace closed her eyes for a moment to block him out. He was right. He'd caught her in a weak moment and she'd done something she knew she would regret. The thing was, she was still waiting for the regret to come. Instead, she just felt more loneliness.

Dammit! She'd told herself she was over this man, the man who had broken her heart at the tender age of eighteen. Why did her pulse have to speed up every time she was anywhere near him? It was ridiculous. She was a twenty-eight-year-old woman, had been around the world, had dined with royalty, and her childhood crush still had the power to render her speechless.

It was beyond irritating.

"Let's start over. I drove all the way out here, and I'm hungry." Before Grace could say a word, Cam ushered the waitress over. "I'll take a cheeseburger with the works, a big helping of chili fries, and a glass of Coke."

"Do you need anything else, ma'am?" she asked Grace.

What the hell? She was stuck there with him temporarily, and now that her mother was gone, she found herself hungry. It wasn't as if Cam was going to leave her alone anyway. She ordered a fresh club sandwich and soup.

"You know, you haven't changed at all—maybe just matured a little in a very appealing way," Cam told her with a look known to melt young girls' hearts.

"I've changed in more ways than show on the outside," she told him. "I've grown a lot stronger over the years. Aside from mistakes at weddings where I've drunk too much and ended up in the bed of a certain ex-boyfriend, I'm not so gullible anymore."

"Speaking of Spence and Sage's wedding, you know she talks about you all the time, telling me you're her oldest friend. She's glad you're spending more time with her."

"You do realize that you should never use the word *old* when talking about a woman, don't you?"

He was smart enough not to reply to that comment.

Grace really wasn't sure if she wanted more to smack this man or kiss him. He was a royal pain in her butt. Still, the more often he forced his company on her the more she wanted to see him, to talk to him. He was just one of those rare guys who could make a girl laugh and cry at the same time.

She couldn't pinpoint what it was about him that brought out her vulnerable side, but it closed her off, made her want to run in the opposite direction. She had no doubt he could bring her to her knees if she let him.

"How's the event-planning business going?" he asked as the waitress set plates down in front of them. While he waited for an answer, he dug in as if he hadn't eaten in a month.

She sipped her soup while she thought about whether or not to answer him. She finally caved. When in Rome . . .

"It's slow, but I have enough clients that it's entertaining."

"Why do you do it, Grace, when you don't need to work?"

"I could ask you the same thing. You have boatloads more money in your trust than I have in mine and you practically live in your law offices, that is when you aren't wrangling cattle," she pointed out. "I work because I'm not some stupid little socialite who wants to do nothing more than sit on her hands all day while the rest of the world truly lives. I enjoy my job, the challenge of it, the opportunity to learn new things, and the chance to meet new people. I get to be creative and I won't ever be like my mother."

She looked down, but she could practically feel his smile burning into her skull. It didn't matter whether she snapped at him or batted her eyelashes.

Cam was an easygoing guy, and it was nearly impossible to ruffle his feathers.

When she looked back up, his smile was gone, but his eyes were hot. He reached across the table and took her hand. She pulled against him for a moment and then decided she was too dignified to struggle with this man in public, so instead she sent him an infuriated gaze and let her hand go limp.

"What do you think you're doing?" she said between clenched teeth.

His eyes traveled over her face, then rested on her mouth, the look so intense, it sent a lingering pulse straight to her core. Her tongue came out and wetted her lips, making his eyes blaze even hotter.

"Why do you continually fight me at each and every turn?" he asked her huskily.

"Because I don't like being manhandled," she snapped.

"Damn! Do you realize how tempting you are with fire shooting out of your eyes? You're magnificent," he said in an awed whisper.

"So I'm cute when I'm mad? Well, you're . . . you are . . . you're insufferable," she retorted, the anger draining. It was hard to stay upset when a man you desired was looking at you as if you were the main course.

"If you really felt that way about me, you wouldn't be so turned on by just a few words and my touch on your hand, Grace. You're fighting yourself as much as you're fighting me. If I thought this was all one-way, I would have dropped it long ago."

For a brief moment, he gave her a glimpse of the boy she used to know. His eyes were full of sincerity instead of arrogance, and his touch on her hand had softened. Beneath his layers of power, he was still the boy who had once been her lover and friend. She had tried to forget that, but she'd found, over the years, that it was an impossible task.

"Maybe I just feel trapped, Camden."

Finally, he released her hand. "I don't think so. I just think you're afraid and that's why you constantly run from me."

"I wasn't the one who ran first, Cam," she said, hating the sorrow this caused her. "But you seem to have quickly forgotten that." So much pain accompanied these words.

"Grace . . ." He trailed off, obviously at a loss for what to say.

There wasn't anything to say. There was nothing he could do to make up for what he'd done to her. They both knew it. She couldn't keep fighting with this man.

"Do whatever you want, Cam, but I'm done with this conversation. Thanks for lunch."

With that, she stood up and did exactly as her mother had done—walked out and left him with the bill. And she couldn't help but feel a small measure of satisfaction at besting him.

5

It seemed that Cam was spending as much time as his brother was at the hospital where Spence was a top-rated heart surgeon. Although at one time the smells and sounds had set off unpleasant thoughts for Cam, now they were a comfort for him. He waited for Spence to focus back on him before speaking.

"Have you ever done anything that you regret?"

Spence gave him a look as if trying to figure out if Cam was serious or not before he considered his words.

"Only about a thousand times," Spence said. But he held up his hand before Cam could speak. "But then I realize that those mistakes I've made along the road of life have shaped me into who I am today. So, even though I might have regrets, I also appreciate those mistakes."

"That makes absolutely no sense," Cam said. "If you regret doing it, then how can you also appreciate it?"

"Because everything we do leads us to where we

currently are," Spence said as if it were the most logical thing in the universe.

"But wouldn't we still get to the end of the road with or without the mistakes?" Cam asked.

"I don't know. Each decision we make impacts us in one way or another. Maybe if you choose one option over another, it will take you on a different journey," Spence told him.

"Argh. I don't know why I bother coming to you for advice," Cam said, throwing up his hands.

"Because you need me."

Spence's pager went off and he looked down before moving over to the phone and calling someone. After a few moments and a few medical terms Cam was beginning to learn, Spence hung up.

"Do you need to go?"

"No. They have it under control. Let's go outside for a minute. I need sun," Spence said. He began moving without waiting for a reply. That's what it was like to be a doctor—constantly moving and jumping to someone else's tune. Cam wondered where the actual glamor was that so many people spoke of when speaking of being a doctor.

To him it looked like a lot of hours and a lot of unappreciative people. But then, once in a while there was a case—that case that changes people's lives for the better. That's what Spence always spoke of.

When Cam still didn't speak when they made it

outside, Spence led him along a path that wound down by the river. It was his favorite place at the hospital—quiet, secluded, where only the sounds of the forest animals scurrying along and crying out to each other could be heard.

"You going to tell me why you're here?" Spence finally said as he leaned down and picked up a few rocks, then began tossing them in the water.

"I don't know. I've just been so frustrated. I had lunch with Grace today. It didn't go well."

"Was it a planned lunch?" Spence asked.

"Well . . . not really," Cam admitted.

"So you once again blindsided her and then expected her to be thrilled you were invading her space," Spence said.

"I didn't do that . . . not exactly," Cam replied, defending himself.

"Come on, Cam. You've been in love with this woman for more than ten years, but stubborn pride keeps you repeatedly making mistakes. You thought she'd just be sitting around, waiting on you while you traipsed around college doing whatever the hell you wanted to do, and then you were pissed to find that she wasn't doing exactly that," Spence told him.

"I wasn't traipsing all around," Cam thundered.

Spence's brows went up. "Well, I wasn't exactly doing that. And since when have you begun taking her side?"

"Since I married her best friend, and I've heard more of the story. We were all asses when we were young, but we've now grown up. It's time to start acting like it," Spence told him.

"Dammit, Spence! I didn't come here to get lectured," Cam told him.

"Yes, you did. You know what you need to do, but you're stubborn and need someone to set you straight. There's no one like your big brother to do just that," Spence said with a laugh.

"Well, you nearly blew it with Sage," Cam pointed out.

"Yes, I did. But luckily I listened to not only those around me but also my heart, and I managed to catch the girl. It's the smartest thing I've ever done," Spence said. He looked at Cam and smiled. "I mean that, little brother, the absolute smartest. I could give up everything in my life, live in some cabin in the middle of the woods with no power, and still I'd be happy just as long as Sage was there by my side."

"Damn, Spence. I'm not sure I can ever get used to this side of you," Cam told him.

"Just wait. You aren't far behind me," Spence said. "But I will say this: Don't let foolishness allow the girl to get away. If you want her to talk to you, then leave her no choice, but don't be an ass about it."

Cam was about to reply when Spence's pager went off.

"Dammit, gotta run."

And just like that, Cam found himself standing by the river alone, his brother's footsteps fading away. Now it was his turn to throw rocks into the water as he contemplated what to do next.

6

"Wake up, Sleeping Beauty."

Grace could hear someone speaking, but she was exhausted. The damn cold she'd managed to catch had been playing havoc with her entire system, and she'd slept more in the last two days than she had in her entire life.

"Go 'waayy . . ." she mumbled, turning over and snuggling back under the blanket, which seemed to be holding her down. She didn't mind being held down. A few more hours of sleep and she'd be right as rain.

"Come on, Grace, wake up. You should know better than to leave your apartment unlocked. Anyone could come strolling on in and do all sorts of things . . ." The person trailed off, and she started to become a little more alert. Then the voice registered, and her eyes shot open.

"Cam! What in the world are you doing in here?" she croaked as she struggled to sit up. She had zero strength at the moment, though, and it seemed an impossible task.

"I came to talk to you. I pounded on the door for a full five minutes. When I saw your car parked below, and there still wasn't an answer, I got worried. I checked the knob and it was unlocked, so I came in to find you snoring on the couch."

Strong hands circled her waist and assisted her in sitting up before he made himself comfortable and sat next to her. Glaring at him as she clutched her blankets, she pulled up her knees and hugged them to her chest. "I do not snore!"

"Out of everything I just said, that's what you pick up on?"

"Well, I don't," she stated. "And as a man of the law, you should realize you're trespassing. I could call the cops and have you arrested right now."

"I'm shaking in my loafers," he said, leaning back and making himself at home.

"Ugh. You're a pig."

"I've been called worse."

"And I'm sure you deserved it."

"Ouch, someone woke up on the wrong side of the . . . couch."

"Oh, my gosh, you always think you're so amusing. Why don't you leave and let me rest before I decide to breathe in your face and give you what I have."

"Baby, you can do a hell of a lot more than breathe in my face if you'd like," he said, leaning too close.

"Knock it off, Cam. This isn't a fair fight. I don't feel good," she said, her heart picking up speed.

"You've always felt good to me," Cam said. "But I'm going to make you a hot cup of tea, and then we're going to talk business. You ran out on lunch the other day, remember." He jumped up from the couch and disappeared around the corner to her kitchen.

She desperately wanted to tell him exactly where he could stick his hot cup of tea, but just the thought of it was doing crazy things to her parched throat. She could have called and asked her best friend, Sage, who just so happened to be a doctor, to come and take care of her, but Grace was independent, and she hadn't wanted to admit she needed to be taken care of.

So she'd been miserable, barely able to move from the couch to the bathroom, let alone bustle around in the kitchen. When the teakettle whistled, she had to fan her face as her eyes burned with tears.

Grace Sinclair did *not* cry. That was unacceptable. She especially didn't cry over something as simple as someone making her a cup of tea. When she was feeling normal again, she'd kick herself, because weak women irritated the hell out of her.

Cam walked back into the room a few minutes later holding her late grandmother's lap tray, a pot with hot water in it, a china cup, a small cup of soup, crackers, and a tomato sandwich, her absolute favorite, cut in half on the diagonal. He remembered, and it took a strength she didn't know she possessed to refuse to let any of this mean anything to her. So he opened a can and boiled some water. Big freaking deal.

"You didn't need to do this," she said, her throat tight. She accepted the tray, though, and didn't waste any time pouring her tea and adding a dollop of honey before she took ravenous mouthfuls of her soup.

"I wanted to do it," Cam told her before sitting back down.

"Thank you," she mumbled.

"What was that? I didn't quite hear you," Cam said, and she sent him another withering look.

"I said, 'Thank you!' " But she sounded anything but thankful.

"You always have had a difficult time thanking people," Cam told her.

"That's because most people do things for selfish reasons, not because they're truly selfless," she said, then frowned when she realized her sandwich was gone.

"Want another one?"

"No . . ." But she drew out the *no*. His attentiveness was sapping her will.

Cam laughed and climbed off the couch, grabbed her plate, then disappeared again. She could have tried to stop him, but the food was giving her some much-needed energy, and she hadn't eaten in . . . hell, it had to be two full days now.

He returned as she was pouring a second cup of tea. He set the sandwich on her tray and sat back down. "Feeling better? Do you need any medicine? I can make a pharmacy run."

"I am feeling a little better. And for real, thank you," she said as she sipped her tea and then began nibbling on the second sandwich.

"Medicine?" he repeated.

"I wouldn't mind some NyQuil," she practically whispered. "It's on the kitchen counter." She had no doubt she was going to have to repay his kindness, but it was so nice to have someone taking care of her, even if only for a little while. A truce was acceptable under the circumstances.

Cam jumped up again and retrieved the capsules, along with some water to wash it down. When she finished her meal, he set the tray on her coffee table before giving her a look that made her instantly nervous.

"We still need to chat, but since you're sick, and slightly stinky at the moment . . ." he said with a chuckle.

"I do *not* stink!" she snarled.

"Okay, I made that up, but I'm sure now that you have a little energy, you would love a hot bath."

Oh, that did sound like heaven, but it was far too much effort. "I'm fine," she told him, although it pained her to say it.

"You forget that I know you, Grace. We may have been apart most of the last ten years, but before that we were inseparable."

"That was a very long time ago, Cam. People change."

"Yes, but not that much, and if I remember correctly, you can sit in a tub until your entire body is a mass of wrinkles—if you have a good book."

With that, he leapt up again, and soon her ears pricked up at the heavenly sound of running water. Her slight food buzz was already diminishing, and she wasn't at all sure she'd have the energy to get up, undress, and bathe, but even though he had retracted his "stinky" comment, she felt disgusting. The cold had left her either shivering or stewing in her own juices, and washing off the sweat sounded better than a million dollars right now.

Ten minutes later Cam came back in the room. "Okay, up you go," he said, and then her cover was being flung aside, and before she knew what he intended, his arms went beneath her and he was lifting her up, holding her securely against his solid chest.

"Mmm, I remember this," he whispered.

Grace felt her chest restrict. Yeah, she remembered it too well herself. He marched into her room, then to the bathroom, and only stopped when he reached the tub. He set her down on the side. "Need help undressing?"

"No! I've got this," she told him.

The adrenaline from being pressed up against him had given her back her lost energy, and she felt her cheeks grow hot at the thought of him stripping her clothes away.

"It's not like I haven't seen it before," he reminded her softly, temptingly.

"That was in the Dark Ages, Cam." Thankfully he didn't remind her of their naked reunion a few months ago.

"Okay, I'm going to leave the door cracked in case you need me," he told her, and disappeared.

Grace undressed, then sighed in complete contentment as she slid into the deep bubble bath and leaned her head against the bath pillow he'd blown up and attached to the back of the tub. Cam had even left a book on the side of the tub, but she couldn't even imagine holding her arms out of the hot water long enough to take it.

With a blissful sigh, comforting food in her stomach now, she closed her eyes and quickly fell asleep.

7

Cam's determination to make Grace listen to him had died the second he panicked at her front door, imagining all sort of horrible things that could have happened to her when she didn't answer, especially since Sage had said she hadn't heard from her in a few days.

When he'd walked inside and found her curled up on the couch, her nose red, her breathing uneven and scratchy, he wanted nothing more than to pull her into his arms and take care of her.

Since her return last year, he'd tried telling himself it was time to move on, that it was more than obvious she wasn't interested in rekindling their romance. If only it were that easy. She'd been his first real love, the source of his best childhood memories, and the girl he'd let slip through his fingers. Their chemistry was undeniable even today.

Now that she was in trouble, there wasn't anything he wouldn't do to protect her. Right now, though, the only thought running through his mind was the fact that she was less than fifty feet from him, soaking naked in a tub full of water and slippery soap.

He groaned as he scrubbed her sandwich plate a little too hard, nearly breaking it when he set it on the towel he'd laid out on her counter. His brothers would really enjoy watching this—Cam cooking, making tea, and then doing dishes. He'd never be able to live that one down.

But what else was he supposed to do? She was sick. And some things really never did change. Grace just wasn't the sort to ask for help, even if her life were in jeopardy. That was just who she was.

Well, Cam had been raised quite differently. He'd been brought up by a man who still believed in helping his neighbors, who wouldn't stand idly by while an elderly person in the parking lot loaded their own groceries, and who would never abandon a friend in a time of need. And whether Grace wanted to admit it or not, she was in need at the moment. Now, if Cam could just convince his body that she was only his friend, and that he wasn't going to be doing anything with her naked body, he would be all good.

When half an hour passed, he decided he'd better check on her. "Grace . . ." No answer. "Grace?" he called again. Still nothing.

Peeking in through the door, he found her with her head resting against the bath pillow, her mouth partially open, and quiet snores drifting from between her slightly swollen, very reddened lips. Even when she was sick, he wanted to capture her mouth with his.

Nope. Shaking his head, he stepped into the bathroom, either very thankful for or maddened by the miracle of bubbles. Although they weren't nearly as high as when the bath had first been drawn, they still managed to conceal all his favorite places on her magnificent body.

"Grace . . ." He leaned in and shook her shoulder.

She didn't stir so much as an inch; she just mumbled and then tried to turn, her head almost slipping beneath the surface of the bathwater. "How much am I going to be tested?" he asked no one in particular.

Grabbing a towel from the rack, he draped it across his chest, then pulled the plug on the bath, and reached into the tub, letting his hands slide against her slick flesh until he got a good hold on her before pulling her straight into his arms.

She immediately began shivering. He covered her as much as he could, then grabbed another towel and draped that over her, too, before quickly stepping into her bedroom, where her bed was a mess of tangled blankets.

Setting her down on one side of the bed, one towel beneath her, the other on top, he then threw her comforter over her. Grace reached out—he imagined it was for him—grabbed a pillow, and snuggled into it.

Camden stood there for a moment trying to figure out what to do next. There was no way he had the willpower to dry her off and dress her. That was asking way too much of him. He'd done his best not to peek while pulling her out of the tub, but a man could be held responsible for only so much.

Turning away to reduce the brutal waves of temptation, he went off to search her linen closet and was thrilled when he found another thick comforter along with clean sheets and spare blankets.

She was curled up in a ball on one side of the bed, so he pulled the sheets off the mattress on the other side, slid the new bedding into place, and tucked it in by her. Then he faced Grace again. He still had the problem of her state of undress. He was sure she was dry now, what with the towels and the thick comforter, but she'd want to wear at least a nightie in case she woke up and needed the bathroom.

He found an indecently short gown hanging behind the door in the bathroom, with spaghetti straps on top and lace around the hem. "Dammit!" Of course she slept in sexy nightclothes. When they'd dated, they'd stolen moments together, never being able to stay a whole night in the same place. He wondered if she'd worn the same sexy undergarments back then.

"Give me strength," he said, looking upward.

Moving back into her room, he draped the gown over her head without moving the blankets, then reached beneath them and pulled it down her body, his knuckles grazing her flesh. Cam was sweating by the time he was done, and it wasn't from over-exertion.

Biting his lip, he pulled her from beneath the now-damp comforter, and she immediately snuggled against him, her breath warming his neck and making his lower body throb in time to the pulsing of his heart.

Laying her on the fresh linens, he quickly covered her up, then moved to the other side of the bed, where he stripped the rest of the old bedding off and quickly fixed the new.

More exhausted than if he'd been herding cattle all day, Cam practically stumbled from her bedroom and made a beeline for her fridge. "Please, please, please," he said repeatedly, then almost felt a tear in his eye when he opened the refrigerator door and found a six-pack of Corona.

Pulling one out, he popped the cap and downed half the bottle in one gulp.

No, he wouldn't be talking to her about anything regarding the file tonight. But because she was feeling so poorly, he also couldn't leave her alone. If something happened to her, he'd never forgive himself.

After finishing the beer, he grabbed another one, then checked to make sure Grace was still sleeping before he settled in on her couch, her mango scent drifting all around him, and his lower brain growling at him for being such a fool. Man, that hurt.

Clicking on the television, he decided to settle in for one very, very long night. And yet, before the first half hour was up, his head was lolling to one side and he was drifting off.

Cam was startled awake by a scratching noise. It took a moment for his eyes to adjust to the darkness, and then he heard the noise again. He was instantly awake. It sounded as if someone were trying to pry open the window.

But they were in Sterling. Who in the hell would break into Grace's apartment? He'd just been ribbing her earlier about her door being unlocked. In this town everyone left their doors unlocked until they went to bed.

When the noise continued, Cam jumped up and moved toward the front door. He went in stealth mode, but the squeaky floors in her apartment probably couldn't help but betray him. He unlocked the door as quickly as possible and thrust it open.

No one was there, and for a moment he thought maybe he'd been imagining the whole thing. But when he looked again, he saw a flat-head screwdriver beneath her window. With narrowed eyes, he looked both ways on the balcony before he stepped up to the tool and bent down.

There were scratch marks on the outside of her window, as if someone had indeed been trying to break in. What the hell? Taking off his shirt, he used it to pick up the screwdriver. With luck, some prints could be lifted from the handle. But the whole idea was absurd. It had to just be neighborhood kids thinking they were being funny. Crime never really happened in Sterling. That's why people chose to live here.

Not able to shed his sense of unease, though, Cam moved back inside the apartment, his rest for the night ruined. When she woke up, Grace was going to answer his questions. This time, he wasn't taking no for an answer.

If someone was after her, he wanted to know why.

8

Her brain fuzzy and her vision unfocused, Grace woke up to the smell of fresh coffee, bacon, and something delicious that she couldn't identify. Sage had to be making breakfast. Grace lay there a moment longer, her lips turning up and her stomach growling.

When she took in a big breath of air, she nearly laughed aloud for pure joy when she realized her nose was no longer stuffy. Wiggling her legs, she still felt aches and pains, but they weren't as debilitating as they'd been the past few days.

Then her eyes snapped back open. Wait a freaking minute. Sage had moved out six months ago. She was married to Spence now—Cam's brother. Cam! He'd been at her house the night before. Thinking hard, Grace tried to call up the last thing she remembered. The tub!

She'd been in the tub and had obviously fallen asleep. Her hand shot to her chest and touched the silky smoothness of her nightie. Slowly lifting the blanket, she peeked underneath. That nightie was all she had on. Her face went crimson as she realized that Cam must have pulled her from the tub, dried her off, and dressed her.

She racked her brain for any other memories, and came up blank. She knew there was no way they'd done anything. As much as she wanted to "monster-ize" Cam, he wasn't a bad guy and he would never take advantage of a sleeping woman, not even if the two of them were in a relationship. So her horror was strictly at knowing he'd seen her naked—again.

Then, with the morning light streaming in through her blinds, she noticed her bedding had been changed. Had he done all of this for her? Why? Since she'd come back to town, not a single conversation had ended without one or both of them either yell-ing or the one time at her best friend's wedding with them ripping each other's clothes off, she thought in shame. So why in the world was he taking care of her now?

"Good morning, Grace. You look much better than you did last night."

Grace froze as she looked to her doorway and found Cam leaning against the jamb with a cup in his hand, smiling at her.

"What are you doing, Cam?"

She clutched at her comforter, pulling it to her chin as she stared at him. Age had only made him better. He'd been so dang handsome when he was in his late teens and early twenties. She'd been in love with him from the time he was sixteen and she was only twelve, and he'd thought of her as nothing but a child.

He was all man now, his cheeks still chiseled but filled out nicely, his shoulders wide and making the perfect upside-down A-frame, and his arms . . . oh, his arms were solid, and looking at them led her gaze down to his stomach and beyond.

Shaking her head, she snapped her eyes back to his, which were, of course, twinkling. "Like the view, darlin'? Need me to turn around?"

"I asked you a question, Camden." She was growing grumpier by the minute.

"I stayed the night. You were so sick and out of it that I was worried about you. And now I just finished making breakfast. You hungry?"

Her stomach growled her answer and he chuckled. She wished she could be stubborn enough to insist he get out, but she really was starving, although she didn't see how she could be after pigging out the night before.

"Would you leave so I can get up?"

"Why? I saw plenty last night," he said with an exaggerated wink.

"That's just plain rude, Cam!" she snapped, sending him a look that should have shaken his confidence, if only a little.

"You weren't thinking I was rude last night."

"I was drugged and out of it. A real man wouldn't have taken advantage of that fact."

He stepped into the room and her heart thudded as she wondered what he was going to do. Slowly, so slowly, he approached the bed, set his coffee cup down on her nightstand, and then leaned down, his face now only inches from hers.

"I showed more restraint last night than could be expected of any mortal man. Now, if you want to thank me properly . . ." he said, with enough of a growl that her stomach was now flipping for reasons that had nothing to do with food.

"I need privacy," she managed to squeak out, but was afraid to move even an inch as his scent enveloped her, making her realize if he were to touch her, she wasn't sure she'd be able to keep from grabbing him.

"As you wish," he said, backing off immediately, picking up his cup, and sauntering out of her room.

Breathing deeply, she lay there until she felt that her body was safely under control, then finally flipped back the covers and climbed out of bed. She couldn't wake up to Cam. It was far too hard on her hormones.

Stepping into her bathroom, she decided a shower was in order. As hungry as she was, she hadn't washed her hair in a while, and until she scrubbed every inch of her poor body, she wasn't going to feel as if she'd beaten the cold that had dragged her down for days.

After she dried off, she peeked in her bedroom—no, Cam wasn't there—then walked over to her closet and selected a warm outfit. Style, for once, wasn't on her mind.

Now clean, clothed, and craving food, she couldn't put off seeing Cam any longer. She emerged from her bedroom and found him sitting at the table, reading her newspaper.

The phone rang before she could say anything. Stepping over, she picked it up and then immediately regretted that decision.

"What can I do for you, Kitty?" she said, trying to have patience. The woman had been her client only for a few days and already Grace was wondering how she was going to get through this wedding. At least she wasn't drawing the event out for a year.

"What did you just say?" Grace wasn't sure she'd heard the woman correctly. But when she repeated it, Grace wanted to slap her.

After a few moments she finally hung up the phone and then was even more grouchy than when she'd come down the stairs, therefore poor Cam was about to get the brunt of her anger.

"Make yourself right at home," she said with a scowl before moving to the coffeepot and pouring herself a fresh cup.

"Don't mind if I do," he murmured, unaffected by her ill mood.

She sat down, refusing to serve herself yet. That

would excuse his behavior. Where in the world had all the groceries come from? She was really a boxed-food kind of gal—who had the time or the energy to cook whole meals? Boring . . . Baking, on the other hand, she absolutely loved to do.

"What was that phone call about? You seem upset," he finally said.

"That was my client from hell," she murmured.

"I'm sure it's not that bad," he said.

"Really?" she gasped. "She was just telling me that her grandmother just had the gall to die on her and so now her seating chart was all messed up. She's demanded a meeting this afternoon to get it fixed."

Cam sat there, his eyes widening as he looked at her as if trying to figure out if she was speaking the truth or not. When she said nothing more, his lips twitched and then he laughed out loud.

"Okay, then. I think you're right. She just might be the biggest bridezilla I've ever heard about."

They both continued sitting there in silence for several more moments, and Grace's stomach rumbled. Dang it! She really wanted to eat, but weren't they in a standoff at the moment?

"Are you going to be so stubborn that you're not going to eat after I went shopping and then was kind enough to prepare breakfast?"

"Are you going to be so needy for compliments that you're going to beg for them and puff up your own worth? Look, I didn't ask you to do that. I didn't ask you to do *any* of this," she told him.

"I know. However, I like taking care of you. You're one of the strongest women I know, Grace, and it's been nice to catch you in a weak moment," he said, his voice soft, although he didn't look up from the paper.

"So you're one of those guys that like weak, simpering little females who can't do anything without a big, strong man around the house?"

"Not at all. I love your strength, but a truly strong person also knows when it's time to ask for a little help, to ask when she needs a shoulder to cry on, and to ask when she's so weak she can't even feed herself," he told her, finally setting the paper down and sending her an intense stare.

"I was doing just fine on my own."

"Yes, you were, and I'm sure you would have woken up today, still weak, but able to get moving again. It was still my pleasure to be here for you." *If only he had been there for her the one time in her life she had needed him the most.* But she would never say that to him. That wasn't a can of worms she was ready to open, one she probably never would be.

"I don't like people taking care of me."

"I'll make sure to not do it too often," he said with a laugh, holding up his hands. "Do you want a little of everything?" He stood up and moved over to the oven, where he began pulling out dishes he'd placed in there to keep the food warm.

"I can get it myself."

"Then you won't be surprised by what I've made you. Enjoy your coffee and be awed by my culinary talents." With that, he grabbed two plates and piled them high. He set hers in front of her, then went to the fridge and pulled out a bowl of fresh-cut fruit and set it out, too.

He'd made a breakfast strata, potatoes, and bacon, along with muffins and the fruit. It looked and smelled delectable, and she wasn't such a fool that she was going to let it go to waste just because she didn't appreciate the way he'd swooped in and saved the day.

Not able to stifle her ecstatic groan, Grace finally looked up at Cam again. "You really went to far too much trouble, but it is sort of nice."

"There's no way I'm getting another thank-you, is there?" he asked.

"Nope. If I gave you another one, you'd think I want or expect this sort of thing, and I don't."

"All righty, then. When you're finished, we can get down to business," he told her.

She took her time eating, because she knew what he was going to say and she didn't want to have this fight with him again. It had been going on all year, and he was starting to wear her down. But it was all so stupid. She hadn't opened that damned nonprofit, so she had nothing to worry about.

The innocent didn't get accused—that would just be wrong, she assured herself.

The two of them finished in silence, and she made sure to be the first one up, gathering the plates and empty dishes and going with them to her sink.

"I'll do those," Cam said, stepping right up behind her, far too close. "You're still not one hundred percent."

"No. You've done enough for me. Sit down and drink your coffee and I'll take care of the dishes. Of course, if you need to go to the office, you can go ahead and take off."

"I don't have a single place to be today," he said, brushing against her back before moving away and returning to his chair. That small contact sent a delicious tingling sensation through her entire body.

She wasn't in any hurry—with luck, he'd grow bored and leave. She knew better, though. Cam wasn't one to give up once he had his mind set on something. When she'd finished with the few dishes they'd dirtied, she poured herself a fresh cup of coffee and returned to the table, where he had that blasted file sitting in front of him.

"There's really no use in going over this again and again, Cam. I didn't open that nonprofit—Youthspiration or whatever it was called—so I'm not worried about facing the law," she told him, pulling her legs up to her chest and hugging them, her way of trying to protect herself.

"I'm not going to tiptoe around this anymore, Grace. Even if you weren't the one to open this thing up, it's in your name. This is money laundering, dammit—it's not Monopoly or Chutes and Ladders—and everything is pointing right at you. You need to talk to me so we can figure this out."

"But I didn't do it," she said, doing her weary best to sound like a broken record.

"Well, then, you need to give me a list of people who you think are capable of coming up with something like this and using you as their scapegoat."

She glared at him for several heartbeats. She didn't like being pushed into this corner, didn't like having to answer to something she hadn't done. But he was right. She hadn't told him she had done so, but she'd finally gotten around to reading through the copies he'd left with her. It really did look like all roads led back to her. Suddenly her shoulders sagged as she looked at him.

When she took too long, he spoke again. "Did you know that in most jurisdictions, embezzling is punishable by prison time and, of course, fines, including the money taken? And do you remember Bernie Madoff, the stockbroker and investment adviser who got away with about sixty-five billion dollars from various investors? In 2009, he was sentenced to one hundred and fifty years in prison. Sure, that's an extreme case, but it shows that the courts aren't smiling on people guilty of fraud, not even the rich ones who can afford lawyers. So you need to tell me, and tell me right now, *who* you think is behind this. I promise you that this is no joke, Grace."

Nausea took up permanent residence in her stomach at the thought of prison time. She wouldn't survive being caged up. No way. No how.

"I have no idea who would do this to me, Cam."

"Somebody did, and it's my job to figure out who. The only way I can do that is if you cooperate with me."

"Why do you even want to help me with this? How do you even know I'm innocent? I could be playing you."

"Innocent people don't make comments like that," he told her with a wry smile.

"Ugh. You think you have it all figured out. Well, you don't. I have no clue what is going on with this, but I didn't steal any money. I don't need to! My grandfather left me a generous trust fund that's more than enough for me to live off. And my poor excuse of a father left me property. I make a modest income from work, but you know that I don't have to work at all if I don't want to." She was practically yelling now. "There's just no reason I would ever need to embezzle money!"

"Slow down. Let's just talk. We'll figure this out. But you're going to have to open up to me. You're going to have to tell me about your life over the past ten years. Well, at least the years that you weren't here in

Sterling," he said, reaching out and patting her hand.

"I don't want to talk about my past. I made a lot of mistakes. It's not something I'm proud of."

"Grace, I want to help you. You have to tell me everything or I can't."

"Really, Cam? Would you like to just open up to me? Do you want to tell me every mistake you've made while you were away from this sleepy little Montana town?" she asked. But before he had a chance to answer, she answered for him. "No. No, you wouldn't."

"If I needed to tell you something so you could help me, I would. As a matter of fact, you would be one of the first people I'd run to," he said.

Her eyes snapped to his. Did he really mean that?

"But we aren't friends," she said, almost begging him to agree with her.

"I want to be so much more than friends, Grace."

The heat in his eyes told her that he wasn't trying to fool her. Another shudder raced through Grace as she fought to keep herself from leaning against him. She'd done her damnedest to convince herself she was over this man, but Grace had a strong feeling that their story wasn't quite finished yet.

9

"Please tell me you just leaned into him and gave him a nice, big, sloppy kiss," Sage said as she zipped down the hospital corridor.

"Sage! I did not kiss him. You know how big a mistake that would be," Grace told her best friend.

"Because once or twice in the last few months was warning enough, and let's not forget the night of my wedding, where a little more than kissing happened . . ."

"I cannot believe you just said that!" Grace snapped.

"Now who's the prude? If a man came into my home while I was sick, then bathed me, tucked me into bed, and fed me, I'd do a hell of a lot more than kissing," Sage told her as she pushed open a door and rushed inside.

"Why are you always moving as if you're preparing for a marathon?" Grace grumbled, finding that she was slightly out of breath.

"Because I could be called to the ER at any time,

and if I don't get some caffeine inside me, and very quickly, I might accidentally slip a catheter into the wrong hole." Sage was already brewing a fresh mocha while speaking. "Do you want one?"

Grace chuckled before replying. "Do you even need to ask?"

"You're lucky I'm asking. It's been the day from hell already and I still have half my shift left," Sage said with a sigh, and grabbed her cup.

"Wait a minute!" Grace gasped. "You can't get away with that earlier comment."

"What comment?" It was typical that Sage had already moved on. With the mind of a genius, she was always moving forward, not backward.

"If a man came into your home and bathed, changed, and fed you, I think Spence might well have to shoot him."

"Who in the hell is planning on coming to my house and touching my wife?"

Dr. Spence Whitman sent a thunderous scowl toward the two women, and they turned and smiled at him. His expression didn't change.

"No one is doing that for me except you, love," Sage said, walking over and kissing him on the cheek. His scowl lessened, if only a little. "Your little brother Cam was doing that for Grace last night," she added before sending a wicked smile Grace's way.

Grace wanted to shoot Sage when Spence glanced in her direction, his scowl completely gone. "Well,

I'll have to pat my brother on the back. He always has been in love with you," Spence said with a wink.

"I am *so* not having this conversation with you, Spence. I was trying to talk to my best friend," Grace told him pointedly. She was praying he'd go away and not tell Cam that she'd been at the hospital talking about him.

"Sure, sure. I'll leave you gals to chat just as soon as my coffee is done," Spence said, kissing his wife one more time before giving his attention to the espresso maker.

"Back to the kissing. After putting out that much effort, you didn't even give him a little cheek action?" Sage asked.

Grace let out a slight growl when Spence turned her way again, and she shot a murderous look at Sage, who just smiled happily in return.

"We'll talk more when we're alone," Grace said through gritted teeth.

"You know that she'll tell me everything when you're gone, right?" Spence said as he added half-and-half to his coffee and leaned against the counter as if he were planning on staying awhile.

"She wouldn't do that, because it breaks the best-friend code of honor," Grace told him. "If she were to break that, we'd be left with no choice but to ensure you came to a speedy death, followed by an unmarked grave so that she could never break the code again by talking to you."

Spence laughed before stepping over and kissing Grace's cheek once again. "Always a pleasure to see you. Let's do dinner tomorrow night. I'll grill steaks, and you bring your famous oriental chicken salad." He didn't leave the room before giving Sage one more scorching kiss, and then finally the two friends were alone.

"How in the world were you so lucky as to find and marry that man?" Grace sighed.

"Hey! Hands off. I chose Spence, you chose Cam. We were supposed to *both* be married by now so that we'd be sisters," Sage reminded her.

"You chose the better brother," Grace grumbled.

"I did do well," Sage said. "But so did you. If you would get over your silly pride and jump that man, you'd feel so much better. He's in love with you, and you're in love with him. You know that in the end it will all work out, so why not skip the melodrama and just get to the *I do*s?"

"Who are you and what have you done with Sage Whitman? Marriage has morphed you into some other human being—certainly not my shy BFF," Grace snapped, exasperated.

"She was a bore. Spence makes me come alive—actually makes me *come* over and over and over again. And when you feel as good as I do, you want everyone you love to feel the same way," Sage told her, a bit smugly.

Grace rolled her eyes. "Oh, my gosh! It's been so long since I've been around people in love, I forgot how nauseating it is," she grumbled. "And Cam and I are certainly not in love with each other. That died ten years ago."

"True love never dies. It may dim, and it may drift to the far reaches of your mind if you allow it to, but all it takes is a spark, a scent, a memory, and in a flash, you're back at the moment your heart fluttered for the first time. You and Cam are meant to be, so no matter how much you fight it, the result will be you in a beautiful wedding gown, and me picking out my *own* maid—no, *matron*—of honor dress. I so don't trust you with that task," Sage said, and just then her beeper went off.

"I wouldn't trust me, either, after the awful dress I had to wear to *your* wedding," Grace growled. "Not that I'm going to be getting married, especially to Camden Whitman."

"Denial, denial. And that dress was from Paris and absolutely fabulous."

"I'll let you think so," Grace said. "Where are we going now?" Sage was once again on the move.

"To the ER."

Grace trailed behind her friend toward the emergency room, knowing their time was about up.

When a child came in on a stretcher, blood pouring down his hand and his parents sobbing as they were led in right behind him, Grace decided that this scene was just too much for her. Especially after the loss she herself had suffered so many years ago.

"I'll call you later. I'm going behind the doors now."

Grace backed away as Sage's favorite nurse, Mo, ran by holding up a Broselow tape, ready to assist in the trauma. "I hope you got some coffee into your friend, Grace, because we're going to need her brain working at full capacity."

"I did, Mo. Good luck," Grace called back before turning to leave.

Before the door shut behind them, Grace watched this superstar team begin work on the small child.

"We have a two-year-old, approximately fourteen-foot fall out of a window. She has a Glasgow coma scale of seven but the medic couldn't get a breathing tube in her because . . . well, frankly, because it's his first day on his own and he sounded like it may be his last. BP is sixty-four over thirty-two, HR one fourteen, RR twelve, and are assisted with a bag valve mask. Oxygenation is ninety-one percent and trending down. The medic got a twenty-two-gauge IV to her left AC and should be arriving any moment," Mo called, ever efficient.

"Everyone in this hospital fears that woman, but Mo sure loves my wife."

Grace jumped at finding Spence next to her. "Is the little girl going to be okay?" she asked, not wanting the answer if it was bad.

"She will be if my wife and Mo have anything to do with it," Spence told her.

"Are we keeping you from something, Cheryl?" Mo shouted at a lab tech, who quickly put her phone away and stood at attention.

"She has a roar but she's got a heart as big as Texas," Spence said.

"I've always enjoyed her. Sage loves her to pieces," Grace replied.

The brand-new paramedic spoke with a shaking voice, preventing Spence from saying anything else for a moment as they both listened. He confirmed Mo's findings.

With that, the medic, who was almost as pale as the patient, finished his job by helping to get the patient transferred to the hospital's gurney and monitoring equipment. He slowly crept to the back of the room as if watching a movie unfold before him.

Sage began her head-to-toe assessment of the patient, calling out her findings. In minutes, the child was assessed, medicated, intubated, and on her way to the CT scan, and out of Grace's sight.

"I don't know how you do this day after day," Grace whispered.

"We do it because we make a difference," Spence told her, his hand resting on her shoulder.

They watched Mo walk over to the medic, who was obviously only still standing because of the counter behind him, holding him up. "Listen, kid, you did great . . . Not an easy call, but you managed everything perfectly." She walked toward Spence and Grace after that. "I think you saw way more than you wanted to see there, darling."

"Yeah. I really shouldn't have peeked in," Grace said, her voice shaking.

"We're here to help people. Sometimes it's messy, but at the end of the day we go home knowing we did everything we possibly could have." Mo walked away without waiting for a response.

"I have to get out of here," Grace told Spence.

Not paying attention to where she was going, she turned a corner and slammed into a rock-hard wall of flesh. She would have fallen on her butt if strong arms hadn't shot out and caught her.

"Twice in one day. I'm a lucky man."

Grace had to crane her head back to look up into Cam's smiling face. Quickly, he lost the smile and concern took its place.

"What's the matter?"

"Nothing. I need to get out of here," she said, her stomach shaking with the control it was taking not to throw up.

"Something's wrong," he told her as he took her arm and began steering her down the hallway toward the exit of the building.

"I just watched a trauma patient come in. It shook me up," Grace admitted as they reached the outside of the building.

"I'm sorry," he said, but she could see he was just humoring her.

She was silent for a moment while she took some deep breaths. "What are you doing here?" she finally asked.

"I came in to talk to Spence and I saw you," Cam replied.

"Well, then, I guess I have bad timing," she told him.

"Or *great* timing," he answered before he pulled her into his arms.

"Cam, stop," she said, but she couldn't seem to pull away.

"It looks like you really need this." That was her only warning before he lowered his head and captured her mouth. Later, Grace would blame shock for needing five minutes before she managed to wobble away on shaky knees.

10

"So, not to be nosy or anything, but usually when you kiss a woman, she doesn't go running."

Cam turned around to see his brother standing in the doorway, a grin on his face. "She had someplace to be. What are you doing out here?" Cam murmured.

"I was looking for Grace. She was shaken up."

"Well, luckily I was here to comfort her," Cam replied.

"Must not have been too comforting by the way she ran away from you," Spence said.

"There wasn't an issue with the kiss. The issue was spending time with you."

"All righty, then. If you say so."

"Don't you have lives to save? As a big, bad doctor, I would think you'd have far more important things to do than spy on your brother."

"Nah, I have a competent staff. Besides, because I'm a married man with a single brother, I'd say your love life is more interesting than babysitting said competent staff who know how to do their jobs well.

At least, that's how I see it," Spence told him. "What are you doing down here, anyway?"

"I wanted to see you, though I'm regretting that choice," Cam said before sighing. "I've been trying to get Grace to talk to me about her case, and she manages to avoid it like it's a freaking plague I'm trying to infect her with. I should just give up, but we both know I won't do that. She thinks if she just runs far enough and fast enough from her problems, they'll all go away. The law doesn't work that way."

"You don't have to lecture me. You may be the lawyer in the family, but I'm the one with all the brains," Spence said.

"Ha! I think you bribed your way through medical school."

"Well . . . Okay, let's be serious," Spence said, all traces of amusement gone. "It's time we talk about who has the better looks."

It took a moment for Cam to realize his brother was still kidding around. "Seriously, how *did* you get through medical school?"

"My good looks, of course. It's how I got the girl, too. Anytime you need any pointers, just come see your big brother."

"You're a pain in the ass, Spence. I should go see Jackson. At least he'll say something worth hearing."

"Ouch. You're wounding my pride," Spence replied.

"Yeah, if that were possible, I'd see monkeys taking over the hospital, too. And now you've kept me here BS-ing with you for so long that I'm sure Grace is miles away. I'd intended to chase her back down."

"Since she's gone, you can join me for some mouthwatering cafeteria food. I'm starving."

"You *look* like you're starving. Or not. Have you . . . put on a few pounds since getting married?" Cam mocked as the two began walking down the hallway.

"My wife keeps me well fed," Spence said with a laugh. "Okay, maybe the cook keeps me fed. Neither Sage nor I have time to mess around in the kitchen. But I'm still hotter than ever." With that, he lifted the top of his scrubs partway up and slapped his solid abs.

"Humble, too," Cam said with a roll of the eyes.

"When you got it, you got it," Spence said. "And boy, do I got it."

"Your humility is one of my favorite things about you, big bro." Just when he finished speaking, Sage ran up and squeezed between them as they walked down the hallway, linking each of her arms in one of theirs.

"Mmm, I don't know why you didn't run away with me, woman. You smell good enough to eat," Cam said, and he leaned in and kissed her cheek.

"I smell like urine and blood, but you can try to charm me all you want," she told him with a smile. "And I would have certainly chased after you, since you're so much younger and more suave than your brother. Sadly, though, your heart is already taken," she sighed.

"Ha! My heart will remain intact forever."

"You can't have something that you've already given away," she told him with a sassy shake of her hips, then she pulled away from the men and snatched up a tray.

"Dang, woman, you in a hurry?" Cam asked while Sage loaded her tray up, leaving them in the dust.

Turning, she threw them a flirtatious smile. "Do you know how many of my lunches have been interrupted? I grab what I can and fill my pockets for later most of the time," she said before reaching the register. Cam had only one item on his tray—a tempting chocolate muffin.

"She's an intern still. She doesn't want to miss a thing," Spence said, moving much more slowly than his wife.

"She's also married to the boss," Cam pointed out.

"And she would never, ever use that advantage. I think being married to me makes her feel she has more to prove."

"The competitive world of medicine," Cam said, sighing, feigning the deepest compassion.

"Oh, like it was any different for you in law school," Spence said as they paid for their lunches and went to join Sage.

"Fine. We're both competitive."

"We're going to have a small party tomorrow

night. Bring the corn and some whiskey," Spence told him, changing the subject.

"Is Grace invited?" Cam asked before taking a bite of his sandwich.

"Yep."

"I'm in."

He stayed for another half hour before Spence was called to the ER. Cam had only one day to think of another approach for dealing with Grace. He wanted to help her with the case—and get the girl.

11

"I don't care about your salad. Yes, you're a genius at making things that don't actually need to be cooked. I want to hear about the kiss that left you weak in the knees," Sage said into the phone.

"How in the world do you know about that?" Grace gasped as she looked around for hidden cameras in her apartment. She wouldn't be surprised to find them there, what with everything else that had been happening lately.

"I know things, especially things that happen in my hospital," Sage told her. "And don't think I wasn't fooled by the fact that you weren't answering your phone last night."

"He kissed me . . . again . . . and then I ran like a chicken from a fox."

"Uh-uh, little girl. I want details. You've been so closed up when it comes to Cam, and that's breaking every code in the best friends' rule book. I want details—now!"

"What do you want to hear? That his warm lips on

mine left me tingling, or that I berated myself all the way home for my self-betrayal? Or how about the fact that I slept horribly last night because that one little kiss raised my body temperature to about a hundred and ten degrees, and I tossed and turned all night?"

"Why don't you just admit that you aren't over this man? That you'll never be over him? Then you can quit suffering and enjoy him to the fullest, or at least he can fill certain parts of your body to the fullest . . ." Sage chuckled.

"You find yourself so amusing, Sage. Look, you know what it was like for me after we broke up. And you know the type of relationships I was in after him. Cam has grown so much more . . . controlling, so demanding. He's not the sweet teenage boy I fell in love with once upon a time," Grace said.

"Of course he's not a silly teenage boy. He's a man who knows how to please a woman, and his sights are all set on you."

"I don't want his sights set on me. I want him to leave me alone."

"You might be able to lie to a lot of people, Grace, but I'm not one of them—poor saps who think you're a woman of the world, tough and independent. Yes, you are amazing, and strong, but you love him, have always loved him, and all you're doing is prolonging the inevitable by fighting against him and yourself."

"Why, again, are we best friends?" Grace asked with a furrowed brow.

"Because I will always tell you how it is, whether it's what you want to hear or not," Sage replied.

"Ugh. That's not your greatest quality. Your job is to drown yourself in misery with me anytime I need a friend to bash men; it's not to tell me I'm in love with the one man I shouldn't be in love with. There are things I can't tell you—that I won't tell you—right now about Cam. I don't want you to hate him. I just . . . I just don't think I can do this again. Wanting him and knowing he's not right for me are two different matters."

"Number one, I wouldn't be your true friend if I said only what you wanted to hear. Only those who want to please you tell you a bunch of crap. A true friend tells you what you *need* to hear. And number two, you know this will kill me not knowing what you can't tell me, but because I do love you, I will be patient and wait it out."

"I do love you, even if you are a royal pain in the ass. Hey, remember what Shakespeare said? 'The first thing we do, let's kill all the lawyers.' You know, we could just shoot all the men in the world and live together happily ever after."

"Trust me, I've thought about that," Sage said, "but I just can't give up the sex. Now that I've discovered it, it's too damn hot to ever let go of."

"Fine, you hussy, be that way. But that's not what I called you about."

"So speak to me. You know I'll be honest, Grace."

"It's strange, really. I think I'm getting Alzheimer's or something." Grace looked around her apartment, trying to see whether anything seemed out of place. Was she just paranoid, or did she have something to be afraid of?

"Um, Grace. You're only twenty-eight. I don't think you're ready for the nursing home quite yet."

"I don't know. It's just little stuff, but it's making me feel like I'm going out of my mind."

"Okay, start from the beginning and tell me what's happening," Sage said, but something in the background started beeping. "Crap! Hold on."

Grace listened in, hearing a lot of frantic movement, and the beeping sound grew more intense, making her pull the phone away from her ear. All of which was followed by a few colorfully unladylike words from her best friend.

A couple of minutes later, Sage came back on the line, and the beeping grew softer. "Sorry about that. I was boiling eggs and I let the damn water evaporate again. The eggs started burning and then exploded onto the hood vent, and the smoke detector went off. I don't know why I attempt to cook. Mrs. Brinkman is going to have my hide when she gets back from her days off."

"You have got to be the only person I know who gets so distracted boiling water that you nearly burn the house down."

"Listen, missy. I clearly remember being your

roommate for a while. I know you aren't any better in the kitchen than I am," Sage reminded her. "Now tell me what's been happening."

"So this morning I ran out to check the mailbox, because it's been about a week, and I could have sworn I passed the newspaper sitting in front of my door, and then when I went back up the stairs and came inside, that paper was sitting on the kitchen table, and it was open. I know I must have done it, but I just can't remember doing it," Grace said, sighing.

"All right, maybe you *are* losing it." Sage laughed, making Grace feel better.

To tell the truth, it had really creeped her out, but she wasn't exactly a morning person, and she could have easily taken the paper in and flung it on the table hard enough that it opened and then forgotten that she'd done it.

"I just have to remember not to even open my front door until I've had at least two full cups of coffee," Grace replied.

"I agree. Sadly enough, I think I drink at least fifteen cups when I'm working, especially an overnight shift."

"Well, your days as an intern are just about up, aren't they?" Grace asked.

"Yes, thank goodness. I only have six months to go, and then we're going to party like it's, well, like it's the end of my schooling forever."

"Good. Now I need to get off the phone so I can

finish making this salad—one of the few items I *can* make—and then get over to your house on time," Grace told her.

They ended the call and Grace crumbled up her crispy noodles, adding them to the salad just as her doorbell rang. Was it Girl Scout cookie time? She pulled the door open to find Cam on the other side. The instant ache in her core wasn't the most positive of signs. Damn this man and the way he made her feel.

"Evening," he said, a big smile on his face.

"What are you doing here, Cam?"

"I thought I'd be kind and offer you a ride out to Spence's house."

"I have a car, thank you," she said, and tried to shut the door.

"Now, don't be rude. You know you're going to want to have a few drinks, and you don't want to drink and drive, do you?" he asked, holding out his arm to prevent her from slamming the door shut.

"I'm not a moron, Cam. I don't do that. It's called restraint," she countered before she realized what he'd said. "Wait a minute. How do you know I'm going out there?"

"I was invited, too," he informed her, and that damnable smile returned—if anything, it was even brighter.

"Ugh! This had so better not be matchmaking," she warned. "Just because we've shared a few kisses in the last year—" she started to say, when he broke in.

"Don't forget about our incredible sex the night of Spence and Sage's wedding."

"I did forget, thank you," she said. By the twinkle in his eyes, she had no doubt that he knew she was lying. Of course she hadn't forgotten. How could she when he was the only man who had managed to make her feel as if she were floating while he traced his fingers across her eager flesh? His kisses since then kept reminding her of how much pleasure he was capable of bringing her.

It was best for everyone concerned—okay, it was best for just her alone if she stayed as far away from Camden Whitman as possible. Her body called her a liar. Her mind told her she was smart to avoid him. And her heart? She wasn't even going to listen to the beating of her heart. It had never steered her in the right direction.

"You can say whatever you want, but your eyes tell me the truth," he said, stepping closer.

"Knock it off, Cam." Her voice was weak as she held up a hand. She knew he could easily overpower her, because they both knew she wanted him.

"I'm just trying to give you a ride, Grace."

"The ride is what I'm afraid of," she said dryly.

Cam laughed and moved in closer, cornering her against the table and lifting a hand to trail it through her loose tendrils of hair. "The ride is the best part," he whispered.

She pulsed deep inside as her womanhood clamored for what his eyes were promising.

"Cam . . . don't . . ." She was seconds away from falling into his arms.

"Okay, I'm sorry." He backed off, disappointing her and yet making her appreciate him at the same time.

Yep. She was certainly crazy. That was the only explanation for the things she was forgetting doing, and her wild emotions she couldn't get a grasp on.

"How many people are going to be at your brother's tonight? He made it sound like it was just a small family dinner. I should have been suspicious," she said, trying to get back on track.

"I think only a few people are coming over."

"How many is 'a few'?" she asked.

"Okay, fine. You know my brother. Probably fifty or so," he answered, finally giving her some much-needed space and walking over to her freshly made salad. He grabbed a fork and dipped in for a bite.

"That's rude, Cam," she snapped, snatching the fork from him before he could double-dip. "Anyway, I don't think I have nearly enough salad, so back off." As her temper rose, so did her attitude. "And who invited you inside, anyway? What makes you think you can barge into my house and make yourself so at home? I'm tired of you using your charm and getting your way every time I blink."

"I'm worried about you," he told her, his voice suddenly hushed.

The actual concern she saw entering his eyes made her tense. "Why are you worried about me?"

"When I stayed over the other night, when you had that cold, I heard something. When I went outside, there was a screwdriver below your window," he said.

Grace knew Cam well enough to know when he was being serious and when he was kidding. She didn't like the true worry she saw on his face.

"And why didn't you tell me about this sooner?"

"Because I didn't want you to be afraid. So I've been keeping an eye on you, on the place, and maybe a few friends are doing the same when I'm unable to."

By the look in his eyes, it was more than obvious that he was waiting for her to lay into him. The problem was that she didn't feel like doing that. She felt . . . dammit . . . she felt a smidgen of fear. What in the world was going on?

"Well, you *should* have told me, Cam. Still, I'm sure it was nothing." But if it was nothing, why was she so alarmed?

"I'm hoping it was nothing, but you live here all alone. I don't think that's wise. I think what would be wiser would be for you to come and share my place. I'm even generous enough to let you share my bed. Let's just say I'm a stand-up guy. The bed's quite comfortable. You remember, right?" he said, taking a step back toward her.

"Stop right there!" She shook her head violently and scurried around to the other side of the table. There was no way she was doing this with him again. If his lips touched hers, the two of them would be going nowhere anytime soon.

"If I promise to lay off . . . for now." He made sure to inject a long pause. "Will you just come to the get-together at your best friend's house?"

She thought long and hard about it before nodding her agreement. That didn't mean she was going to ride with him. They could argue about that in the parking lot.

"Good then. It's all settled. You can sit by the fire, have a few laughs, and if you get too cold, I'll make sure to keep you warm," he said with a wink.

"You just said you were going to lay off," she pointed out.

"I said 'for now.'"

"Ah, you're always such a gentleman," she said, rolling her eyes. "Let me tell you, though, that if I need warming up, I am perfectly capable of finding someone . . . else . . . willing to do it."

The flare in his eyes told her he didn't like that response at all. That was just too bad for him. It made her feel a lot better to get under his thick hide.

"Don't forget your coat. The sun's almost down. It's going to cool off within the next hour."

Before she could get it herself, Cam was gathering up her coat, handing it to her, and pushing her out the door. They reached the top of the steps together, and for once, Grace was incredibly grateful Cam was there, because her foot slipped, and she almost went tumbling down the solid wooden staircase.

If it hadn't been for Cam's quick thinking, she didn't know what would have happened. He dropped her salad bowl but caught her, and the two of them teetered for a few terrifying seconds while he regained his balance.

"What the heck?" she cried out as she clung to him.

"You're not usually so klutzy," he said, his voice a little breathless. "That scared the hell out of me!"

"What did I slip on?"

Cam backed up, still holding on to her, and they both glanced around for the culprit. Something green and slimy was on the top step. "What is that?" Cam bent down to take a closer look.

"Jell-O?" she asked.

"I don't know, but if your neighbors drop something, especially right here, then they should have the decency to clean it up before someone else comes along and gets seriously hurt," he said, looking both ways down the open walkway. "Give me your keys. I'm going to run inside and grab some paper towels. We don't want someone else to stumble on this."

With that, he took her keys and did exactly as he said he would, getting the mess cleaned up in no time at all. "This is what I hate about apartments. The low maintenance is great, but the shared space isn't so wonderful."

"When have *you* ever lived in an *apartment*?" she asked with a pointed look.

"I lived in one all through college," he bragged, as if proud of himself.

"What? No mansion on the hill? I thought the privileged Camden Whitman would simply insist on taking over one of the frat houses."

"Come on, Grace, you didn't exactly grow up in a cottage," he told her with a raised eyebrow.

"Yeah, but I wasn't nearly as arrogant as you've always been."

"Ha! I didn't live in that big house on the hill until my father adopted me," he reminded her, his bravado dropping away, and for a moment the lost little boy who'd been found by Martin Whitman showed up in his beautiful eyes.

Grace could have kicked herself. How in the world had she forgotten that Spence, Jackson, and Cam had all been adopted by Martin after they had saved his only biological son, Michael, from drowning? Of course, no one ever really thought about it, because

Martin didn't treat them as adopted children at all. They were just his sons.

"Sorry," she mumbled feebly.

"Don't start. I hate it when people do that. I was far more fortunate than most, because I got out of the system and was taken into a home full of love. And I got three brothers out of the deal as an added bonus. Not even a tiny percentage of kids in the system get it as good as I did."

"Okay."

"Now, Grace, back to this apartment situation . . ." he began.

"It doesn't really matter. My house is going to be finished next week. I've lived in these apartments for over a year now, so it will almost be sad to leave," she said before turning and giving him a smile. "I'm totally lying. I can't wait to have a huge tub and a deck I can sit on while I drink my morning coffee."

"If you had decided to build when you first came back, you could have been living there now."

"I wasn't ready then to make that decision, Cam. I wasn't sure if I was staying here or not."

"So you've decided to stay for good?"

The hope in his eyes was almost too much to take.

"Or maybe I just want a good investment and I'm going to rent the place out," she told him flippantly.

"Come on, you know you're moving into the place you designed," he said, a frustrated sigh escaping his lips.

She decided to give him a break. "Yes, for now I'll be moving in there."

"In that case, I'll be sure to come help with the boxes."

"Don't worry about it. Sage and Spence are helping, and I don't have a lot of stuff."

"When someone offers to help you, Grace, the polite thing is to say thanks and give a grateful smile," he said before leering at her. "And, of course, to jump into their arms, wrap your legs around them, and lay a big, fat, juicy one on their waiting lips."

He opened the passenger-side door of his car and stood close enough that she had no choice but to brush against him as she climbed in.

"Do you think about anything other than sex?" she asked him.

"Not really. I've got the proverbial one-track mind."

"You're impossible, but if I need a favor that I'm supposed to repay with kisses, I'll have to remember that the next time Mr. Longsteine offers to take down my trash for me," she said as she made herself comfortable in the passenger's seat.

"Isn't he something like eighty years old?"

"Yep, so I'll probably give him a heart attack."

"You're an evil woman, Grace."

"I try."

Cam shut her door and was climbing into the driver's seat within seconds. It wasn't until they were on the road that she realized he'd kept her so busy, she'd forgotten that she hadn't wanted to ride with him in the first place.

Camden Whitman was too smooth for her own good. What on earth was she going to do about it?

12

A get-together at any of the Whitmans' places wasn't just a casual dinner and small talk around a table. Oh, no. It was laughter, music, noise, children running around, and hardworking people letting go on a Friday night.

Cam and Grace walked inside the mansion her bestie Sage referred to modestly as a "house," and people were scattered throughout.

"Let's head to the back. That's where the real fun is," Cam told her, and before she could refuse, he was taking her hand and leading her through the maze of hallways.

A brightly burning fire, at a safe distance from the house, caught Grace's immediate attention, and the smell of barbecued meat filled the air. She hadn't felt hungry up until that very moment and she was surprised when she began to salivate and the muscles in her stomach started to constrict and growl.

Surveying the tables to the right, she winced

slightly—her salad hadn't made it to the event when countless other delightful dishes had.

"Grace. You're late," Spence said as he came up and pulled her away from Cam. She missed the wink he sent his brother, but she didn't miss the scowl Cam shot him.

"I dropped the salad and almost fell down the stairs. It's a long and boring story. I'm sorry," she told him as she gave him a quick squeeze to return his embrace.

"Bummer. I love your salads, but I'm certainly glad you didn't fall and break something. Of course, with two excellent surgeons here, we would have fixed you up in no time."

Cam guffawed. "Any chance to brag, huh, brother?"

"Well, of course," Spence replied, feigning innocence as he kept his arm around Sage.

Sage felt as if she were in a battle of wills, and she wanted no part of it. She shifted on her feet and planned her escape route.

"Grace, you're acting like a fish out of water. Knock it off. You know everyone here," Sage said as she joined them.

"I don't know what's wrong with me. I guess I've just been sort of antisocial the last few months," Grace said with a laugh, grateful for the interruption.

"It's about time that ends." Sage was emphatic.

"I agree. I never see you anymore." Alyssa Whitman, Jackson's wife, broke through the crowd and gave Grace a hug. "We haven't done a girls' night in what seems like forever."

"Maybe because you're about two years pregnant," Sage replied.

"I know! I think this baby is protesting the whole idea of coming out," Alyssa said. "I warned my doctor that if she doesn't enter this world on her due date, I'm leaving her no choice."

Jackson spoke now. "I want you both safe and healthy, but I have to admit, I'm pretty excited about meeting my new daughter."

"Wow, Jackson, three girls in one house. You're getting overrun," Spence teased.

"And I'm loving every minute of it. Angel is the biggest blessing I could ever imagine, and this new little girl is going to wrap me around her finger, too." His eyes softened instantly as he talked about his daughters. The world thought Jackson was so hard, but he was a puddle of mush when it came to his family.

"Yeah, she'll have us all wrapped," Cam chimed in.

Against her will, Grace felt her heart begin to melt even more at Cam's confession. One thing she'd always considered pretty amazing about Cam and his brothers was the deep bond they shared with their neighbors, friends, and children. The world didn't seem to grow men like that anymore.

Shaking her head to clear those thoughts away,

Grace tried to tune back in to the conversation again. She didn't need to be thinking about what a great guy Cam was. Sure, he was wonderful, but their time together was long past. They'd given it a shot when she was a teenager and it hadn't worked. They'd both be much better off looking ahead and not behind.

"As much as I love my husband," Alyssa said, "I've had enough of his overprotectiveness this last month, so let's ditch the men for a while and see what treats the neighbors brought." She took Sage and Grace's arms and led them away.

"It's only because I love you!" Jackson called out after them, and the three women grinned at each other.

"I can't believe how much I adore that man," Alyssa said with a sigh. "But my back is on fire, and I haven't seen my feet in two months, so when I do deliver this child, I don't think I'm going to be loving him so much."

"At least it's a healthy pregnancy and this little girl is going to come out chubby and smiling," Sage replied.

"Amen to that. I have never been so scared as when Angel came too soon. I didn't even know babies could be that tiny," Alyssa confessed, her expression somber.

"She's still a petite little thing," Grace said, "but with those blond curls and big brown eyes, she's about the cutest little girl I've ever seen."

"Yes, I agree, but then, I'm pretty dang biased," Alyssa said with a wink.

"Enough about food and babies. I want to know what the deal is with you and Cam. You guys drove here together?" Sage asked.

"How do you know we didn't just get here at the same time?" Grace replied, with one eyebrow raised but otherwise giving nothing away with her features.

"Um, pretty obvious when you walked back here hand in hand," Sage told her with a knowing stare.

"Crap. You would have to notice that," Grace moaned. "He just showed up at my apartment and told me I was riding with him, then I almost slipped down the stairs, he caught me, and I suddenly found myself in his car. I didn't plan on riding with him."

"I almost miss the days when Jackson was chasing me," Alyssa said with a laugh. "Wait, he still chases me around, so I don't really know what's changed except that we sleep in the same bed every night now."

Sage had to put in her two cents' worth. "I fought like crazy not to fall in love with Spence all over again. But it was a lost cause from the beginning because I never fell *out* of love with him. We can put our love on hold, as I've told you, Grace, but once you feel true love, you can never push it away again. You might as well just admit defeat now."

"He just wants to be friends," Grace insisted, and the other two women rolled their eyes. "Okay, he might want to be 'friends with benefits.' But a happily-ever-after is completely out of the question. It's come and gone."

Grace needed to believe what she herself was saying right then, and the problem was . . . she didn't.

"Well, then you might want to alert Cam to that fact, because right now the man is drinking in every part of you with his eyes. He can't seem to look away."

"You two are horrible, and I refuse to stand here and fight when I'm sure to lose. So let's talk about kids, childbirth, the government—anything other than Camden Whitman," she begged with large pleading eyes.

"Fine," Sage told her. "We'll be good for at least fifteen minutes."

"I'll be happy with fifteen minutes. Because that gives me time to consume at least two drinks, and then I'll be numb to whatever you have to say." Grace injected her words with a syrupy sweetness, and she batted her eyelashes to heighten the effect.

The three of them got something to eat and drink and went in search of a comfortable place to sit—not an easy task for Alyssa, with her belly sticking out a mile.

"You lush," Alyssa told her with a pout. "It's just not fair that someone in my condition can have only *virgin* drinks. The boat sailed on my virginity a long time ago."

"My heart bleeds for you," Grace countered. "Your life with Jackson must be a living hell. But this is goooooood. I don't know what's in this so-called jungle juice, and I probably don't want to know."

"Stop trying to torment me. I'd kill for just a glass of wine," Alyssa groaned.

"I'll have one for you. I'm not on call tonight." Sage smiled broadly.

"You're just too kind."

"I know, Alyssa. Oddly enough, I get that a lot."

The three women sat back, and soon Grace did feel better. She let her worries drift away and simply basked in the pleasure of spending time with her friends. Soon she wouldn't even notice that Cam was there. Even if she had to lie to herself and play tricks on her mind. The brain was a powerful tool, one that you could program to do what you wanted. At least if you were determined enough.

When there was a murmuring in the crowd, Grace didn't pay the least attention. There were dozens of people around, so a little chaos was expected. But soon her eyes shot open, when her foot was kicked, making her jump and causing her to spill some of her much-needed drink.

Looking up, she found Kitty standing before her, clutching two pieces of blue fabric in her hand, murder in her eyes. What the hell?

"Kitty? What are you doing here? Were you invited?" Grace asked as she sat up and stared at her client from hell.

"No, I wasn't invited to this hillbilly festival," the woman snarled, and looked around in disdain.

"Then what in the world are you doing here?" Grace didn't notice the crowd quieting so they could all listen in.

"I couldn't reach you on your cell, which I find quite disturbing, since you are working for me, so I called your mother to find out where in the world you were," the woman said, looking Grace over to find the device.

"I don't have it on me. When I'm with my friends, I find it rude to play with my phone," Grace told her.

"It's your job to be available to me 24/7, Grace. And there's an emergency," Kitty snarled.

"What possible emergency could there be? The wedding is over a month away," Grace reminded her.

"Does this look like Persian blue to you?" Kitty practically screamed as she thrust one of the pieces of fabric in Grace's face. "Does it?"

Grace was so caught off guard she didn't know what to do or say. Her cheeks heated as the display continued in front of her friends.

"When I called the supply house, I told them Persian blue, and it said Persian blue on the tags, so I assumed that was exactly what it was," Grace told her.

"This isn't Persian blue," Kitty snapped. *"This*

is," she said, holding up a piece of fabric that looked identical to the one she was waving about in anger.

"Honestly, they look exactly the same to me," Grace told her.

"How can you call yourself an event planner if you can't even tell the difference between Persian blue and whatever the hell this color of blue is?"

Grace was quickly losing her cool. Finally, she stood, going face-to-face with Kitty. She had to tell herself to remain calm. No matter how bad the client was, she was still a client, and it was Grace's job to make her happy.

"I'm so sorry, Kitty. I will take the two swatches to the supply house and make sure we fix this mess."

When Grace spoke calmly, it calmed Kitty somewhat. She was still practically shaking with anger, and it took all of Grace's control not to snap, but somehow she was beginning to defuse the situation.

"Okay, then. I'll leave you to it. This smoke from your little bonfire thing is hurting my delicate skin."

Without saying anything more, the woman turned and walked away, most likely to find the broomstick she'd come in on.

"What in the hell was that?" Sage asked as she came to stand by Grace.

"That's my hell. Kitty Grier, so far the worst client I've had," Grace said with a shudder.

"Damn, Grace. You really need a new job." Sage laughed before taking the nearly empty cup Grace had been holding and replacing it with a full glass of pure goodness.

"You know what I need," Grace said before taking a long swallow.

"Forget about her. Let's go back to relaxing," Sage wisely told her.

Soon, Kitty was forgotten, so Grace resumed her position in the chair and closed her eyes. She would eventually get one day—just one, that's all she was asking—when there was absolutely zero drama.

Unfortunately, today hadn't been that day.

13

Cam felt as if he were in a trance. His eyes were drawn to this incredible woman, and he was hopelessly captivated by every little thing about Grace Sinclair. The way she tipped her head back and filled the air with the sound of her contagious laughter—it stopped him in his tracks. And he wasn't the only one who was spellbound.

Surveying the room quickly, he found many admiring eyes. *Endearing* was the word for her. As she sat back in her chair, unconscious of her charms, she twirled her long strands of hair in her finger and tilted her head to the side, eyes wide while she listened intently to the conversation bubbling around her.

It had been so long since he'd held her in his arms, sunk deep inside her body. Their coming together again was inevitable, and it was the last thing he should be thinking of at this moment. Something bad was going on in her life, and he needed to focus on helping her. But who said he couldn't offer up a little temptation along the way? They had once been good together. He was positive they could be that way again.

"You and Grace have sure been spending a lot of time together," Jackson said as he followed Cam's line of sight and smirked at the target just before taking a swig of beer.

"Yeah," Spence added. "Having little kissing sessions in the hallways of hospitals, catching her from falling at her apartment, even staying the night and nursing her back to health. Hmmmm."

"Shut up, both of you," Cam grumbled, pulling his gaze from Grace so he could focus on his brothers. He knew that if he let them get too out of hand, he'd be saying something he shouldn't—something he wouldn't be able to take back.

Yes, he wanted Grace, but his feelings ran much deeper than that, and those feelings were for him to think about and analyze. They weren't to be put on display for all the world to see, especially not for his brothers.

"What? We just want to help you out," Jackson said far too innocently.

Michael joined the group. "What am I missing?"

"We were just telling Cam how good Grace looks and how we noticed they've been spending a lot of time together," Spence piped up.

"And she belongs to me, so back off," Cam told them. Hell, he couldn't lie to his brothers. The situation would only grow worse if he did.

"Didn't you tell me earlier you were simply trying to help her with a case?" Michael asked.

"I *am* trying to help her with a case, but there's . . . history between us. The situation isn't exactly black-and-white," Cam said. "Enough, okay?" He was really hoping they would now drop their line of questioning.

He could hope, but that had never gotten him anywhere.

"Just throw her over your shoulder and take ownership," Jackson said with a laugh before looking over his own shoulder to be sure his wife hadn't heard him say that.

"Mighty big words, Jackson. They'd have more impact if you didn't look so worried right now," Spence said, grinning widely. "Talk about whipped."

"You're one to talk. I would love to know what Sage would think about some of the comments *you* just made, big brother," Jackson fired back.

"Okay, truce. Our wives would kill us," Spence said. "I'm not ashamed to admit it—not in the least."

"You know what? I didn't ask for any of your opinions, and I certainly don't want them," Cam said between clenched teeth. Then he zeroed in on Michael. "Why have you been so secretive lately?"

Michael froze before looking around, acting even more suspiciously. "I have no idea what you're talking about," he finally said.

"Come to think of it, I haven't seen you around much. Where have you been?" Jackson asked.

Now all the brothers were gazing at the youngest Whitman, who was shifting in his seat.

"Is there a girl involved here, Mikey?" Spence asked.

"No," Michael shouted before lowering his voice. "I don't want a girl. I like being single," he finished.

"I don't believe you," Cam said. Obviously something was up.

"I'm done with this conversation. You guys need to get a life of your own if you're so freaking worried about the love lives of other people." Michael stomped off.

"He's got a point," Cam said. Then he hotfooted it toward the cooler, where he grabbed a fresh beer and decided he was better off sitting by the fire to brood, alone, until the steaks were done.

"WOW, IT APPEARS as if two of your sons are pretty upset," Joseph Anderson said with a congratulatory clap on Martin's shoulder.

The two old men had witnessed the brotherly banter and they were grinning like fools though trying to remain hidden by the large oak tree in Spence's backyard.

"Yep. I knew setting that file on Cam's desk would do the trick. Grace kept on shooing him away and he wasn't moving fast enough for my liking," Martin said. "But now I'm also curious about what's going on with Michael."

"I have to say, you learned from the best, but you might just be exceeding me when it comes to match-making," Joseph replied. He had to struggle to keep his naturally booming voice low.

"I'm just glad you were able to make it down this weekend. I have a lot to fill you in on," Martin told him.

"Yes, phone calls get mighty old after a while," Joseph agreed.

"What are you two doing hiding behind this tree?" Maggie asked, making both men jump.

"Quiet, woman, or you're going to get us caught," Martin warned her, holding a finger to his lips to silence her further.

Maggie jerked her arms across her chest and let out a huff. "Don't you shush me, Martin Whitman, or I'll smack you."

"Are you three insane? You're starting to draw attention to yourselves over here," Eileen said in exasperation as she approached with Bethel. "How are we supposed to sneak away for our secret meeting if all eyes are on us?"

"Maggie started it," Joseph grumbled.

"I most certainly did not," Maggie replied haughtily. "And a gentleman would never shush a lady."

"You're right, darling," Martin said. "We weren't

being very inconspicuous. Let's go back to my place and get to planning. We'll give Cam and Grace a little more time to pull themselves together, but if they don't start moving faster, we might need to poke them along. We also need to start making plans for Michael. I can see something is up. I want to know what it is."

The group began moving toward their cars.

"What is going on with Michael?" Bethel asked. "I must have missed something."

"He's been disappearing for weeks at a time and he's being very secretive about it," Martin grumbled. "I just don't like it, especially after the display tonight."

"Well, don't you worry about it, Martin. We'll get it all worked out," Eileen assured him with a pat on the back.

"Of course we'll figure it out. I have no doubt of that with you all here," Martin said, and he gazed at Eileen long enough that a slight blush suffused her cheeks. "Did I tell you how beautiful you look tonight?"

"Oh, Martin. You're such a flirt," Eileen said with a youthful giggle, instantly shaving twenty years off her age.

"Only with you," he told her with a wink that made the blush turn into a full-blown flush.

"You two done flirting? It's cold out here," Bethel growled, but she softened her remark with a smile.

"We weren't flirting," Eileen insisted as they reached the car and climbed into the backseat.

Maggie chuckled. "Oh, come, now, Eileen, it's more than obvious that the two of you have been flirting for years now."

"You girls just hush. I don't want Martin to hear you, and he's about to open the driver's-side door."

"Maybe the two of you need some meddling done on *your* behalf," Bethel offered. The wheels were turning behind her eyes as she looked at Maggie.

"Don't you dare!" Eileen snapped, and playfully slapped Bethel's knee.

Then they couldn't say anything more, because Martin and Joseph climbed into the car. The women hoped the two men didn't notice the sudden silence.

"Hold on, ladies. We're going to take the back way home," Martin said with a laugh.

The group of lifelong friends had been through thick and thin together, and they were just barely tapping the surface of their adventures.

14

After a couple of hours, the crowd had thinned slightly, but the music had been turned up, and the party seemed to just be getting started. Grace knew she should try to sneak away, catch a ride back into town with someone, and let Cam figure out later that she was gone. But for some reason she didn't want to. What she wanted to do was enjoy the slight buzz drifting lazily through her body, sit by the glowing fire, and have Cam sitting right next to her. Her mind began to wander.

That most likely wasn't the smartest thing she could be doing. But why should she be smart all the time? Wasn't it okay to be naughty once in a while? Everyone thought Grace was the experienced one, the person who had the world in the palm of her hand.

She'd grown up with a wealthy family, in a beautiful home, and she'd traveled. Man, how she'd traveled. She'd gone to Europe, Australia, Japan, Russia, and so many other places, she couldn't even name them all. And she'd done most of it alone because she'd been running, either from her parents or from the ache in her heart after men had betrayed her. But one thing was for sure—Grace was sick and tired of running away.

Yes, she'd grown up with money. But she'd also grown up without love. She had thought she'd found love with the Whitmans, and she knew she shared a kindred love with her best friend, Sage, but Grace was so much more careful now when it came to such a crippling emotion.

Because aside from Sage and Grandma Bethel, Sage's grandmother, no one else she had ever loved and who had professed to love her in return had actually stuck around—not even Cam.

Maybe she had rejection issues, to use shrink-speak, and maybe she had issues with being controlled. But the reality was that it didn't matter what psychological problems she had or what she was afraid of. Because reality didn't lie, and the reality was that people she loved eventually always disappeared. Her heart couldn't handle any more bitterness or despair.

So it was much easier to put on a face, be the life of the party, and let the people around you think you were an unstoppable force. It was much easier not to get hurt when you wore a mask.

"Are you in a food coma?"

Grace was too relaxed at the moment to even tense

up at the sound of Cam's voice. He sat down next to her and lowered the back of his lawn chair, then turned on his side so he was facing her. Even though there were people milling all around, only the glow of the fire cast any light on the two of them, and the scene felt intensely intimate.

And with the crackling fire and the slow country song "Who I Am with You" playing, Grace felt her eyes drift a little as she looked at the boy who had turned into such a fine-looking man. Her resistance was zilch at the moment. She really should have tried to catch a ride home.

"I don't think I'll need to eat for at least a week," she finally said when she realized how long she'd gone without answering him.

"That was nothing. You've been to one of my dad's feasts," he said with a laugh.

Grace grinned in response. "Yes, I have, and you're right. I don't understand how people can prepare that much food, let alone eat it all."

"It's ranching country. We get hungry," he said with a wink.

"Camden Whitman, you sit behind a desk all day. If you're not careful, you won't be able to fit there with all the food you've been stuffing into that belly."

"Hey! I work out," he said as he rubbed his impressively ripped belly. "And I love cattle roundup time."

"Yeah, I have to admit, I missed that when I was

in the city. I even missed the smells here, if you can believe that," she said with a fond smile.

"I certainly believe it, Grace. I was away for seven years during college, only home for the holidays and part of the summer. I missed little old Sterling like crazy. It's insane, really, to miss this place when there's so much more world out there, but I think when you know home is somewhere else, you can never be happy no matter how glamorous or important you think your life is."

He sounded so uncharacteristically serious. Grace really wanted to ask him what the story was behind that last statement, but they weren't in a place in their lives anymore where she could sit and talk to him for hours about their hopes and dreams. She'd once known this man better than she knew herself, but that was a long time ago.

"I didn't know where home was for a really long time. That was pretty dang hard. After we left here, even though my parents based themselves in Missoula because of my father's company, we traveled the world. Then I was on my own, and I traveled even more. I honestly didn't think I would ever return here. I don't know why I did, really . . ." She looked away now, unable to look Cam in the eyes anymore.

"You came back because you know this is your home, Grace."

She didn't even try to fight it when Cam reached

out and grabbed her hand. What troubled her was how right it felt in the security of his palm.

She'd always felt safest when she was with Cam. How she wished she could turn back time. Turn back the horrors she'd faced over the years, turn back the last time she and Cam had said good-bye, turn it all back so she wasn't this empty shell she feared she had become.

"I don't know, Cam. I love being with Sage again, but she's in a different place in life than I am. Maybe I shouldn't have come back." She knew she'd hate herself in the morning for this moment of weakness, of opening up to a man—especially if that man was Cam.

"You're where you belong, Grace. I assure you of that. Sage adores you and so does my entire family," he said, squeezing her hand. "What happened while you were away? What won't you tell me?"

"I don't want to do this, Cam," she said, feeling tears choke her throat.

"I swear that all I want to do is help you, so if you just tell me your story, you can get it off your chest and it will help with this case hanging over your head," he said with such warmth in his voice that Grace found herself unable to hold back.

"I can't talk about this here," she whispered. "I don't want anyone to overhear us."

"But you will talk to me?" His voice showed a hint of excitement, and hope glinted in his soft eyes.

"I can't seem to keep fighting you on it, so, yes, I guess I will talk to you," she said. The strangest thing happened once she'd gotten those words out—a weight she hadn't known was there lifted from her chest.

Maybe Cam was right.

"Let's go to my house. It's just over the hill and we can talk all night if you're up to it," he said, standing and reaching out a hand.

"Your house?" she said, her stomach tightening. "I don't know if we should do that."

Red flags waved and loud sirens clanged inside her mind.

"Come on, Grace. I don't want you changing your mind in the time it will take to reach your place," he said with a laugh. "I promise not to bite you the minute we walk in the door."

And with that, he gave her no other choice. Without even letting her say good-bye to her hostess and best friend, he led her around the front of the house and practically stuffed her into his car. The motor was revving and they were heading down some tree-lined back road she'd never been on before. Within minutes were pulling up to Cam's place.

She'd never been to his place before, and as the beautiful three-story log home rose before her, Grace felt her insides stir. She wasn't strong enough to be alone with Cam here.

When she'd left New York, she vowed to quit

making mistakes. And she kept making them. So after Cam opened her car door and helped her climb out, she was berating herself all the way up the path to his front steps. Grace had zero doubt that she was making the mistake of her life by coming to her one-time lover's home—where they'd be all alone.

15

Cam saw a stern-looking man staring back at him in the bathroom mirror. He had to play this one carefully. No, *play* wasn't the word he wanted. He'd finally managed to win a modicum of Grace's trust, and he wasn't going to blow it because he couldn't keep his pants zipped and his constant erection where it belonged.

Dammit! It really sucked being a man. A little romance, a little wine, and the right words—that was probably all it would take, and he'd get her into his bed in no time flat. But that would make him just as big an asshole as the people who'd treated her so poorly that she was afraid to be open and honest anymore. And what if he was one of those people— one of the many who had made her feel that she needed to hide who she really was? He couldn't be sure that he wasn't one of them, and it scared the hell out of him.

Yes, they had both messed up when they were teenagers, but she shouldn't bear this much hostility toward him—not after ten years. He would hear her story. After that, he would be open and honest with her. He would tell her that he would be taking her to his bed soon. Very soon!

"Business first," he mumbled, shifting where he stood, hoping like hell he could get his body to listen to his mind. "Nope. Apparently not going to happen," he mumbled as he shifted again, so he gave up and left the bathroom.

He hoped she wasn't asleep.

"What took you so long?" she asked when he stepped into the living room.

"Did you miss me?"

"Hardly. I've grown quite accustomed to you disappearing, Cam." The words came out like a joke, but there was an underlying pain to her tone that made him stop for a moment where he was.

"I never meant to disappear on you, Grace."

"It doesn't really matter, though, does it?"

"It matters if, after all this time, you're still holding on to your resentment."

"It was a long time ago. But you know what they say . . ." She gave a bitter laugh.

"No. Not really. What do they say?" He couldn't help bracing himself for her answer.

"You never forget your first love. Your next lovers will never be privileged enough to get your entire heart, because you've already given a piece away."

How in the world had they gotten to this place so quickly?

Before he could respond, she laughed. "Lighten up, Cam. You want to talk business, so let's talk business."

Cam was almost unable to keep up with her. One second she displayed a sliver of vulnerability, and the next she was hiding behind dark humor and the shutters were over her eyes. This wasn't getting them anywhere.

"Good. Let's talk business," he said. He might as well go along with her on this, he told himself, so he switched gears.

"What do you need to know?"

"I need to know it all, Grace, even the stuff you might not think is relevant. You need to walk me, step by step, through the past ten years, especially the time you were gone from Sterling. Someone in your past used you, and it's my job to figure out who that was."

Cam sat down and put a small laptop on his knees. He wanted to pull Grace to him, show her just how sorry he was for breaking her heart and prove how he could love her the right way if she would let him. But he knew the only way to truly help her was to give her some space, allow her time to dig deep within herself to call up details and divulge her story.

"I guess I'll start from the time I left, then." She

paused for a moment and he could see she was thinking.

"Why don't you start right before you left," he suggested. "Weren't you involved with Jimmy Wells, my father's ranch hand?"

A shudder went through her. She really didn't want to talk about what had happened with Jimmy. She couldn't tell Cam the entire truth. She still felt too much shame about the situation, even though she knew she shouldn't.

"Grace. I know this isn't ideal, speaking with your ex-boyfriend about another boyfriend, but he could be the guy setting you up, so I need to know the truth."

"The truth?" Grace laughed a humorless sound that echoed in his large living room.

"Yes, the truth," he said quietly. Grace couldn't look him in the eyes, couldn't know what he was thinking or feeling about this. She decided to give the modified version of the story she had rehearsed for years.

"Yeah, I was with Jimmy."

He had his own feelings about her being with Jimmy. Never would he forget how that had made him feel. But this wasn't about him, it was about her, and he needed to keep his feelings to himself.

"I met Jimmy after you went off to law school. He was charming and silly, and he made me laugh when all I felt like doing at the time was crying. I was working for your dad, too, that summer before my senior year, and I didn't know what I was going to do with my life. Sage had plans for after graduation to be premed, and even though Bethel said I could stay after Sage left, it wouldn't have been the same. You were gone, everyone was going away, everyone had plans—everyone except for me."

She stopped again, her eyes closing briefly, and it took everything in him not to set aside the laptop and pull her into his waiting embrace. But he was afraid that if he interrupted, she was going to clam up again.

"So I worked alongside Jimmy all that summer, all the while missing you. He was nothing more than a friend, but one day he took it too far and kissed me behind the barn. I immediately told him I was involved with you, and he backed off, so I thought he was a stand-up kind of guy."

"Wait! What?" His own feelings of bitterness rushed through him, but he pushed them aside. This wasn't his time to tell his story. Maybe someday, but for now he needed to just listen. He should have bitten his tongue, because her eyes snapped to his and she looked at him quizzically. "Don't mind me, Grace. Please continue."

"Um . . . okay." She looked away from him again, recalling memories she had tried to bury. "Then I got the call from you that you weren't coming home for the summer after all, and I was devastated. You told me a long-distance relationship was too hard, and you thought we should see other people."

She hated this part of the conversation, hated that he'd so coldly dumped her. But that was a long time ago. It didn't matter now, did it? Yes, it mattered a lot, actually, because so much bad had happened after that.

"When he found out that you and I were no longer a couple, he figured I was fair game, I guess. That's when he became a little more persistent, and I was worried that if I pushed him away, I would lose his friendship."

"You still had Sage at that point," he reminded her.

"I know. But I was feeling abandoned by her, even though she wasn't leaving for another year. I was trying to prepare myself for that. Plus, she was working at the doctor's office that summer, so we really weren't seeing a heck of a lot of each other. It sucked."

"Then what happened?"

"Eventually I let him kiss me again, but he was pushing for more and more, and I wasn't willing to do that."

"Did something more happen?" His fists clenched at the pain he saw on her face. Maybe he didn't want to hear the rest of this story.

"Not that summer. His dad was transferred out of state and then he was gone and my senior year started. I didn't see him again until the next summer . . ."

That was the summer from hell for her. If she'd thought the one before had been bad, it was nothing in comparison.

"The year had flown by, and then my nightmares were coming true. Sage left to intern for a doctor in LA, and I'd pulled away from most of the other kids in my class, just feeling sorry for myself. I worked for your dad again that summer, and a couple weeks in, Jimmy showed up. He said his dad's job hadn't worked out and they were back. I was actually excited to see a familiar face, one that wasn't judging me for not having future plans."

"I can understand that," Cam said quietly.

"So it was a mellow summer, lots of work, and I found myself laughing quite often, which was something I was missing so much. Then you came back . . ."

Both of them remembered that moment well. They'd made love for the last time, and Grace had thought it was all going to be great . . . That was until he'd so coldly walked away from her again.

"Grace . . ." What could he say? Nothing.

"Don't say anything, Cam. It doesn't matter. The bottom line, though, is that I was in a vulnerable spot. Jimmy showed up with a couple of bottles of wine. I don't know where he got them, but he said it was really good stuff. So we went down to the swimming hole and had a picnic . . . and drank all the wine. I remember lying there on the blanket, my head sort of spinning, and then Jimmy was climbing on top of me . . ." She stopped again, and Cam felt like he wanted to break something, preferably Jimmy's face.

"I must have blacked out. Because one minute he was on top of me, and then the next, I woke up and it was the middle of the night. I was so cold, and Jimmy wasn't anywhere around. My body was sore, but my clothes were on."

"Wait a minute!" Cam exploded. "Are you telling me that he raped you?"

Grace was quiet for several tense moments. "No," she said, but Cam didn't believe her. He knew now wasn't the time to push her, so, sitting there tensely, he waited for her to continue.

"I felt really sick, but somehow I managed to make it back to your dad's property and to my car, and I drove home. I climbed into bed and the next day I still didn't feel good, but it wasn't as bad as the night before." She stopped. He waited.

"Did you speak to him again, Grace?"

"Yes. I did. It was a few days, and when I finally found Jimmy, he apologized, said that I'd gotten too drunk and passed out. He said he had tried to wake me, but I wouldn't budge, and his mom had been expecting him home, so he had to leave."

"Are you freaking telling me that the guy leaves you out by the lake, passed out, and then just tells you sorry but he had to go?" Cam asked with murder in his voice.

"I was young, stupid, and didn't care about him enough to even question what he said."

"So was that the last time you saw him?"

Shame filled her eyes when she looked at him again. And silence accompanied his question.

"Grace, did you see him again?" Cam growled.

"Yes, I saw him again," she finally answered.

"You still dated him after that?" Cam was incredulous.

"No. It was definitely over after that," she told him.

"Then when did you next see him?" Cam was frustrated with how much he needed to push her to get any information from her.

"We moved to Billings, and a couple years later I was finding a small measure of peace, and we met up again," she admitted. "I'd prefer not to go into that right now," she told him, shame filling her at what she'd allowed Jimmy to do to her.

"For me to help you, you have to tell me everything," Cam told her.

"Please, Cam. I can only give so much right now," she said.

"Continue with what you're willing to talk about, then," he told her gently.

She continued speaking before she wouldn't be able to. "One day when I came home from work early, I heard strange noises upstairs. I opened my mother's bedroom door, because no one was supposed to be home. I found her and Jimmy together, and neither of them looked like they were having a bad time."

Cam was stunned speechless. "Your mother and your ex were having sex?" he gasped. "What in the hell . . ."

"Oh, yeah, they were having sex—pretty wild sex, from the sound of it. I couldn't move. I was telling myself to shut the door, to turn around and walk out. But for some reason I couldn't do it. My mother was screaming—not in pain, mind you—and then Jimmy, well, Jimmy must have found his happy moment," she said, her voice suddenly void of emotion. "I must have made a sound because they both turned toward the door and saw me. Jimmy looked so damn cocky, which is what I would expect of him," she said. "But my mother, my darling mother—I'll never forget the look on her face. It was . . . triumph. I never asked her about that look, that verification of how much she despised me. I finally managed to get my feet to move, and I calmly shut the door and walked to my room. Within minutes, I packed a bag of clothes and a few other items I didn't want to leave behind and then I walked away from the house. I never went back."

"Did you ever talk to him again? Have you and your mother reconciled?"

"Jimmy tried calling me for the next month. He finally gave up. I didn't speak to my mother for three years. Finally, for the sake of my father, I came home.

He never knew. I didn't tell him and neither did my mother, of course. Our relationship was forever altered that day. We now talk once in a while, but it will never be more than obligatory meetings. I decided it was best if we came to a mutual understanding. We're more like acquaintances than anything else. I'm a party planner, and she has a lot of contacts, so she'll send business my way. I walk in the door, she gives me air kisses. We're stiff and formal, but so are a lot of other families."

"I don't know how you could even look her in the face after that," Cam said. He was completely blown away. What in the world was wrong with her family?

"I was never in love with Jimmy. It's just . . ." She stopped herself from whatever she'd been about to say. "Never mind. It's not even worth talking about. The bottom line is that I climbed in my car that day and drove to New York. It took me several days, but when I arrived, I thought at first that it was the greatest place on earth."

"But that didn't last, either?"

"No. After a few months I was extremely homesick. But the problem was that I didn't really have a home. I couldn't move back in with my parents. My only true friend was off in college, and I didn't feel like there was anywhere I belonged."

"Grace, I'm so sorry you ever felt that way."

"It doesn't matter. I went to college, got a degree

in hospitality, and then started my event-planning business. But I realized after a few years that New York was just too much for me. So I came back home to Montana, but I decided to settle here in Sterling rather than in Billings."

He waited, but she was quiet for several moments. "Did you meet anyone of importance in New York?"

"I had one semi-long-term relationship in New York, with Vince. The sex was good—your standard hot Italian lover, you know—but there was no emotion," she said with another laugh.

Her comment stung more than Cam would ever admit. No, he hadn't been a saint since they had parted ten years ago, and yes, he'd had other relationships, but none had worked out. How could they when his heart wasn't his to give to another?

Cam didn't know why, but for some reason he had pictured Grace back in Sterling waiting for when he was done with his degree. He'd wronged her in the way he'd left, but he would never forget that summer that had broken him apart.

"Your New York guy is still a lead. I need his information."

"Really? I haven't heard a word from him since I left New York. What would he matter?"

"If you dated him, he's a suspect, Grace."

"There's not much to tell. He was from a wealthy family, but he was trying to be an artist, all living free and stuff. We shared a tiny loft, and after a while

I realized he was perfectly content to live off either his daddy's money or mine, and I grew tired of it. He didn't even fight me when I left. He cheated on me, of course. But it was just something I expected at that point in my life. And I didn't have enough emotion left in me to care. He was the last relationship I've been in."

"Dammit, Grace. You are worth so much more than you can ever imagine."

"Then why do I keep getting left?" she asked.

Cam was silent as she looked down and reined in her emotions. Cam felt like the most disgusting of human beings at that moment. He'd hurt her so badly, and he didn't know how he was going to make it up to her. He might not be able to.

"Grace . . ." He didn't know what he planned on saying.

"I don't think I can talk about any of this anymore tonight, Cam. I'm so tired." The painful memories seemed to choke her voice.

Even though she resisted, Cam put down the computer and then pulled her into the cradle of his arms. "I'm sorry, Grace. I'm so sorry for what you've been through."

Her entire body was stiff for several tense moments, and then, finally, she rested her head on his shoulder and he felt a shudder pass through her.

"It was a long time ago. I just learned that I can't trust anyone," she whispered.

"That's no way to be. I think you'll learn to trust me again—in time."

She said nothing, but it didn't take long before he felt the steady, shallow breaths on his neck indicating she'd fallen asleep.

Cam eased himself carefully up off the couch and stood with her in his arms, then headed to his room. She might wake up angry in the morning, but he doubted it. Tonight she needed someone to hold her and let her know she wasn't alone in the world.

Tomorrow they could go back to their battle of wills.

16

The rhythmic sound of a heart beating beneath her ear was what pulled Grace from her slumber. It took a moment for her to realize where she was, and then the smell of Cam drifted through her and she had no doubt she was lying in his arms, in his bed.

She should be upset, but instead she felt comforted. The night before had taken a lot out of her, and although there wasn't even the tiniest glimmer of light peeking through the curtains, telling her it was the middle of the night, she still felt like it was a new day, like it was almost a new beginning.

She hadn't wanted to share her story with Cam, but doing so had freed up something inside her, something that had needed to be released for a long time. Was she over everything that had happened? No, she certainly wasn't. But at the same time, some of her anger had drained away.

"How are you feeling?"

She wasn't even startled by the sound of his voice.

She'd heard the shift in his breathing and knew he was awake.

"Better," she told him.

"Grace, I don't know how many times I can apologize for what happened in the past, but I hope if I do it enough, then someday you'll believe me and forgive me," he said, his hand coming up and caressing the back of her head.

"You hurt me, Cam. You hurt me more than any of the others because you were the one I loved," she told him.

Maybe it was the security of darkness, or maybe it was because she'd already opened up to him, but for some reason, it just felt right to tell him how she really felt.

Besides, right now all she seemed to be feeling was the warmth of Cam's bare chest, warm beneath her hand. She should be pulling away, leaving his arms and reaching for the blankets to cover herself, letting him know this wasn't what she wanted. So she didn't understand when, instead of leaving his arms, she fluttered her fingers against his chest, the feel of him too enticing to stop.

"I was so young and stupid and running on pure hormones," Cam admitted.

"Yeah," she said with a sigh. "But still, I thought I meant more to you than just any girl who could be easily forgotten."

He stiffened beneath her before his hand continued caressing her head, before moving lower and rubbing against her back.

"How could I ever forget you?" he finally said. His fingers slid below the hem of her shirt and traveled up bare skin, reaching her ribs, the tips circling around and brushing the side of her breast, making pleasure heat her core.

"What are we doing here?" she asked quietly, but even as she spoke, she pressed her hips forward against his hardness, seeking relief.

"We're talking," he murmured. He moved his face toward hers and gently caressed her lips, just a whisper of movement, just enough to make her entire body tingle in anticipation of what was to come.

"You're seducing me," she moaned.

"I'm not doing anything you don't want me to do," he countered, sliding his fingers down her back now. How she wanted to have those fingers where they had been, so he could cup her swollen breasts.

"I didn't say I wanted this," she panted.

"Your body is telling me exactly what you want. If you need me to stop, just say so," he said against her neck, tracing the smooth skin with his tongue and scorching her with his touch. His hand trailed over her behind, and she cursed the panties that barred her from skin-to-skin contact.

Grace refused to tell him how much she wanted him, but she also couldn't tell him to stop, so she lay there quietly, small whimpers escaping her open mouth as his hand moved down the back of her leg and then circled her knee and began gliding slowly up the inside of her thigh.

When his fingers stopped at the elastic of her panties, then retreated, she moaned her disapproval. He rested his hand on the inside of her thigh while his mouth made a trail of kisses from her neck to her collarbone, making her stomach tighten, her breasts tingle.

"Please . . ." she moaned, too desperate, too needful now to keep from begging.

"What do you want me to do, Grace?"

"Don't tease me. Don't offer me something you won't really give me."

"I've been trying to give this to you for a while," he said as his lips traced the top of her neckline and he dipped his tongue beneath her shirt, but not reaching the place she wanted it most.

"Have some mercy, Cam," she cried, pushing her hips into him again before reaching for his head and dragging it downward.

He opened his mouth over her nipple. The cotton of her shirt prevented him from tasting her skin, but when he sucked through the fabric, her body sang anyway, and need poured through her.

He moved his hands down to her behind and then she was on her back and he was on top of her, pressing his hardness against her while he sucked harder on her straining nipple. Their clothes were a maddening barrier between them.

"More," she demanded.

Letting go of her peaked nipple, he ran his tongue up her throat and finally kissed her the way she was meant to be kissed, possessing her mouth as he pulled against her hips and ground himself against her core.

"I need you, Cam," she murmured into his mouth.

He released her lips briefly. "I've wanted to hear that for so long," he said, and he lifted her shirt away and then ripped the side of her panties to free her for his easy exploration.

Sliding his mouth down her throat, he at last circled first one nipple and then the other, wetting them, hardening them, making her scream out her passion. When she was at the point of madness, he kissed his way down her quivering stomach and spread her thighs apart with his hands.

Grace arched off the bed, into his mouth, greedy for what he was about to bring her. His tongue toyed with her swollen folds, and she felt her pleasure hanging right on the edge as he flicked his tongue around the one point of her body that cried out for him the most.

"Now, Grace," he groaned before sucking her swollen bud into his mouth at the same time that he pushed two fingers inside her.

She didn't disappoint either of them. Her body

let go, explosions of pleasure ripping through her, making her call his name over and over again until there was nothing left inside her. He slowly climbed back up her body and let his hips—still clothed, dammit—rest against hers, making her burn once again, and even hotter than before.

"I want to do that over and over again," he said, his lips touching hers so softly, with so much control.

"Mmm," she murmured, in complete agreement.

"Tell me you won't pull away. Tell me this isn't just one more time, and then six months will pass again without you allowing me to touch you."

He cupped her chin and forced her to look at him. She tried not to, but he wouldn't let her go, his passion-filled gaze nearly undoing her.

"I can't make that promise, Cam," she said, her lips quivering as she reached for his hips and pulled him against her. "I just can't do it, so please don't make me. You want me, so take me."

She tried reaching for his lips again, but he wouldn't kiss her. He just lay there, poised above her as his hips ground against hers and the two of them stared at each other.

"All you have to do is admit you're mine, Grace, and I will continue to make your body sing," Cam said.

He shifted his body slightly to the right so he could reach up and cup her still-aching breast and trace her nipple with his thumb. She had to bite her lip to keep from groaning.

"You're only punishing yourself by withholding, Cam," she told him as she pressed up against him once more.

"Yes, I'm punishing myself," he said, then pressed hard against her, showing her how thick and full he was, showing her how good it would feel if he cast aside his shorts and thrust inside her. "But I want more than to have you only once in my bed."

"This is all I can give you right now," she said. She nearly cried out when he pulled away from her. "Don't do this, Cam. You want me."

He paused next to the bed and looked down at her, something burning in his eyes that she couldn't comprehend, couldn't imagine being for her. It appeared to be love, but there was no way he loved her. No one ever had.

"I do want you, Grace. And I *will* have you."

With that parting shot, he left her alone and aching in his bed.

17

"Thank you for the ride home."

Grace climbed stiffly from Cam's car and tried to scurry away, but he was right on her heels. "I'll walk you up."

"Not now, Cam. I don't want to talk to you anymore."

This morning had been traumatic enough, and she was still reeling from their intimate talk in the middle of the night and then waking up that morning in his arms. But mostly, she was mortified about what had followed. The way he'd walked away had nearly killed her, but she wouldn't beg him, and she definitely wouldn't commit to him. What had her on edge more than anything else, though, was the fact that it had felt so right being there with him.

Not just the sex, or almost sex.

But also his scent, his expert hands, the feel of his warm chest beneath her fingers. All of it had been what she'd pictured waking up to every morning for the rest of her life. But some dreams were meant to die, and that was one of them. She wouldn't let a man control her ever again, and Cam was incapable of relinquishing control, especially to a woman. All the Whitmans were that way. Maybe all men were.

"You're running away, Grace. You do it every time you think there's even the slightest chance of a connection."

"If I may remind you, you were the first to run. Back then, I wasn't going anywhere, Cam. And I'm not running anywhere now. I'm just . . . I'm tired, that's all," she told him as she reached her door and inserted her key. "So go home."

"Dammit, Grace—" But he didn't get any further, because she gasped as the door swung open, with a perfect view of her kitchen.

"What in the world?"

Cam stopped what else he'd been about to say and pushed past her. Grace was right on his heels. "Are you doing some rearranging?" Cam asked, but his eyes were narrowed.

"No. I didn't do this." It was odd, because the scene before her should shock her, at least a little bit, but only mild curiosity piqued her brain.

"What happened?" Cam asked.

She walked inside the room and looked at her small kitchen table, which had been turned upside down on the floor, the chairs sitting against it as if there were nothing wrong.

"I don't know. Maybe this is Sage's idea of a joke," Grace said slowly.

"Sage isn't in town," he reminded her. She'd left that morning for a conference in Seattle. "And do you really think she'd have driven over here after her party and done something like this, even if she hadn't had an early flight?"

The scene certainly wasn't malicious—not at all—but it was strange. And the only person Grace was aware of who would possibly have a key was her best friend and former roommate. Sage could have done this before leaving, but, as Cam had just pointed out, why?

She pulled out her cell phone and dialed, then waited to leave a message. "Hey, Sage, call me when you get this. I just wanted to know if you stopped by."

"I don't think you should be here alone, Grace. Too many strange things are happening."

"I've been on my own for a lot of years, Cam, and in New York, too, where the crime rate is slightly higher than in Sterling, Montana. I'm not too worried about an overturned table. It's a joke, that's all. Someone thinks they're very amusing."

"I don't find this amusing at all, Grace. Someone broke into your apartment and wasn't even subtle about it. They wanted you to know they were here. If it doesn't scare you, it sure as hell should." He started walking down her hallway.

"Where are you going?"

"I'm making sure no one is still here," he told her.

She caught up to him. "I don't need you to ensure my safety, Cam."

"What gave you the impression I was asking for your opinion?" he shot back as he looked into Sage's old room first, checking the closet, the small bathroom, and even under the bed.

"Really? Under the bed?" she asked with a laugh.

"Under the bed is a great hiding spot for serial killers," he said casually.

A small tremor rippled through her, but she forced it to subside, refusing to be as paranoid as Cam just then. Once he was sure that room was secure, he moved into her room and went through the entire routine over again.

She relented, and finally returned to the kitchen to make a fresh pot of coffee. She'd leave the panicking to a mere man. When she opened a cupboard, something moved, and Grace let out a scream and then sprinted faster than she had since middle school track.

"What's wrong? Who's there?" Cam nearly collided with her right outside the kitchen doorway; his eyes were darting this way and that.

"There! There!" she screamed, and pointed to her cupboard, her entire body shaking.

Cam, in a fighting stance, crept into her kitchen, grabbed a knife from the block on the counter, and looked frantically around. "I don't see anything," he told her, but his eyes were still whipping in every direction.

Then the brown mouse came scurrying from the cupboard, scampered across the counter, and skidded down the back of the stove. "Get it!" Grace shrieked.

Cam's entire body sagged. He must have been holding himself so tightly that she was surprised he didn't snap in half. "A mouse? Really . . .?" he asked, turning in her direction.

When she saw the merriment in his eyes, she saw red, finding herself barely able to keep from flying at him with claws fully extended.

"I've never had a mouse in this apartment," she told him, still standing outside the door.

"It happens, Grace. Just set out some traps, or get a cat."

"I'm only going to be here another week, though I don't think I'm going to be able to stay here at all now," she said, eyeing the stove the mouse had disappeared behind.

"It was just looking for some food."

"I don't leave food out," she told him.

"Well, you did this time. There's a box of spilled crackers in here, and the mouse was having a field day," he pointed out, looking into the cupboard the mouse had come sprinting out of.

"What? I don't remember even buying crackers, let alone leaving them opened." Was she really losing her mind? Was she sleepwalking? Maybe she had done all of this to herself and she couldn't remember.

She'd been told stress could make you sleepwalk, could make you do things you couldn't remember doing.

"You really don't remember buying the crackers? Like you didn't remember picking up the newspaper? Spence told me about that." When she mouthed a silent *no*, he stood there for a moment. "I see. And I'm starting to find all of these small coincidences suspicious. Are you okay, Grace?"

Cam came walking back toward her. She didn't appreciate the concerned look in his eyes. The one thing she resented more than love was pity. Grace considered herself stronger than most people, and she refused to have anyone feeling sorry for her— ever! She wasn't going to give in to her fears—or to his, dammit.

"I'm fine, Cam. And no, now that I think about it, I don't find any of it suspicious. I just think I haven't been getting much sleep lately. I recently finished dealing with a fiftieth wedding anniversary party, and the client was an absolute nightmare. I'm going to turn off my phone until next Wednesday, when I meet with my new client. That way I can sleep for days on end and get all caught up. Then things will stop happening that I can't remember."

"Tell me everything that's been happening," he demanded.

He had that alert look in his eyes again that she didn't like one little bit. She was going to put the kibosh on that right away.

"You're overreacting, Cam, and you know it. You need to drop this."

Cam's eyes turned into slits as he stared her down. Sadly enough, she was still standing in the kitchen doorway. Bravery with rodents wasn't her strong suit.

"If there's something you're not telling me, then you'd better spit it out now, Grace."

"Does that tone really work on people, Cam? Tell me. Because I *guarantee* that you're not scary," she said, putting her hand on her hip and tapping her toe.

"Oh, it works when I want it to."

He was only inches from her, and a tremor ran down her spine, but it wasn't caused by fear. He'd already left her needy and achy once today. She wasn't about to let him do that to her again.

Cam let out a low growl, then turned on his heel, moved to her table, and easily set it upright. It was done before she had a chance to tell him she could do it herself. The problem she wanted taken care of was the damn rodent, not her table.

"I'll check on you later," Cam said as he moved back over to her front door.

She watched in horror when he stepped outside and began walking away. "What about the mouse?" she yelled after him.

"Feed it some cheese."

He quickly climbed into his car and left. It took ten more minutes for Grace to talk herself into going back into her apartment. The first thing she did was throw away the crackers and then all the cheese in her fridge. There was no way she wanted Mr. Mouse to think her apartment was a vacation rental.

18

"Can you and Axel meet me for lunch in half an hour?"

Cam waited for Bryson Winchester's reply while he was parked on the side of the road only a block from Grace's place.

"Sure. Is everything okay?" Bryson asked.

"I don't know. I want to talk to both of you, and then we can evaluate the situation together."

"You know I'll help where I can," Bryson assured him.

"Great. Let's meet at Jackson's bar." He hung up and began driving in that direction. He wouldn't mind an early-afternoon beer. His stress level was a bit too high right now.

His friends Axel Carlson and Bryson Winchester, who were both former FBI agents, weren't long behind him.

"I'm glad you could make it," Cam told them as they sat down and picked up their menus.

"You don't ask for help unless it's serious," Axel said, putting his menu back down.

"What can I get you boys?"

They put in their order with the waitress, and as she turned to leave, Cam looked into the expectant eyes of Axel and Bryson.

"It might be nothing. I really don't know. But my brother made a comment the other day that Grace mentioned strange things occurring, and then, when I took her home a little while ago, we walked inside her place and her table was upside down and there were crackers in her cupboard she doesn't remember buying. When I stayed over one time, it looked like someone was tampering with her window. Now, if it was just one thing, I might be able to brush it off, but it sounds like several little things have been going on, and I'm beginning to worry. On top of all of this, there's the fraud case that I can't discuss the details of, but there are some players in her past . . . well, I wouldn't put them above using underhanded methods to scare her into silence."

"What else has happened that you know of?" The way that both Axel and Bryson were giving him their full attention worried Cam. If they thought this was a joke, they'd be laughing it off. There was no laughter, not even the slightest of smiles.

"It's really nothing major, but she made a comment to Sage that she went to check her mail and thought she'd left the paper in front of her door, but when she came back, it was opened up on her kitchen table. The window has me more worried than just about anything . . . well, that and the fact that someone seems to have easy access to her place, and they aren't afraid of showing her that."

"The only way for us to know for sure what's going on is if we install some security devices— cameras, microphones, a good alarm system," Bryson said.

"I don't think she'll go for any of the above," Cam replied.

"She doesn't need to know about all of it," Axel told him with a wink.

"Dammit, Axel, you can't say that to me. I'm an attorney," Cam said with a glare.

"Not right this minute, you're not. At this moment, you're just a concerned boyfriend," Bryson said.

"Not quite that yet, either," Cam grumbled.

"Isn't she moving into her new house in a week or two?" Bryson asked.

"Yes, I think at the end of this week or early next week."

"My buddy is doing the final inspection. I think we can get a few things installed before she gets in there," Axel said. "In the meantime, we need to make a 'disaster' happen at her place so she has no choice but to leave the apartment."

"It's an apartment. What can we possibly do that's not going to ruin the entire place?" Cam asked.

"Leave that up to me," Axel said with a wicked smile.

"Maybe it's better if I don't know. That way I can truly be shocked. But remember, there are good people living there," Cam told him.

"I wouldn't do anything too illegal," Axel said.

"Damn, if only your old bosses at the FBI could hear you now," Bryson remarked with a grin.

"I'm going to get disbarred by the end of this, aren't I?" Cam said.

Bryson laughed. "Possibly, but your girl will be safe."

"I need better friends," Cam groaned.

"Oh, come on. You know you love it," Bryson told him.

"Now that business is all taken care of, I have some news to share," Axel said, beaming as he looked at the two men.

They waited. He said nothing else. "Spit it out," Cam finally growled.

"Ella and I are expecting our first baby." The normally composed Axel looked like a kid in a candy store as he shared that piece of information.

"Congratulations, buddy!" Cam stood and smacked him hard on the back.

"Thanks. Okay, sorry we got off topic," Axel said. "Let's get back to your girl now, since mine seems to be doing a whole lot better than yours at the moment."

The men finished their lunch, and when Cam left, he wondered whether Grace was ever going to talk to him again. The way things were going, she might be in deeper water with him than with whoever thought it an amusing pastime to pester her.

He just wanted to keep her safe, he reasoned. It had nothing to do with his wanting to spend more time with her—nothing at all to do with that.

19

Grace gazed at the modest yet beautiful home sitting in the exact same place the old monstrosity of a house she'd been raised in had once sat. This house was much smaller, but she'd played a big part in its design, and had picked out every single piece of the house personally.

She didn't know what she was trying to prove by building a cottage right on the site of her parents' mansion, but it gave her pleasure to picture her mother's face upon seeing this.

She'd wanted to burn her parents' home down, to watch the fingers of dark smoke rise into the air and have a chance to say good-bye to all the miserable things that had happened in that house. She'd gotten her wish with a "burn to learn" from the local fire department when they'd burned her house down while training new recruits. But not before she'd donated all the usable pieces of the house, the windows, fixtures, expensive chandeliers, and even the flooring. She'd gutted the house, and it gave her pleasure knowing that a number of lives would be made better from the proceeds of her parents' property. Something good needed to come out of at least one thing they'd created.

After Cam had left her at the apartment, she was paranoid for the next hour about the dang mouse, so she decided she was better off walking around the property she would soon be living on. At first she didn't think about the fact that there were thousands of mice hanging out in the fields she was wandering through.

But then the idea started gnawing away at her brain. Yes, she knew in theory that they were more frightened of her than she was of them, but those things could fit in all sorts of places, and they could move much too fast. What if she slipped on her shoe and felt mouse whiskers against her toes? Heart attack city! A shudder ran through her at just the thought of those beady little eyes staring up at her.

Still, she couldn't avoid going home forever. Her furniture was being delivered next week, and if she slept in the house right now, she'd be on the floor anyway, where a hundred mice could easily crawl over her.

Not ready to go to the apartment yet, she walked behind the house, listening for little squeaks all the while, and made her way gingerly down the overgrown path that led to her grandparents' original homestead. A soft smile turned her lips up as she pushed against the door and walked inside.

When she'd come home last year, the building had been filthy, but since then she'd cleaned it all up, brought in a new rug, and hung crystals in the windows. Sitting down in the rocking chair in the corner, she thought about how many nights she and Sage had slept in the loft, how many times they'd completely freaked each other out by telling ghost stories.

One memory drifted through her, one that took her back in time to a warm summer day when the nights were short but memorable and love was floating through the air.

She and Sage were eighteen at the time, and after a full day at the lake, they camped out in the cabin, telling stories of alien abductions in the mountains. Then they heard scratching outside, and they instantly fell silent.

When a light passed by their window, the two girls had screamed bloody murder, thinking they would certainly be the next to be taken into the great beyond. When the door opened, Grace thought for sure her life was over. She and Sage clung together, telling one another how much they were loved.

When Cam's laughter had drifted up to them, she wasn't sure what she felt more strongly: happiness that she was going to live or anger that he would do something like that to her. But when he pulled her outside and kissed her into forgiveness, she had stars in her eyes.

They'd had so many nights like that, dragging their feet in the water at the dock, holding hands while walking in the moonlight, and the stories he told her—oh, how those stories mesmerized her. He talked of the places they would go and the life they would have.

She had truly believed it would last forever. But Cam went back to college, and they drifted apart, and somehow she lost her childhood love. Yes, he was back, but it would never be the same.

Her communing with the ghosts of her past had just turned too depressing, so Grace decided she was done with being alone in the woods. Leaving the cabin, but still dragging her feet about going home, she drove to the small diner in town and had a late lunch. When she finally did decide to head back to the apartments just as the sun was beginning to fall from the sky, worry filled her when she spotted the fire chief's SUV in front of her building.

She hoped Ms. Jenkins from three doors down hadn't had another fall. The ambulance came at least once a month for her. She should have gone into a retirement home a long time ago, but the stubborn woman said she'd lived in the apartments for thirty years and she dang well wasn't going to move. Sadly, at some point she'd be left with no choice.

But Hawk Winchester, fire chief, wasn't at Ms. Jenkins's door. He was at Grace's.

"What's going on, Hawk?"

He was posting a sign on her door. Before she had a chance to read it, he turned to her. "Hi, Grace. I didn't realize this was your place," he said.

She didn't notice he wasn't exactly looking her in the eye while saying that.

"Yes, it's my apartment. What's the matter?"

"There's been a report of a gas leak. I can't let you stay here until we investigate it," he told her.

She fired off anxious questions: "A gas leak? Is the entire apartment building being evacuated? Why aren't the trucks here in case it explodes? There are things in there I need. Can I just run in real quick?"

"If you tell me what you need, I can get it," he offered.

"How long will this last?" she asked instead.

"Could be a couple of days. Could be, I don't know, a week," he said, shifting on his feet.

"All week?" Crap. This was just her luck. "I have to get in there, Hawk. I can't go a week without some clothes and my computer."

"I can help with that, Hawk. We can be in and out and you can leave the front door open," Cam said as he joined her in front of the door.

Grace turned all her attention and frustration on Cam when he joined them. "What in the heck are you doing back here, Cam?"

"I heard about the gas leak and was coming to check up on you," he said, way too much innocence in his eyes.

"I told you: I don't need anyone checking up on me, Cam."

"And I told you: *Too damn bad*."

Hands on their hips, they faced off until Hawk cleared his throat . . . loudly.

"Listen, I don't want to get in the middle of your fight, but if you hurry, you can go on in and grab some items."

She decided to ignore Cam and instead turned back to Hawk. Maybe then her nemesis would take a hint and go the hell away. "How long do I have, Hawk?"

"Don't take too long" was his only reply.

"The place isn't going to explode if I open the door, right?" Grace asked.

"No. Not at all," Hawk told her.

"I'll be right behind you," Cam said.

She ignored him once again and slowly made her way into the apartment, which seemed just fine to her. But didn't some gases have no odor, and didn't people just die in their sleep because of them? Who was she to argue with the fire chief?

The gas leak could have waited one more week, dammit. The big question on her mind was: Where in the heck she was going to go now?

20

"Do you know the amount of trouble I could get in for this?" Hawk growled.

"Hey, there was a leaky pipe," Cam defended.

"Yeah, but it will be fixed by tomorrow. If she decides to investigate this, I am throwing you under the bus, Cam," Hawk said, not a smile to be found.

"You agreed with me that something is going on," Cam reminded him, "and you've known Grace her entire life and know what a pain in the ass she can be. She won't admit it when she needs help. This was the easiest way for me to keep an eye on her without having her scratch my eyes out."

"I'm only doing this because I care about Grace, and I *will* throw you so far under the bus, they won't be able to identify the body," Hawk told him.

"You wouldn't do that to your friend, now, would you?" Cam said, giving his best buddy-buddy look.

"Hell yes, and I'll do it with a big smile, knowing you're going to get your ass kicked. If Natalie hears about this, I'll be staying in your house, too," Hawk warned him.

"I always have a room open for friends," Cam said with a laugh.

"Just hurry up and get out of here so I can go home and see my wife. I want a last supper before this gets out."

"It won't ever get out, Hawk. I guarantee it," Cam said.

"Yeah, somehow I'm not believing that," Hawk told him.

Cam walked into Grace's apartment, ready to do more battle if need be. It was a great space, actually, even if he did hate apartments. She'd decorated the place well, tastefully but not over-the-top, and a person felt welcome the moment they stepped through the front door.

He walked into her room and found her pulling things out of the closet and slipping them into a bag. She turned around and jumped.

"You should have said something, Cam," she said with her hand on her heart, and she took a deep breath. "You nearly scared me to death."

"Sorry about that. Why so jumpy?" He moved over to her dresser and opened the top drawer, incredibly happy with his find.

"Anyone would be jumpy to see a giant standing where no one had been a moment before," she told him as she turned to grab another shirt.

"Mmm, so you like what you see," he said before picking up a lacy red thong. "Nice panties." He held them up and enjoyed the look of horror on her face when she turned back to him.

"Stay out of my drawers," she snapped as she rushed over to him, grabbed the delicates, and slammed her drawer shut.

"But, darlin', I've spent years trying to get into your drawers. Anyway, I'm just trying to help you move faster. Hawk said not to linger," he told her as he opened another drawer, striking gold again with what had to be the matching bra.

"Camden Whitman, have you no decency?" She snatched the bra from him, then reached in and grabbed the clothes in the top drawer and shoved them into her suitcase.

"Get the items in that next drawer, too," he said with a wink.

With a smirk, she opened that drawer. "Gladly." She scooped out a bunch of socks.

"Come on, Gracie, you know there has to be lingerie in one of these drawers," he practically growled.

"I don't think I'll be needing any of that," she assured him.

"You're right. I'd just rip it right off."

"Really? I don't think so. You had a chance this morning and turned me down flat," she practically snarled.

"I want more than a one-night stand. What are you going to do, sue me?"

"And I don't like being controlled."

"You're not being any fun at all right now," he said with a pout.

"That's just too bad for you. I'm not exactly in a playful mood. I haven't even had time to figure out where I'm going to go. I'd call Sage again, but she and Spence won't be back from the conference until Tuesday."

"You're going to stay with me," he told her, opening another drawer against her wishes and finding jammies, although not the ones he'd been hoping for. Still, he grabbed some and placed them in her bag.

"Staying with you isn't an option," she told him before grabbing a few more items and then zipping the bag closed. "Now be a good boy and take this out for me. I have a few more items I need to pack."

Cam decided not to argue with her. He'd just place her things in his vehicle and she'd either have to follow him to his place or go without her clothes. That sounded perfectly reasonable to him.

She packed two more suitcases, and they were done within fifteen minutes. "I just want to do a final sweep to make sure I've got everything I'll need for the next week or so," she told Cam as he grabbed her last bag.

"No problem. I'll wait for you outside." He moved

down the stairs and loaded up the last case, then leaned against his truck and chatted with Hawk.

"I really would like to be there when she finds out what a meddler you're being," Hawk said as he chewed on a toothpick.

"Well, she's not going to find out, so we don't have to worry about that, do we?"

"We'll see, Cam. In a perfect world, you just might be correct. But since when have our lives ever gone as smoothly as we've wanted them to go?" Hawk chuckled.

"Okay, I've got what I'll need for the week, Hawk. My house is going to be done this coming Friday, so there won't be a problem with me staying here after that anyway," Grace said. She was being far more polite to the town fire chief than she was being with Cam.

That only grated the tiniest bit.

"Sounds good, Grace. I hope your night goes a lot better from here on out," Hawk said before climbing into his vehicle and taking off.

"Okay, follow me home," Cam said as he moved to the driver's side of her car and held the door open for her.

"I told you I wasn't going to your house, Cam. You really need to learn to take no for an answer," she snapped at him.

"Well, your luggage is loaded in my truck, so if you need anything, you might want to follow me home," he said with a lazy, crooked smile.

"You're not amusing me. I'm hungry, tired, and not in the best of moods right now. So be a gentleman and move my luggage over to my car," she said between clenched teeth.

"We can discuss it over dinner. Climb in," he told her, pointing to her seat.

"Seriously, Cam, you're pissing me off," she growled.

"Good. I like it when there's fire in your eyes."

He decided talking was doing him no good, so before she had a chance to blink, he pulled her into his arms and lowered his head. He was planning on kissing her into submission.

The tables quickly turned on him, though, and within seconds she was the one who was controlling him. The softness of her lips molding to his, the scent of her subtle perfume drifting between them, and the barely audible sigh slipping from her throat had his body hard and aching, and he was wishing they were already home.

After a minute or maybe twenty—time didn't matter—he pulled back and looked into her smoldering eyes. "Follow me home, Grace."

He didn't give her time to answer him, just assisted her into her car and shut her door. Then he moved over to his vehicle and climbed in the driver's side. And waited.

Five minutes passed, and he wondered if the stubborn woman would sit there all night just to punish him. Grace Sinclair was certainly tenacious enough to do just that. But then her car started and he gave a sigh of relief. Maybe he should follow her, just in case she tried to change her mind and give up on her bags.

She pulled out, and he let out a satisfied breath when she turned in the direction of his house. Cam had no illusions that she was suddenly going to comply with his wishes. Still, his anticipation grew the closer they got to home.

21

What a controlling jerk. Why was he doing this? Why did everything seem to be going wrong at once? Her life was in an uproar, and it had all started the moment that stupid fraud file had shown up on Cam's desk.

Yes, Grace could see that he was trying to help her, but he was royally ticking her off. The thing was, though, that she didn't really know where to go, and the only place in Sterling was a down-at-the-heels motel.

If she had the choice to stay there or in one of Cam's spare rooms, though, she would probably choose the motel, because staying at his house left her open to temptation that would be hell to fight.

She had practically begged him to take her this morning, and as much as he'd wanted her, he'd said no, not unless she gave him all of her. She just wasn't able to do that. If she did, she knew where she would be left standing—if she were still standing—when it all came to an end.

And she had no doubt that it would come to an end. He'd left her before. He would leave her again. This time, though, she was weaker. There weren't enough pieces of her left to pick up, not after the stuff that had happened with her mother and then with the guy in New York. He'd used her. Gotten what he'd wanted and then left her broken. It seemed to be the story of her life. She'd been kicked back down too many times to be able to keep getting back on her feet. A person could only withstand so much before they were completely broken.

But even having those thoughts upset Grace tremendously. She wasn't a quitter. Tightening her grip on the steering wheel, she drove on doggedly toward Cam's house. If he wanted to play games with her, she wouldn't just sit idly by while he held all the ace cards up his sleeve.

Cam had no right to try to take over her life, to try to tell her how to live and what to do. If only she were able to get that point across to him, she'd be a very happy woman. As she pulled up in front of his house, she threw back her shoulders and put her player's face on. He would listen to what she had to say.

"You drive like a grandma, you know," Cam said as he approached her at the car, holding two of her suitcases.

"I drive safely, unlike most of the cowboys in this area," she replied, going to the back of his truck and climbing on the tire to reach the last bag.

"I'll get that," he told her with a frown.

"I am more than capable of getting my own bags. Just leave those in the foyer. I'm not unpacking here." With that, she led the way up his steps.

"Nah. I don't like things cluttering up my entry hall. We'll just take them to your room—unless you want them in mine," he said, ascending the stairs as well.

"You don't perform to my satisfaction. I'll take my own room," she told him with a smirk.

"Ah, baby, you know that isn't true. When you pull your head out of your cute little arse and admit how much you want me, I'll perform all night and all day," he told her, opening the door directly across from his own bedroom.

"Don't you have a ton of spare rooms in this monster-sized house?"

"This is my favorite guest room, reserved for only the most elite of visitors." He proceeded through the doorway and set her bags in an amazing walk-in closet.

"No one needs this much space," she scolded him, hoping he wouldn't notice the way she was salivating at the floor-to-ceiling shoe racks. "Especially in a guest room."

"I like big spaces. It comes from a time when two other boys and I shared a room that was smaller than the average linen closet."

His tone may have been joking, but she heard the underlying pain.

"I'm sorry, Cam. I always forget that your life didn't start out as well as it's ended up." She turned to him and held his arm for a moment.

"My life is great, Grace. But it doesn't matter how good it is now or how good it's been for the past twenty years. There are some things that will never be forgotten."

"You know, Cam, you can talk to me about it anytime you want." Grace was almost surprised when those words popped out of her mouth.

"I might take you up on that offer, Grace. But I'm far more worried about what's going on in *your* life right now."

He walked from the closet and moved toward another door. When he opened it, she had a hard time holding in her gasp. The bathroom was the size of her last bedroom, which she'd considered pretty dang roomy. A soaking tub sat in the middle of gray granite, and the double vanity was a woman's wet dream come true. The shower looked big enough to fit ten people, with multiple spray heads and smooth granite walls.

"Wow. I've never had a chance to see your bathroom. I can't imagine what it looks like if this is the guest one," she said, unable to keep the awe from her tone. Maybe she had been a little too hasty in building such a small home.

No. This was more than any person needed. Her new house certainly wasn't too small. It was more than enough space for a single person. She hated cleaning, and couldn't imagine how long it would take to clean this house. Not that a guy like him would clean it himself.

"I'll show you my bathroom right now," Cam said, holding out a hand.

"I think I'll pass. It's been an eventful day. I'm going to shower and go to sleep." She turned away from him, not wanting to be tempted once again that day.

"Grace, it's early yet—only six thirty—and before we drove out here, you said you were hungry. Take your shower and come downstairs. I promise not to attack . . . for tonight, at least."

He didn't try to cajole her any further, just turned around and walked from the room, leaving the decision to her. She appreciated that more than anything else at the moment. Even if she had just half an hour to gather herself together after having so much thrown at her in one day, she might begin to feel a little more human again.

Grabbing a pair of her most unsexy flannel pajamas, she went into the bathroom. She took a little more than half an hour, though, because after the heavenly shower, she couldn't resist soaking in the giant tub, and to get out before sitting there for an hour would be a waste of good water.

She wasn't going to admit even to herself that she was putting off the inevitable. Cam was downstairs waiting for her, and her resistance was zilch. Would they finish what they'd begun that very morning?

When Grace was all out of thoughts about how to avoid him, she sat up in the tub, an evil idea taking place in her mind. He'd left her reeling this morning. Wasn't payback a bitch?

22

Cam sat on the couch trying to read a legal thriller he'd had lying around for the past four months, but he just couldn't get into the story. Was Grace ever going to come back down, or hide out in her room? He knew she had to be hungry, and although his meal of sandwiches and chips wasn't the best dinner ever, it was still food and it was sitting on the coffee table, waiting.

He would have had his cook, Mrs. Bateman, come out and fix up some meals, but he'd been in and out so much that he'd given her a few days off. Bad timing.

Cam finally tossed the book aside. Why even pretend to read? He leaned back and tried to listen for the sound of Grace's footsteps.

He shouldn't care if she didn't come down tonight. They would talk tomorrow. Well, they would if she climbed out of bed before he went in to the office. He had meetings and couldn't play hooky all day—although he'd like nothing better than to lie around with Grace, eating his meals off her delectable body.

The first creak of the staircase had him sitting up straight. He shouldn't be this anxious around a woman, but after this morning, his body was still hurting. What in hell had possessed him? Why had he tried to get more from her than just the pleasure of the moment? She'd wanted him, and he'd been a fool to want more.

And now he was paying.

When she came in, Cam felt as if all the oxygen had been sucked out of the living room. "Grace?" His voice was little more than a croak as he watched her saunter toward him.

"Yes, Cam?" she asked with far too much innocence.

"What are you doing?"

She smiled the smile of a woman who knew who she was, and knew exactly what she wanted, and what she was going to get. Her long, dark hair hung down her back; her eyes—so dark, so exotic—were bright and enchanting. Hell, even her toes were turning him on as she moved closer and closer.

She stopped a few feet from him, her short silky robe held together only by a slim belt that looked a little too loose. Yes, he'd seen her naked—that very morning, in fact—but her peaked nipples poked tantalizingly through the thin fabric and were making him pant like a dog.

Raising her arms, she ran her hands through her hair; her head fell back, and she sighed. Cam couldn't have spoken if his life had depended on it. She had him in a trance, and if this was the show, he prayed it would never end. Maybe he'd really just fallen asleep and this was his fantasy invading his dreams.

Reaching down, he pinched his leg, sending sharp pain shooting through him and proving he was actually awake. Thank the powers that be, he thought as she finished running her fingers through her hair, brought them to her neck, and began playing with the lapels on her robe, slowly sliding her fingers up and down the edges, opening the robe just a little bit more with each pass.

He'd been holding his breath, but it all rushed out in a gasp when she pulled one side of the robe open, revealing a perfectly round breast with a dark, pointed nipple. Then she revealed the other side, ran her hands across both those treasures, and moaned as she felt the pleasure from her own caress.

He was afraid he might actually explode without a single touch from her if she continued her jaw-dropping performance. "Grace . . ." he gasped again.

She pressed one finger to her lips and shook her head, those sensational eyes twinkling as she took another step toward him, her other hand trailing between her breasts, down the line of her toned stomach.

Cam had dated Grace for only one year, made love with her for months, and had thought he'd seen and done it all. But she had never stripped for him, not once, and she'd never looked as gorgeous as she looked now.

The breath escaping his lungs felt like fire, and his erection was so hard, he had surpassed the point of pain.

"Grace, I can't take a whole lot more, not after this morning," he groaned. To hell with commitment. They would fight about that another day. Right now, he just wanted to feel her body take him within its warm grasp.

When he reached out to her this time, she undid the robe, freezing him where he sat, and then surprised him when she stepped forward and then climbed onto his lap. Without a word, she pressed against him, took his hair in her hands, and leaned forward, connecting their mouths in a clash of power and hunger.

Cam immediately opened up to her as she rocked her hips against the denim of his jeans and moaned into the kiss, her fingers tightening in his hair and pulling hard, anchoring him exactly where she wanted him.

He wound his arms around her back, slid his hands beneath the short hem of her robe, and gripped her bare ass, groaning into her mouth at the realization that the only thing stopping him from plunging into her right now was his jeans. And, dammit, he couldn't get to them right now.

Breaking away, he gasped before attempting to speak again. "Let me deal with the jeans."

Instead of granting his wish, she grabbed the edges of his shirt and yanked it apart, making buttons fly in every direction. Then she bent down and sucked on the skin of his neck before moving farther downward. Now his hands found her head, and it was his turn to anchor her.

She twirled her tongue across his nipples as her hands found the front of his jeans. Cam groaned as her deft and delicate mouth moved down the planes of his stomach, his arousal pleading for freedom as she took her own sweet time unbuttoning him.

"I need to be inside you, Grace," he cried, tugging on her hair as he tried to pull her back up.

Slipping from his grasp and kneeling on the carpet in front of the couch, she undid the final button on his pants, reached inside, and pulled him out, the touch of her fingers nearly sending him over the edge as she gripped him. Pushing herself between his thighs, she looked up at him and licked her lips before focusing entirely on the bead of moisture welling up on the tip of his arousal.

"Please, Grace. Please."

"Mmm. Who's begging now, Cam?" she murmured. Before he could even try to comprehend her words, she leaned forward and circled his thickness with her hot mouth. That almost sent him shooting off the couch.

Any and all thoughts fled Cam's mind as she held the base of him in her hand and slid her lips up and down his length, letting little moans of pleasure escape her throat. He was fighting desperately to avoid releasing too quickly.

Cam had almost forgotten what it felt like to have Grace's hands all over him, her mouth taking him to other worlds, her body telling him she was his and only his. How could he ever have forgotten the magic only she could bring him?

Her touch was unlike any other woman's, and he desired her, and only her. And from the way she was touching him, tasting him, he knew she felt the same. There was no reason for them to fight this any longer.

"Climb on me, Grace," he begged, reaching for her hair again and tugging.

She shook her head and stayed right where she was, sucking even harder. He felt the pressure building, felt the inevitable explosion coming on. No. He wanted to be buried in her core when he came, not in her mouth. He had to stop this.

But her hot satin mouth moved farther down around him, and when his sensitive tip touched the back of her throat, he nearly lost his mind.

"Gracie . . . your touch . . . it's . . . I can't . . ." He couldn't even get coherent words to exit his throat as she moved faster, her mouth sucking him hard while one hand squeezed his flesh and the other ran up his stomach and glided over his nipples.

And then she looked up, their eyes connecting as she slid her mouth down him, then slowly back up, letting him pop out so she could lick her lips and then lick the fluid from his tip. It was the most erotic thing he'd ever watched.

His entire body tightened as he tried frantically to withhold the orgasm that threatened. Sweat beaded all over his body and he tugged on her once more. But then she took him into her mouth again and sucked while her tongue circled his tip, and the battle was over.

It felt like fire ripping up and through him as wave after wave of his hot pleasure spilled into her mouth. His entire body locked up as he felt himself pump over and over again, and with her lips clasping him tightly, she swallowed his essence.

Shouting her name, he gripped her hair and shook until the last drop slipped down the delicate curve of her throat. Their eyes connected again as the last of his ecstasy began to ebb.

"This isn't over, Gracie. I still need to be inside you," he sighed, suddenly weak from the pure pleasure she had just given him.

She sucked him once more, her red lips holding him until the very last second, and made him jump from the sensation of it. Cam tried to gain his breath, tried to move, but he needed just a moment. He hadn't had that powerful an orgasm in . . . not since he'd been with her eight months earlier.

"Only you, Grace. You're the only one who can make me so weak," he told her as he reached for her.

Before he could take hold, she backed up and then stopped, tying her robe and looking down at him with satisfaction.

"Was that good, Cam?" Her question was so sweet.

"It was amazing. Let's go to my room. It's not nearly over," he said, already feeling his body stirring again.

"Good. We're even."

Cam sat there a moment, totally baffled. She was halfway up the stairs before he figured out exactly what was happening. Payback from this morning.

"Grace!" He caught up to her and pinned her against the railing, his arousal already growing again. "I just said this, and I'll say it again: This isn't over."

"Yes, Cam, it is. You can be the one to suffer now. I wanted you inside me this morning, and now you can think about the fact that you could have had that."

She leaned in and kissed him hard, her lips demanding against his, making him forget what they were talking of or fighting about. He didn't seem to know anything anymore, she had his mind so messed up.

Surprising Cam once again, she pushed away from him and climbed to the top of the stairs, and the last thing he heard was the click of her door shutting and the sound of the bolt slipping firmly into place.

He moved to her door and leaned against it. "You're going to suffer just as much as I will tonight," he called out to her.

"It will be well worth it," she called back.

With a groan, Cam crossed the hall to his room. Hot damn if she wasn't the sexiest woman he'd ever known. There was no way in hell he was letting her get away from him.

⚖️ 23

Grace should have felt better, should have felt some sense of peace. After all, she'd finally gotten one up on Cam. But her victory was hollow. She'd spent just as much time as she was sure he had in just the same way—aching, lonely, needing to feel *something*.

So her victory had been short-lived. There was now no doubt in her mind that she was on a fool's errand, trying to fight against the man who had stolen her heart so long ago. But what did time matter, when it seemed so endless?

After throwing on some clothes, she made her way down the stairs of his impressive home, all the while listening for the sound of his voice. It was soon obvious that she was here alone. Her shoulders sagged in relief as she walked into the kitchen and made a fresh pot of coffee.

After a few hours, she paced Cam's place restlessly. This was ridiculous. She certainly wasn't a prisoner. Just because he'd insisted on her coming there, that didn't mean she had to stay. Her best friend would soon be home, and she could go there if she couldn't return to her apartment.

For that matter, she was sure that Sage would let her stay at her place even though she wasn't home. Why hadn't she thought of that sooner? Putting on a jacket, Grace stepped onto the front porch and looked at the sky, seeing clouds gather in the distance.

A spring storm seemed to be brewing. No matter. She'd been through many of those before. After making her way to her car, she slipped her key into the ignition and turned. Nothing. She tried again. Again nothing.

"Dammit!" Hitting her hands on the steering wheel in frustration, she pulled her cell phone from her purse and dialed Cam.

"I hope you slept as poorly as I did last night" was how he answered.

"You tampered with my car? Really, Cam? Was that necessary?" There was no time for pleasantries.

"I didn't touch your car, Grace. Maybe it's just old and the battery died."

"I don't believe you. For some reason, you're trying to keep me trapped at your place." With that, she hung up, knowing it wasn't going to do her any good to argue with the man.

But she wouldn't be held captive. Stepping from the car, she looked again at the sky. Yes, it looked ominous, but she'd been born and raised in Montana, and a little rain wasn't going to kill her.

Sage's property couldn't be that far away. They'd driven from her house the week before and it hadn't taken them long to arrive at Cam's. She looked in each direction, smiling when she spotted the road she was sure they'd come in on.

She began her walk, too stubborn to wait for a mechanic to come and fix her car. She noted the trees were starting to change from ugly brown to new green, buds reaching for the sun, wanting to open, and animals peeking out from the burrows that had kept them safe during the snowy months.

Montana winters could be harsh and cruel, but the spring, summer, and fall were full of wonder and activity, and out of all the places she'd lived over the past ten years, no place had felt like home as much as this sleepy country town did.

Looking around at the scenery as she walked, her body fighting off the cold suddenly ripping through the air, she enjoyed the sight of a flowing stream, a source that ran year-round and kept the cows hydrated while also nourishing the plant life.

The farther she moved from Cam's house, the more she was able to focus on the sounds of the woods. She kept going, listening for the chirping of the birds and the scratching of chipmunks in search of food.

A chill ran through her, and Grace looked around as another layer of clouds covered the sun, making the shadows deepen and sending a streak of fear through her. Maybe this wasn't the best idea she'd ever come up with.

No, it was fine. As long as she followed the road, she would reach Grace's house. And by doing this she was letting Cam know that he couldn't control her, couldn't tell her how to live her life or where she was supposed to be.

When the first touch of cold settled upon her nose, Grace looked up, and a new shiver of fear raced through her. It was spring, a time for birth, for new beginnings, for the ice of winter to melt away. But as she stood there in amazement, snow soon dotted her shoulders, and Grace knew she needed to hurry this up.

How long had she been walking? She wasn't sure. It had to have been an hour, maybe a little more. She'd been so lost in her thoughts, she hadn't paid attention. Her only goal had been to reach Sage's welcoming house, where she could go inside, warm up, and have a nice hot cup of coffee.

That plan had failed. Grace turned around and began following the road back, fear a constant as the path that had been laid out before her quickly filled with new snow. Within fifteen minutes, she stopped.

The road was covered, as was the forest floor around her. She could no longer tell where the road ended and the forest began. If she stepped off the pavement, she'd be lost in the woods. But if she didn't keep moving, she had no idea how long it would take someone to figure out that she'd gone walking toward Sage's house.

She knew it didn't take long for frostbite to set in. She had to forge ahead. The road was a winding one, though, and without being able to see it, she might go straight instead of making a necessary turn. She might wander farther inside the woods and end up making them her eternal home.

How foolish she'd been in her anger. No wonder the birds hadn't been singing, the forest had been so quiet. The animals had been smart enough to keep hidden from the encroaching storm. They knew not to get caught in the unforgiving torrent of snow that weighed heavier and heavier upon her shoulders, making each step so much harder to take.

Uncontrollable shivers racked her body as she bent her head and moved forward with as much momentum as she could, but when she turned back around to see how far she'd come, she wasn't able to tell. Her footsteps were quickly erased by the layers of fresh snow on top of them.

Her fingers shaking, she reached into her pocket. It was time to admit defeat and call Cam, to let him know she was wandering in the woods. Even if she was lost, he would know how to find her. He knew this area far better than she did.

Nothing in the first pocket. When she reached in the other, her fingers came up empty. Had she really left her phone behind? What the hell was she thinking?

Grace didn't give up, didn't call defeat, not ever. But as the piercing cold took a new turn—her body was not even able to shiver anymore, it was so exhausted—she knew she was going to lose this battle.

Wanting nothing more than to sink to the ground and let the snow bury her the same way it was burying her path home, she still trudged along, moving slower than she'd ever moved before but knowing there was no way she would give up without one hell of a fight. Her clothes were heavy, the cotton feeling permanently plastered to her skin. When a strange warmth spread through her, Grace was too tired to panic.

She'd taken survival classes. She knew it wasn't a good thing that she wasn't as cold as she'd been a few moments before, or that all she wanted to do was close her eyes. She moved ahead, her eyelids feeling as if weights were dragging them down. Closing them for just a moment, she took another step, and another.

And then Grace smiled, because the sun broke

through the sky and shined down on her, warming her from the outside all the way in. It was only a small break in the sky as she glanced around at the falling snow all around her, but in her one special place, it was warm.

And she was no longer hurting. She was no longer moving . . .

24

"I need both of you to quit fighting long enough to try to let me mediate here," Cam said with a heavy sigh.

"Listen to me, Camden Whitman, you were a stubborn, pigheaded pain in my butt not too long ago, so don't you dare use that tone of voice with me."

Cam had to fight hard not to smile as the retired city librarian, Darcie Stuller, who had to be somewhere in her nineties, and her equally opinionated neighbor, who was in the same age bracket, squabbled over dog poop.

"Don't you listen to her, Camden. She lets little Toby come into my yard and poop on purpose. Do you hear me? On purpose!" Linda Reedy shouted as she shook her arthritic fingers in the air.

"I would never do such a thing. Toby is good to Linda. He wouldn't do such a tasteless thing as . . . do his duty . . . in a yard," Darcie said with a vicious glare.

"It's not the dog who has a problem; it's you!"

Linda shouted. "Ever since my rose beat your rose ten years ago in the county fair, you've had it in for me."

"Ladies, this is getting us nowhere. Do you realize the cost to go to litigation over this matter?" Cam said as calmly as he could manage.

There were times he loved living in Sterling, because it was a small town where crime was virtually unheard-of. But at times like this, he didn't exactly enjoy his job.

"I heard there's a place that can swab the dog's mouth and then test the poop and prove beyond a doubt who the culprit is," Linda said with triumph.

Cam had to really fight a smile. "Yes, Ms. Reedy, there are labs that will do this, but it's very expensive. It would be much better for both of you if we could simply solve this matter right here, right now," Cam told them, looking each of the women in the eye.

"If I don't take a stand now, she won't stop terrorizing me," Linda insisted.

"What if we can agree right now that Ms. Stuller won't let Toby come into your yard and that she'll make sure to have the dog walker pick up all feces from here on out?" Cam asked, praying this would end.

"I want an apology, as well," Linda insisted.

"I'm not apologizing to that old bat! I did nothing wrong," Darcie snapped.

"Listen!" Cam interrupted before this got heated again. "You two were best friends for most of your lives. Now you're letting minor disputes harm that friendship. I know that you both love each other, though it's buried very deep down right now, so if you don't do something to fix this before it's too late, you're going to have severe regrets. Neither of you is getting any younger."

"Did you just call us old?" Darcie gasped, her wrinkled cheeks flushing.

"Don't you speak to us that way, young man. You're never too old to get your ears boxed, you know," Linda added.

"Let's get out of here, Linda. I don't want to listen to this nonsense anymore. Young men thinking they're so smart just because they hang a piece of paper on the wall." Darcie got slowly to her feet.

"I agree, Darcie. I'm sorry. It was probably that snotty little kid's dog from down the block. We'll sit out there all day if we need to, so we can catch him and call the sheriff," Linda said.

Cam sat there motionless as the two women left his conference room. When he was sure they were gone, he tossed down his pen, and finally let out the laughter that had been bubbling up for the past hour as he listened to the women bicker.

Had he known all it would take was to allude to their age, he would have done it ten minutes in. At least he wasn't going to have to stand before the judge explaining DNA evidence of dog poop anytime soon. There were some things to be grateful for.

Finally, he stood and moved to his office, where he looked out the window with a frown. When had it begun snowing? He should have been paying better attention to the news. At least he didn't have to worry about Grace out there driving in it, not after her strange call a couple of hours ago about her car not working.

"Cam, you have a call on line one." His assistant popped in and back out again.

Maybe he should just head home for the day. His mind certainly wasn't on work. No, it was on a certain brunette who had his heart racing and his blood boiling. Her staying in his house might not have been the smartest decision he'd made in a while. If he didn't make love to her soon, he was afraid certain parts of his body might well fall off.

"Camden Whitman here. How can I help you?"

"Cam, I'm sorry to bug you at work, but little Gracie took off over an hour ago on foot, and then the snow started. It's really coming down now and I'm worried about her. I sent some men out, but I thought you'd want to know." When Shawn, his foreman, stopped speaking, Cam felt his heart stop altogether.

"Damn stubborn woman!" Cam shouted. "I'm on my way now. Get my horse ready."

Cam hung up, then walked from his office, told

his assistant to cancel the rest of his appointments, and rushed to his vehicle.

Since Grace's return, his neighbors, father, brothers, and just about everyone else in the entire town of Sterling had been poking and prodding into his business, asking if he and Grace were going to renew their epic romance, if he was going to finally make an honest woman out of her and settle down, have a few kids . . . The questions went on and on.

At first, Cam hadn't known what to think. Grace was the one to get away. But they were young and dumb, teenagers who thought they held the world in the palm of their hands. When the real world kicked in, they weren't able to hold on to each other. They went eight years without speaking, and they didn't do a hell of a lot of talking in the last two years—it was mainly just fighting, actually.

Cam had told himself many times that he was over Grace Sinclair, that their time together hadn't been anything like "epic." The problem with that, though, was that every time he was with her, he couldn't seem to keep his hands or his mouth to himself.

As he drove home much faster than he should with the roads covered in a layer of fresh snow, Cam knew their story wasn't finished. But he just didn't know how to begin anymore. So much had happened.

Sliding to a stop in front of his barn, Cam leapt from the truck, thankful to see Shawn on his own horse, with Cam's horse saddled and waiting. "Which direction did she go?"

"She headed down Watkins Creek Road. I figured she was just going for a quick stroll. Then the guys and I got busy buckling things up for the unexpected storm. By the time we figured out she wasn't back yet, I got real worried," Shawn replied.

"We'll find her," Cam insisted, and they took off down the road.

They went down about a mile, the snow falling thicker and thicker, and Cam felt real panic grow within him. If she hadn't stayed on the road, she could be anywhere. If she'd stopped walking, holed up beside a tree, anything, she could be buried in snow by now.

"Have you called the sheriff?"

"Yes. There have been four auto accidents already in town. There are a lot of people visiting for spring break or something, and people who have no business driving in snow are out driving. But he said if we didn't find her in the next hour, he'd get a search and rescue going."

"Dammit!" Cam was panicking more by the second.

That's how he almost missed it. Something off to his right. It wasn't much, just a slight flash that caught his eye. "This way!" he shouted, and raced through the trees toward it.

"That's her."

Leaping from his horse, he jumped down in the snow and ran up to Grace, who was curled up in a ball, the snow nearly covering her. The flash from her bright blue coat, a small piece of it still showing, was all that had caught his attention.

If he had missed that . . . No! He couldn't even think that way.

"Grace! Wake up! Grace!" He shook her shoulders before lifting her into his arms and pressing his ear to her mouth. "She's breathing, but barely. We need to get her back now. Call the men, have them get my room ready. I want heated blankets, the fire going— that room has to be a freaking toaster oven."

"Shouldn't we take her to the hospital?" Shawn asked while still pulling out his phone right after helping Cam get Grace on the front of his own horse.

"It's too far, and the roads are too bad now. I need to warm her up."

The ride took only ten minutes on the way back, but it felt like hours as he cradled Grace inside his coat, holding her tight, hoping like hell he could get some heat back into her system. Stopping his horse right in front of his back door, he pulled her off the saddle and rushed into the house with her in his arms, knowing Shawn would take care of the animals.

He didn't care what it took. He wasn't letting her go.

25

Grace felt as if she were falling into a cloud of pil-
lows. She was warm, and so very tired. Someone
was talking, but she didn't care. Her body wouldn't
move, and she had no desire to do anything so difficult as to open her eyes.

Her lips felt parched, but she didn't care about
that, either. All she cared about was the fact that she
felt warmth, and softness, and the voice sounded too
far away to bother her, so she snuggled back down
and felt the voice fade farther away.

Then something jolted her. She groaned, wishing
she had the energy to push whoever was bothering
her away. Why was it such a difficult concept for
people to understand when someone just wanted to
sleep?

"Open your lips, Grace."

"No." Was that her voice? She could have sworn
she'd spoken, but that most certainly wasn't her
voice.

Something hard and hot was now behind her.

It felt good, so she nestled into it and took a deep breath, the scent raw and spicy—absolutely delicious. But something was pressing against her lips. She tried shaking her head, but even that movement was too difficult, so she gave up.

When the offending thing against her lips wouldn't go away, she parted them just slightly, and then wished she hadn't. Fire shot down her throat, making her eyes fly open as she began to cough.

"More. Drink this, Grace."

The cup pressed to her lips was tilted up again, and more fire ran down her throat. She coughed and complained, and finally it stopped, but only for a moment. The glass was back and she tried to refuse, but she didn't have the strength.

This time, though, it was cool and refreshing and she gulped it down.

"The whiskey will warm your insides. The water will hydrate you."

"Cam?"

"Yes, it's me." It took a moment for her to process his words, but he sounded angry—furious, in fact. Why was he so upset? She was too tired to try to figure it out.

Then she noticed that Cam was sitting behind her—in his bed—and she was stark naked.

"Wh . . . what is going on?" she croaked out.

"I barely managed to find you—do you realize that? You were lying on the ground damn well covered in snow. You've been in and out of consciousness for two hours, and you nearly gave me a freaking heart attack."

It took several moments for his words to sink in, and then she remembered her walk—her bright idea of making it to Sage's house after he'd disabled her car.

"I wouldn't have been outside walking if you hadn't messed up my car," she mumbled, leaning back into the warmth of his bare skin. She wasn't even concerned at the moment that they were both pretty much naked.

"Once again, I didn't tamper with your car!" he growled. "You're from here, Grace. You know better than to walk around when there's a storm brewing."

"I didn't know a storm was coming," she said, turning just a little so she could snuggle more deeply into his warmth.

"The clouds were as black as they come, Grace. You know better!" he thundered.

"Stop yelling," she said, but her voice was so weak, it didn't hold much authority. "I thought it was just going to rain. I've gotten wet before."

"Even if it had been rain, you could have gotten pneumonia at the very least."

"I'm a Montana girl. I'm tough. It just started snowing so hard, and I lost the road, and then I couldn't find my way forward or back. It was so cold, and then it wasn't cold anymore, and then . . . I just remember something warm, and that's all I remember."

"You remember warmth because you were suffering from hypothermia, you stubborn little fool."

At least he'd stopped yelling.

"I made a mistake. You don't need to be such a jerk," she told him, a flash of anger whipping through her.

He was quiet for a moment. She guessed he didn't like being on the receiving end of a sharp tongue. Well, too dang bad for him. She might be craving his warmth at the moment, but she certainly wasn't going to be berated for making a small mistake. Okay, a big mistake, but it was over and she was now safe.

"Dammit, Grace, I was scared to death."

"Do I still have all my fingers and toes?" she asked in an attempt to make a joke. She wiggled all of her digits to make sure she did, in fact, have them.

"I don't find you amusing," he said, but he was much calmer as he ran his fingers slowly up and down her arms. "And, yes, you have all your body parts."

"I'm sorry, Cam. I knew I was in trouble when it began coming down so quickly, but I couldn't find my phone and I couldn't get out of it." Her voice was now choked with tears that she didn't want to give in to. She was afraid that if she did, she might never stop.

"I shouldn't have yelled, Grace. I was just so damn terrified," he said as he pulled her more tightly to him and kissed the side of her forehead.

The soothing action was making her eyes drift shut again. She was still so very tired.

"I just want to sleep," she told him, turning slightly, laying her head against his warm chest as he caressed the side of her face.

"That's because your body was working so hard to keep you alive. It's probably the equivalent of running a marathon," he whispered.

"I've always thought people who run marathons are fools. Why in the world would you punish yourself like that? I find it much more enjoyable to sit with a glass of wine and watch an episode of *Scandal*." She couldn't quite get out a laugh.

"I'll stick with the whiskey. My gut is still tied in knots."

"I'm naked," she pointed out. Should she be mortified that she wasn't more embarrassed about it?

"Yes, you are," he said with a laugh.

"Don't you think it's pretty bad to take advantage of a sick, knocked-out girl?"

"I needed to get you warm, Grace," he said with a sigh. "So I stripped us both—your clothes were soaked anyway—and held you for a good hour under about a dozen blankets. I think I sweated off ten pounds, but you eventually stopped shivering. Then

I changed the bedding around you and washed off before coming back in here."

"That's kinda nasty," she said with an attempt at a giggle. It sounded more like a dying frog.

"I kept you alive," he reminded her.

"Thank you, Cam," she said, her laughter gone. "I mean it—thank you. I don't want to imagine what might have happened if you hadn't shown up."

"I could never let anything happen to you, Grace. You realize that, right?"

He moved from behind her, and she wanted to moan her displeasure, but he pulled her so she was lying back down, then crawled in with her, holding her tightly.

"You've always been a hero," she told him, curled up against his chest, enjoying the warmth of his arm across her back.

"I'm certainly no hero, and I will be the first to tell you that I'm not having heroic thoughts with you lying here naked in my arms," he said with a strained voice. "But right now I need you to close your eyes and get more rest."

Grace did exactly as he asked and shut her eyes, his scent and warmth carrying her off into a blissful slumber.

26

Out of bed at last.

Grace dressed in her warmest pajamas, threw a blanket around her shoulders, and slowly made her way down the staircase. Cam was nowhere to be found, so she wandered out to his sunroom, where she was entranced by the winter wonderland before her.

Snow covered the land, the buildings, the trees, and mountains. It made everything look so fresh, so clean. In the heated sunporch, she could gaze at the beauty while staying nice and warm in her small cocoon. Why didn't the sight of snow make her afraid now? The human mind was sure hard to figure out.

"Is it safe to come sit with you, or are you still grouchy because I woke you and made you drink that tomato soup?" Cam asked as he joined her.

"Yes, I'm still a little steamed about that. You'll have to take your chances."

"Okay, but only if you share that blanket." He pulled the blanket open, making her grumble, then sat next to her, stretching his legs out and throwing his arm along the back of the sofa as he got comfortable.

"Brave man," she groused, unwilling to admit that the sofa had just become a heck of a lot more comfortable with him sitting there next to her.

"Yes, I'm quite the stud," he said. "I've been known to save lives."

Grace couldn't help but laugh. "Your ego is certainly in check," she told him, then swatted his hand away from her thigh. "And you can keep your hands to yourself."

"I like touching you. You used to like it just as much as I did," he reminded her, his fingers running along the top of her thigh, causing a shiver to rush through her.

"I can't say I remember liking that," she lied.

"You liked more than my touch, Grace. You loved my kisses, too."

"They were okay," she said, now completely lying. They were always fantastic.

"Ha!" he chuckled, bringing his arm around her and twining his fingers in her damp hair. "I remember when you used to chase me."

"I most certainly did not," she informed him huffily. "You were the one chasing me."

"That's not how I remember it, Grace. I seem to recall you hanging out at the ranch a lot during roundup season. I think you just wanted to take a look at me after work, when I was shirtless and sweaty."

This time an almost girlish giggle escaped her. She just couldn't pretend that wasn't true. She and Sage had loved hanging around the Whitman ranch, where the boys would be working, half the time without shirts, and, man, had the view been perfect! If only she could go back to those days of innocence.

"I was only here to look at your brothers. They filled out much quicker than you."

"Well, it's true that Sage's eyes never strayed far from Spence," Cam said. "But, Gracie, yours were all over me. Right from the beginning."

"You were scrawny, as I recall." She wasn't admitting defeat.

"The secret is that I put a little more effort out when you were around. I had to make sure to show off, because watching you waltz around in your tiny tank tops and short shorts had my mouth watering. Damn, it still makes my heart thud to remember those days."

Her own heart began pounding just thinking about that time, the time before the first kiss, when flirting was second nature, and she'd felt so feminine and powerful in her young womanhood. She'd watched him gazing at her, and she'd loved the power of knowing she was turning this handsome guy on.

"Do you remember our first kiss?" he asked as his

fingers slid against her neck. She stopped trying to brush him away.

Revisiting the past like this was a terrible idea, but she couldn't stop herself from enjoying the journey while Cam was at her side.

"There were so many, I don't know if I can remember the first." Of course she did. What she really was fishing for was to see whether he remembered.

"It was just before you turned eighteen, and if I recall, that was the summer you decided to wear clothing that showed all your curves," he said, looking at her and giving a salacious wink.

"Yes, before that, I was horrified by my curves," she said. She could feel herself blush even after so many years.

"Believe me, I was enjoying the more confident you," he told her. "You and Sage, always inseparable, came walking up to us with a couple other girls—I can't remember their names—and you were carrying a bottle of Sage's grandma's lemonade. That stuff was to die for. I think you were practicing a new way of sashaying, 'cause your hips were swiveling and shaking the entire time, and I could barely tear my eyes away."

"I was not doing that!" she said with another laugh.

"Anyway," he went on, "you said you wanted to talk to me about something, and I was more than willing to break away from the group. We walked to the other side of the barn, and you asked me if I was going to the barn dance that Friday."

"Oh, my gosh, I forgot about that part," Grace said. How much more forward could a young girl get?

"I said that I was going if I could take you as my date," he said. "And then you handed me the bottle of lemonade and told me I looked hot. I was burning up at that point. You looked up at me, licked your lips, and I was your slave from that moment on. I leaned down and stole the kiss I'd been dreaming about for the past month straight."

His fingers continued caressing her neck the entire time he told the story, and the way he said the words made her stomach quiver and her heart race. He hadn't forgotten a single detail of a moment that had meant so much to her.

"I can't believe you remember all that," she sighed, leaning into him without even realizing it.

"That was the day you became my girl. I asked you out again that night at the dance, and then we had many more barn kisses . . . not to mention other things later on."

"I must say, you were quite patient, Cam. I moved pretty slowly."

"It was enough to just hold you in my arms and taste your sweet lips," he whispered, leaning down and kissing her cheek, causing another shudder to pass through her.

"Some days I wish we could turn back time and

live in those moments forever, the moments when young love was so powerful, and summer nights were something to treasure."

"You don't have to let go of those moments," he told her. "You can hold on to them forever."

"But you have to grow up, Cam. You have to become an adult. The real world demands that we don't live on love and dreams alone," she said with a sad shake of her head. "We have wins and losses, and sometimes the losses are too much to bear . . ."

"Who says that?"

"Everyone. I can't name a specific person."

"Well, they're all stupid. Because I think you can live on love and dreams alone. Sure, you have to work, and you have to be responsible, but then you get these moments, these perfect moments in the day, when the rest of the world falls away, and you close your eyes, and you remember the past, and look ahead to the future. To lose your dreams is to lose a piece of your soul, and no one should give that up."

Grace was quiet for several moments as she tried to process his words. How she wanted to believe what he said. But hadn't her life shown her that dreams had never been enough? Once she'd wanted nothing more than to be Cam's wife and to live the fairy tale forever. But her dreams had been shattered, forever changing her.

"If we all lived in a dream world, then nothing would ever get done," she said sadly.

"I came to see you once when you were in New York."

His words stopped her from what she'd been about to say. She repeated them back to be sure he'd said what she thought.

"When?" she finally asked.

"You'd been there for about a year. You were going to school, and I stopped by your campus. I was going to surprise you. I'd just finished my law degree and it had been years since we'd spoken, and I was in New York for a conference. I was too close not to see you." His voice faded away.

"Why didn't you follow through? Sometimes New York was pretty rough. I think I would have really loved seeing anyone from back home." She didn't want to give too much of herself away—didn't want to tell him that he was the person from home she would have most liked to see.

"I found you on the campus, but you were with a group of people and you were laughing. I thought you looked really happy. I didn't want to risk interrupting that. I'd heard you'd had a rough go of things for a while."

"Yes. Even without me saying a word, I'm sure the gossip stretched all the way back to Sterling," she said with bitterness.

"It's not that people like to gossip. It's that they

care about their own when you're from a small town, Grace."

"I didn't need them to worry about me, Cam. I was doing just fine."

"In two seconds flat, you go from open and trusting to instantly closed off again. I was once your friend and your lover. You don't need to shut me out," he told her, turning her head and forcing her to look at him.

Grace had to fight the sudden urge not to cry.

"Well, Cam, I think our 'stroll down memory lane' is over," she said, untangling herself from him and standing.

"Why do you always run the second you start feeling something?" he asked, not chasing her but sitting there and holding her gaze.

"Because I learned a long time ago that to open myself up only hurts me. I learned that dreams are for fools, and the past is best left where it belongs."

She had no more strength to talk about this. Walking quietly away, she went back to the guest room she'd stayed in before her ordeal in the snow.

Grace knew she wouldn't get much sleep after that talk—not when she knew how close Cam was, and especially when she knew that his arms would be open for her if only she were brave enough to step into them.

27

Grace sipped her tea and enjoyed the warmth of the rays of sunlight beaming through the large living room windows as she worked on her laptop. She was changing the dinner menu for the fourth time, since the bride now seemed to have a vendetta against seafood. Instead of getting upset, she decided to just continue working, reminding herself the paycheck was a good one.

At least the snowstorm had come and gone, and this would be her last night in Cam's house. So she certainly had that to look forward to.

She should have gone over to Sage's place—Sage and Spence had rushed home as soon as they heard about what had happened—but she was using the pretense that she had to do some more work with Cam and it would be easier to just stay there. Her new house would receive its final inspection tomorrow, and her furniture was being delivered as well.

She could finally leave the apartment and have beautiful views of the Montana countryside once again. Not that she didn't have spectacular views at Cam's place.

When the front door opened and she heard foot-steps across the floors, she thought nothing of it. Maybe one of the hands needed something, or possibly it was Sage coming to visit. She could have gotten off work early. It was doubtful, but miracles did happen.

Turning around, she instead found Martin Whit-man walking into the room, and she couldn't help but smile. It had been months since she'd seen him, and usually she was so busy fighting with Cam, she didn't get to enjoy one-on-one chats.

"Mr. Whitman, what a pleasure to see you," Grace said as she stood up and went to him. "Cam isn't back yet. He's running late with a client."

Martin was truly a kind man and one of the most giving people she'd ever known. He was the first to jump in and help a neighbor, and the last to leave when something needed doing. His laughter was in-fectious, and so many times during her childhood she'd envied the Whitman boys for having such a father. She'd always wondered what it would be like to grow up in a house so filled with love.

"I came to see you, Gracie," he said, stopping in front of her and then pulling her in for a bear hug. "You've been running around so much, I keep miss-ing you. When I found out about your scare in the snow, I told Cam I must come over and see for myself that you were all right."

After Martin held Grace long enough that she was afraid he'd squeezed all the oxygen out of her lungs, he drew back and looked at her. "You have circles beneath your eyes, young lady. You're not getting enough rest. Did Spence give you a full checkup?"

The love and worry was evident in his eyes and tone of voice. It choked her up for a moment and she was unable to answer him. Blinking rapidly so she wouldn't show him how much his parental concern meant to her, she turned her head and took a deep breath before looking him in the eyes again.

"I have to admit, I was pretty scared out there in the snow, but it all worked out. Cam found me, got me warm, and force-fed me for two days. I'm still a bit worn-out, but I'm tough. I'll be back to a hundred percent by tomorrow."

"You've always been a fighter, Gracie. I remember your determination to lift those hay bales every summer. If the boys could do it, then you were darn well gonna do it, too. That first summer, you sure had some sore muscles, but you also earned the respect of every one of my ranch hands," Martin said as he led her to the couch and the two of them sat down.

She laughed. "I've never liked being one of those girls who just sits on the sidelines while someone else does all the fun stuff."

"Sitting on the sidelines isn't all that bad. You get to watch all the chaos that is sure to happen if you wait long enough."

"You've always enjoyed a bit of disaster," Grace

said, a big smile lighting up her eyes. "But you're always the first one in to help clean it up."

"I sure missed you all those years you were gone. I hope you're planning on staying for good now," Martin told her with a stern look. "I understand the need to go out there and find yourself, but this is your home. Once you live in a place like Sterling, there's no leaving. The town gets into your blood and it will always call you home."

"That's because wonderful people like you live here, Mr. Whitman. I've been to a lot of places, and I've never felt as happy as I do here."

"I can't believe no one managed to snatch you up in the years you were away," he said with a laugh. "You've always been such a kind and beautiful girl. You know, I always hoped that you and Cam would marry so I could call you my daughter."

"I would have loved to have you for a dad," she said, avoiding the rest of his statement. "Are you hungry? Thirsty? I know this isn't my place, but I can't believe I didn't offer you something the moment you came in."

"I know how to find things around this place. Cam is actually pretty organized," he said before standing. "I think I'll have coffee and something sweet, if you have it."

"I'll make a fresh pot. I could use some, too. And Cam's cook just made a Bundt cake that's the best thing I think I've ever eaten."

The two walked into the kitchen, and Martin sat at the table while Grace made coffee and pulled the cake from the fridge.

"I'm going to miss Sally," Grace told him as the coffee finished percolating and she poured them each a cup. "The creative ways she turns ordinary food into masterpiece dishes is out of this world. She's spoiled me rotten in a few days' time. I wish I'd learned how to cook better." It was just one more disadvantage she'd had in growing up in such a cold home. "My mom wasn't the milk-and-cookies type," she said with a brittle laugh. "My dad wasn't so hot in the kitchen, either."

"I know you don't like to hear this, Grace," Martin said after she joined him at the table. "But you're strong enough to know that you're important. I know your parents have put you through the wringer, but you have to remember that you're a survivor and what your parents have done or said, or didn't do or say, doesn't define who you are."

"I was just making a joke, Mr. Whitman. I know that." Grace wished she had just kept her mouth shut.

"There are a lot of truths in jokes," he told her.

"Sometimes," she said, then lifted her coffee cup to her mouth to keep herself from saying more. Why did she want to bare her soul to this man? It had always been that way. She blamed his eyes, his beautiful, soulful eyes.

"I'm not going to push you, Grace. And I know you

have Sage, and Spence, and Cam, and even Michael and Jackson. Our family loves you as one of our own. As long as you know that, you'll always be just fine."

"I do know that," she said, her voice quiet.

"All right, we've gotten that out of the way. Tell me what you've been so busy with lately."

Grace somehow managed to switch gears, and spent the next fifteen minutes telling him about her event-planning business. It was easy to talk to him because he seemed genuinely interested in what she had to say.

". . . so I am locked in to planning Kitty Grier's wedding. She's a spoiled socialite who wants her way about everything. I haven't even met the groom, and most likely won't until the wedding day. In those circles, the wedding isn't about the man, it's all about how much the bride can outdo her so-called best friends' weddings. I'm not saying I don't enjoy large weddings. I'm just saying that sometimes it gets a little over-the-top."

"I like over-the-top weddings. But the groom most certainly is a part of the ceremony," Martin said, chortling.

"Yes, yes, he is," Grace said with a sigh.

"You will make a beautiful bride one day, Gracie," Martin said, taking her hand again.

"I don't know if I'll ever marry. It wasn't like I had a good example of marriage from my parents."

"No, you didn't, but, oh, how I loved my wife before she left this world. It was far too soon. And I have many friends in beautiful marriages," he told her. "And just look at how happy your best friend and Spence are right now."

"Yes, I've never seen Sage so happy, but that's because Spence puts her on a pedestal. That man would die for her," Grace said with only the slightest taste of envy on her tongue.

"I've seen a certain person look at you in exactly the same way that Spence looks at Sage," Martin said with a raised eyebrow.

Grace didn't know what to say, and she was saved from having to answer by Cam, who picked that moment to walk through the door.

"You both went silent awfully fast when I came in," Cam said, and his lips quirked up at the corners.

When he gave his dad a hug, then kissed her on the cheek, Grace was shocked to realize that, yes, she wanted him to gaze at her the way Spence did at Sage. How sappy could she get?

But at the same time, that thought terrified her. Because if he did, she would have to let down the walls of protection around her heart. And Grace didn't think she could do that—because if she let them down and her heart was broken again, it would never be repaired.

28

"I've enjoyed the visit, Grace—and tell Sally that her cake was the second-sweetest thing in the house—but I must run," Martin said. "I have a date." He stood, then bent down and kissed the cheek opposite the one Cam had just grazed with his lips.

"Leaving as soon as I get in, Father?" Cam asked.

"I always want to visit with you, son," Martin told Cam. "But time is money—for you, at least. Don't you do anything to my girl." And then he was gone, leaving his son alone with Grace—exactly where Cam wanted to be.

"I wonder what he thinks I'll do to you," Cam said. Hell, he wouldn't mind doing all sorts of things to or, better, with her. First and foremost, he'd like nothing more than to carry her upstairs to his room and finally make proper love to her. Those teasing sessions they both seemed so set on were getting a little old, although they were better than nothing.

"You've been known to play less than fair," Grace

told him as she picked at her barely touched slice of cake.

"You know that man has always loved you, don't you?"

Cam sat down and grabbed an extra fork from the table, then took a large bite off her plate. Grace pushed it toward him. She'd lost her appetite.

"Yes, and I've always had a soft spot for him. Your father is a kind and gentle man," she said, adoration shining in her eyes.

"He has his grumpy days . . . but not too often." Cam finished off the cake in no time before getting up and pouring himself a cup of coffee.

"I can honestly say that I've never seen your father in a bad mood. I don't believe he's capable of it."

"The time my brothers and I decided to make a long rope of his expensive silk ties and climb from the second-story window—I'd say his language was pretty darn harsh," Cam said, thinking back fondly. The "rope" had broken halfway down, with Cam landing on what would be his very bruised ass.

"I would have loved to see that," Grace said, laughing.

The sound enchanted him. There was nothing quite like it.

"I need to go and meet with the guys, Gracie. The new barn is going to be done soon and I'm really looking forward to having more horses."

"Where are you building it, Cam? It's not visible from the house."

"It's on the west pasture. There's great grazing land out there. Come with me so you can see the setup." He stood up and held out his hand.

"I have a new client I'm meeting with in two days. I need to pull some things together for that," she said. "I'll see it later, maybe when it's finished."

Cam knew a brush-off when he heard one. And he was done with letting her push him away. There was a lot going on in Grace's life, and whether she wanted to admit to it or not, she needed him. And he was finally unafraid to admit that he needed her, too.

Maybe their story had ended ten years earlier. But that didn't mean that they couldn't begin a new story together. They would never know if they didn't give it a try. Sure, she wasn't ready to hear that yet, but Cam was a determined man, and he would get what he wanted out of this even if he had to beg or just steal her time.

"You have the rest of the night. It won't take long." When he didn't back down, he saw the surrender in her eyes.

"I need my coat," she told him.

After she bundled up, Cam led her outside to his truck, then drove down to the barn. He was happy with the progress. They'd been building for a month, but the walls were finished and painted, the roof done, and the enormous front doors opened.

"They still have a lot of work to do on the inside—the stalls need to be finished, for example. The arena is going to be a thing of beauty. My brothers are now thinking of copying me," Cam said as he led her inside.

"It's quiet. They aren't working now?" she asked as she looked around at the large space.

"They're done for the evening. No one can work 24/7, Grace."

"There are times I work half that—seven days a week, twelve hours a day. It just depends on how difficult my client at the time is."

"Yes, I've had cases like that when sleep is considered a luxury item."

"Well, this is beautiful, Cam. I remember how you talked about breeding horses when you were young. I figured that was over, now that you're a studly attorney."

"The best dreams are those we discover when we're young. People give up on those only if they give up on themselves."

"Sometimes we're foolish to try to recapture our youth," she countered.

"There's a difference between reliving our youth and ensuring that we keep alive the dreams we've always had," he said as they entered the waiting area of the arena, the only part that was finished.

Beautiful teak hardwood floors led up to a large river-rock fireplace centered on the back wall. A bar was set up in the corner, and two couches and a recliner surrounded the fireplace.

"Are you planning on living in here?" she asked with a laugh.

Cam hit a button and the fire leapt to life, instantly heating the area and drawing Grace into it.

"Every stable needs a comfortable lounge for customers to relax in," he said.

When he looked at her profile, the flames from the fire casting a glow on her lovely face, he felt his heart warm, too. "You are so beautiful, Grace, that it takes my breath away," he whispered, making her turn and look at him.

The moment stretched on for several seconds, both of them lost in a river of emotions. He took a step toward her, needing to feel her in his arms.

"Not now, Cam," she said, and her panic was evident.

He knew she was pulling back because it was too much. Sex she could almost handle. It was emotional intimacy that she couldn't deal with.

He stopped only inches from her. "You've protected yourself for so long that you won't allow good things to happen. If you would just quit fighting me, you'd see that we're supposed to be together."

"I don't want this," she whispered as he reached for her and pulled her to him.

"I can't stop it."

Talking hadn't been getting them anywhere. Although his words couldn't make her believe the love he had for her, she wouldn't be able to deny it in his touch, his kiss.

The smallest contact with her lips had him floating; his body always responded instantly to her touch, smell, taste. It didn't matter how much lost time there was between them. It didn't matter if either of them fought it. What they had together was too powerful to deny.

She held back for only a moment and then wrapped her arms around him and clung for dear life, clearly needing him as much as he needed her. She might not be telling him what she wanted in words, but she was telling him with her body. Cam knew she couldn't lie to him while in his arms.

When they were young, they'd fumbled with their youthful passions, each learning how to please one another. They weren't kids anymore, and the way they kissed right now showed that.

But it wasn't just passion that Cam felt—his heart was also melting just a little bit more. Each time he was with Grace, at each intimate moment they shared, he gave a little bit more of his heart to her.

If she ever allowed him to—*when* she allowed him to—he would give it all. There had never been anyone else but Grace. Yes, he'd had other girlfriends. But Grace was the only girl who'd ever truly had him.

His thoughts spooked him just a bit, and he pulled

back, unable to breathe. He cupped her cheek and decided he wouldn't allow this to scare him. And he also wouldn't allow her to turn away. He was shaken, but she looked absolutely terrified.

"Do you really understand what you do to me, Grace?"

Her face lost all color as she gazed wide-eyed at him. "I'm not trying to do anything," she murmured.

"That's the thing, though, Gracie. You don't have to try," he said, almost choking up with emotion. "Just being with you sends my world spinning."

"Cam, we've been over a long time—too long to renew this."

"But we didn't get to finish—we didn't get our closure. Maybe this will all fade, but right now I don't want to let you go."

"Some wounds can't ever heal, Cam." She tried to pull away from him, and this time he yielded.

"I want to be with you, and if I thought it was over for you, I would let you go, no matter how painful that might be," he said to her back. She stopped walking but didn't turn around. "But you do want me, Grace. You're just too afraid to admit that. It's a losing battle. The sooner you accept that fact, the easier both of our lives will be."

She was quiet for several moments and he wondered if she was going to just walk out or if she'd respond to him. Finally, she turned, her face composed, but there was still a spark in her eyes.

"You hurt me once and now you want to control me. I don't consider either of those things acceptable, Cam. So, yes, I do want you—I've always wanted you. But I can resist the urges of my body because I value myself and I won't be fooled by any more men."

With that, she stalked out of the barn. His house wasn't far, so he allowed her to go—for now.

29

Cam sat in his office across from Axel and Bryson as they looked through the security footage and all the notes Cam had collected in the last month.

"I'm about ready to punch through a freaking wall, I'm getting so damn frustrated," Axel said as he swept his hand across the table in front of him and scattered several papers.

"We're getting closer. I feel it," Bryson told his friend, the calmer one of the group.

"Dammit, I feel like we're right there but we just can't find that final piece of the puzzle," Cam said.

"What about the lead in Chicago?" Bryson asked.

"I'm still working on that one. I think that's going to be our big break," Cam told them.

"What name did you find?"

"It's not a name. It's a business. But what I don't get is how it can possibly connect to Grace," Cam told them.

"If it's come up several times, then there's got to

be a connection. You know neither of us believes in coincidence in our line of work," Bryson said.

"Neither do I. All I know is that the person setting Grace up isn't stupid and they know her well. They know her spending habits, what she likes, what charities she donates to, everything," Cam said with a sigh.

"Well, that's how most counterfeiters are. They don't go into this stupidly. They want to get away with it. So we just have to keep on digging until we find the final pieces to the puzzle," Axel declared, calming down as he gathered the papers he'd just scattered.

"I'm meeting next week with Maverick, a buddy of mine who has a knack for tracking people down. He's done several off-the-books things for me in the past. I have a feeling he's going to find something we've all been missing," Bryson announced to the group.

"Good. Then we're all on the same page. The cameras are up and working at Grace's new place, and I have tracking on the car. If she ever figures out any of this, we are all dead. I just think it's fair to warn you," Cam said.

"Yep. We have no doubt about it," Axel said with a laugh. "Life was easier before I got married, though, 'cause if my wife finds out, I'll be moving in with you."

Although he was chuckling, they all knew his

wife would be furious. When Axel had been assigned to babysit Ella, she'd been livid, and had fought him every step of the way. She wouldn't take too lightly to him now spying on a good friend of hers.

"I'll try my hardest to keep us all out of the hot seat," Cam said.

"Good. 'Cause Misty would put me in the dog house," Bryson told them. "Still, she would be even more upset if something did happen to Grace. The women have all become a lot closer as they've wrangled us in over the years."

"Yeah, I think you were doing a hell of a lot more chasing of your wife than she was of you," Cam said.

"Hey. Isn't there a code of men or something that you're not supposed to say something like that?" Bryson reminded him.

"Yeah. I guess there is, but I'll tell ya, I've been chasing after Grace ever since she moved back to town and it's not doing me a hell of a lot of good."

"Then maybe you need to chase a little harder," Axel told him.

"Yeah, if I do it any harder, I'm going to be behind bars for harassment," Cam said with a laugh.

"Maybe you can be there together," Axel added with a wink.

"With some handcuffs," Bryson said with a leer.

"Okay, this meeting is officially over. You two aren't any help at all," Cam said, rolling his eyes.

"Hey! We aren't getting paid for this," Bryson reminded him. "So our only enjoyment is making you squirm."

"I'll remember this the next time either of you ask for a favor," Cam said with a pointed look.

"And you know we'll be the first ones here," Bryson said.

That was a fact. No matter how much the men ribbed one another, they would give up their lives for a friend. It was why Cam knew he was never alone. That was something money could never buy.

30

People passed by in a blur as Grace waited in the hospital lobby for Sage to come out. Too much quiet time allowed her mind to wander. That wasn't good. Because it reminded her that it had been three days since she'd seen or talked with Cam. Three days, which meant three nights—three very, very long nights.

After their little tiff in his barn, she'd marched up to the house, gone straight to her room, and sat there sulking for a while. It wasn't that she didn't want him, didn't want to be with him, didn't love being in his arms or sitting there talking with him.

Grace had no doubt what this was about. He'd looked at her with something shining in his eyes that seemed far too much like love, and she had run. She could keep repeating to herself that it was to protect herself, to guard her heart, to avoid being controlled by a mere man ever again, but it still boiled down to that one uncontrollable emotion—fear. Illogical, irrevocable fear.

"Sorry I took so long. I was supposed to be out of here an hour ago, but then a car-versus-biker case came in, and you know how that goes . . ." Sage trailed off when she saw the look on Grace's face. "What's wrong, sweetheart?"

"I'm fine. Let's get out of here. I don't know how you work in a hospital sixty-plus hours a week. The smell alone would drive me crazy."

"There's definitely something wrong, but I can beat it out of you on the way to dinner. I think I could eat an entire cow right now, I'm so hungry."

The two women walked from the hospital and climbed into Sage's shiny red SUV, a gift from her husband, who had said there was no way he was allowing her to end up on the wrong side of the hospital bed. Sage's old car had hardly been the safest of vehicles.

Three minutes of silence followed before Sage let out a deep sigh. "Okay, woman, I'm trying to give you time to gather your thoughts, but you know that patience isn't one of my virtues, so spill your guts already."

"It's really nothing that matters, Sage. I mean, I'm the one who asked for it, and I'm getting what I want, so I don't see why I'm so dang upset about it. Maybe it's hormones, or maybe I'm slowly going insane from years of living with horrific parents. Cry me a river, cue the violins, and all that. I don't know. I finally get what I want—silence—but instead of being happy about it, I've been on the verge of tears for three days."

"All right, darling, normally I can decipher crazy talk, but I have to admit that right now I'm completely clueless. Could I ask for a translation?"

"It's fine. *I'm* fine." Then to Grace's utter horror, her eyes filled with tears, and before she was able to blink them back, they flooded down her cheeks.

Sage found a place to pull over. She turned to Grace with such a look of horror on her face that it brought out a wobbly smile.

"I'm so sorry," Grace said. "I know, I never cry. And usually I'm the one who's giving out the advice and saying 'Suck it up' or something equally drill sergeant–like, but right now I feel like I'm coming apart completely," Grace sobbed. Much to her horror, the tears kept right on falling.

"What in the world did Cam do to you?" Sage asked, menace in her eyes. "I swear, if he did something—and he *had* to have done something—I'm going to find him and . . . and . . . beat the crap out of him. I'll damn well use something more effective than defibrillation paddles, too."

The pure fury on Sage's face broke through the tears and made Grace laugh. The thought of petite Sage going up against Cam, who easily weighed twice as much and who towered over her by a good twelve inches, made Grace's day.

"Have I told you how much I love you?" Grace said with a sniffle.

"I love you, too, sweetie, which is why I need to kick someone's ass for doing this to you."

"No one did anything to me. This is all on me," Grace said with a hiccup.

"Please, for the love of all that's holy, tell me what is going on," Sage demanded, throwing her hands in the air in frustration.

"I had 'almost sex' with Cam twice, and some hot kisses off in the shadows, and then, of course, real sex months ago, and . . . and . . . I'm letting him in, letting him get to me." The tears started all over again.

She waited for Sage to tell her what a fool she'd been, waited for her best friend to tell her that it could never work, that her and Cam's time was over. She waited for Sage to tell her all the words she needed to hear in order to get over her high school crush.

So when her best friend started chuckling, then full-out laughing, it was such a shock that it instantly dried up Grace's tears. She sat there and watched Sage guffawing so hard, she snorted a few times. When Grace could speak again, her tone was less than friendly.

"What in the world is wrong with you, Sage? I'm speaking from my heart and you're laughing at me?"

"I'm sorry, Grace. I really am. I'm trying to get it

under control, but this is so dang funny. First, that you think you can actually resist the love of your life; second, that you're so ridiculously upset about having real feelings for the man; and third, that you're pissed off over crying. I've known you for a lot of years, and you are my absolute best friend, but to see tears on your cheeks, puffy eyes, and a swollen upper lip is the joy of my life. You are too beautiful for words and, even crying, you look like a heroine waiting for her knight, but you can have real emotion without the world stopping."

Sage's laughter was reduced to a few chuckles again as she was giving her little speech. The rest of Grace's tears dried up as she glared at her friend.

"I'm glad you're enjoying my pain," she snapped.

"Oh, it's not your pain that I'm enjoying; it's the fact that the seemingly unflappable Grace Sinclair can actually get her feathers ruffled at least once in her life. I cried so much when I didn't know which way was up and which was down with Spence. And you're always so in control . . ." The last of Sage's giggles died away.

"*I'm* in control?" Grace gasped. "You have a certain order to everything, even in decorating a Christmas tree. You're OCD personified. I, on the other hand, live life by the seat of my pants."

"That's so not true," Sage said. "No, you may not feel that you have to be as organized as I do, but you're always in control of your emotions, or you try to look as if you are. I love seeing you going a little crazy. It's really good for my ego."

"Ugh. I shouldn't have told you any of this. I already feel like a fool for sitting here, bawling my eyes out."

"It's perfectly human to cry when you're sad or frustrated, Gracie. It doesn't make you a weaker person, and it doesn't make others think less of you—well, unless you do it morning, noon, and night, seven days a week. But we cry for a reason—so we're not holding all of that emotion inside us. It's perfectly healthy and normal."

"I just want him to leave me be. I was doing perfectly fine without him—I was for years."

"Maybe if you were honest with yourself, and honest with Cam, you would actually work some of this out," Sage told her. "You can sit there all day long and say you were fine, but I see the way you still look at that man, and you know as well as I do that you're in love with him. Always have been and always will be. Quit fighting yourself, and him, too."

Grace was surprised by the sudden firmness in Sage's voice. Her friend wasn't normally so forceful, at least not when it came to matters of the heart. But then again, Grace didn't often discuss personal matters with anyone, even her BFF. It was something very difficult for her to do.

"Why can't you just be a normal best friend

who tells me exactly what I want to hear?" Grace grumbled.

"Because then I wouldn't be your best friend. I swear I've told you that before. Have you ever told me what I want to hear?" Sage asked with a meaningful look. "Or do you tell me what I need to hear?"

"That's different," Grace said.

"How so?"

"Because this is about me and that's about you."

"Grace, you're a pain in the ass. I hope you realize that," Sage said before reaching out and giving her a big hug. "Look, you've been keeping secrets from me since I got back to town and found you here. I hope you aren't doing the same with Cam. Unlike me, he can actually help you with law-type stuff. I can help you with the emotional stuff."

"Or you can just laugh at me," Grace murmured.

"I can laugh at you and still help you. And I don't charge a thousand bucks an hour." Sage started the car again and pulled out on the road as they made their way to Billings.

"What if this is all just about sex for him?"

"Aren't you the one who used to tell me to get it wherever I could?" Sage asked.

"Yes. But you know that was mostly for show. I don't take sex as lightly as I pretended to when I was teasing you."

"Don't you think I know that? Again, I'm your best friend, Grace. I know you better than any other person on this planet. And that's a stupid question, because you know Cam and you know it's not just about sex."

"I know. But I let Cam hurt me once and I won't do it again. I lost myself for a while. I never want to be lost again."

"Maybe you're his soul mate and he knows you're scared. Cam's not the type of guy to stand around with his thumbs in his pockets. If he wants something, he'll go after it. I don't think he wants to run anymore. No way."

"Or maybe it's because I'm the woman who got away and he's just a man who doesn't like being told no," Grace growled.

"That could be true as well. The offer is still there for me to kick his ass if you want me to." Sage said this so seriously that Grace couldn't help but chuckle.

"I might take you up on that, sweetie."

Sage was quiet for a few moments and Grace pulled herself together.

"There's so many bad decisions I've made in my life, but the worst decisions have been choosing the men I've been with," Grace finally said.

"We all make bad dating choices, Grace."

"Jimmy raped me," Grace quietly admitted.

"I'm going to kill him," Sage said, so much fury in her voice.

"That's not the worst of it, Sage. While I was

drugged and unconscious, he took pictures of me—
bad pictures. Then he used those to blackmail me for
a couple of years. I told my mother about it, but she
reamed me up one side and down the other. She said
I would disgrace the family if I ever said anything."

Grace stopped, hating to admit this ugliness to her
best friend.

"That wasn't your fault, Grace. And that woman
you call 'Mother' doesn't deserve that title. She never
has. How dare she shame you!" Sage looked as if she
wanted to punch something.

"After I found him in bed with my mother, I
stopped paying him the money. If she could sleep
with a man who had done what he'd done with me,
I was no longer worried about shaming her. He was
too much of a coward to keep coming after me when
I refused to pay him anymore, but as if one or two
mistakes weren't enough, then I met Vince."

She stopped again, hating to confess her shame
even more.

"I remember you speaking about him. But you
never said anything bad," Sage said. They were still
driving as the sun dropped from the sky, and soon
they entered Billings. The car stopped but neither of
them moved.

"Your life was so good. It seemed that everyone's
lives but mine were good, so I glamorized it all, made
it sound like I had this amazing hot Italian lover who
rocked my world, but in reality he was demeaning,

demanding, and horrible to me. It took me a year to get away from him. I just always make the wrong choices, it seems. I don't want to keep doing that. I want to be stronger."

"Ah, honey, you are so much stronger than you think. Don't continue to berate yourself for trusting people or protecting people who should love you unconditionally. And always remember that I love you no matter what," Sage told her as she reached across the seats and pulled Grace close for a hug.

"I love you, too, Sage. Thanks for listening to me. It does feel better to get some of this off my chest," Grace said.

"One more piece of advice," Sage added before pausing. "Don't push Cam away. For years I've watched you push people away for fear of getting hurt. Don't do it with Cam. He really is one of the good guys."

"I don't know if I'm qualified to tell who the good guys are anymore," Grace said.

"You will know if you search your heart. But I won't keep preaching at you about it," Sage told her.

She didn't say anything more, just got out of the car and waited for Grace to join her. Grace didn't know what she was going to do next. But it was much too late to push Cam from her life, because no matter what she told anyone, she knew that she really did love him.

31

Grace used to love watching movies, because they allowed her to sink into a world of make-believe and live, if only for a couple of hours, anywhere but in the here and now. She was suddenly the heroine of the story, traveling through space and time, or having a man do that all for her, just to be with her. Real life wasn't nearly that simple or nearly that happy. If only it were.

She was home. Finally. And she loved her place, a nice cottage-style home nestled in the trees and only steps away from the slow-flowing creek that she loved so much. The place was only about two thousand square feet, but it was an open floor plan with wonderful views of the hills, the water, and the forest all around her.

The spacious kitchen boasted an island and a built-in oven where she might actually find some enjoyment in cooking. The living room was off the kitchen and she'd lovingly picked out deep-chocolate-colored leather furniture that was both beautiful and comfortable and had already hung colorful splashes of artwork on her walls, making the interior feel welcoming.

Her favorite part of the home was the large master bedroom with a king-sized bed, deep-purple bedding, and, again, large windows she could open up and listen to the birds sing through. It wasn't the size of Cam's place, and she'd certainly love to own his bathroom, but she hadn't wanted to be extravagant and remind herself of the home she'd grown up in.

She was more than willing to give up some luxuries to have peace of mind. And that was exactly what she should have been feeling. Unfortunately, she wasn't.

A full week had now passed since she'd last spoken with Cam, and she was beginning to think he'd given up on her, but that morning a bouquet of flowers had arrived with a simple note attached: *Call me when you're ready.*

The words were simple, and she'd read them a thousand times over, trying to inject meaning into them, but the bottom line was that she couldn't find fault with them. He wasn't suddenly trying to make her do something she didn't want to do. He was leaving any decision up to her.

And she didn't know what to do with that. She didn't know how to handle this new way he was choosing to communicate with her. So she'd sat at home and watched movies since noon. Along with her movies, she'd eaten a few bowls of heavily buttered popcorn and drunk a little too much wine. Talk about a glamorous Friday night.

And still, unlike the endings of the movies she had chosen to watch, she was feeling distinctly unhappy. During the course of the evening, she'd grabbed her phone about two dozen times and tried desperately to work up the courage to call Cam, to tell him she was ready to talk. But each time she put the phone down without dialing.

Finally, her eyes were drifting shut, when there was a knock on her door. Jumping up, she glanced at the clock, noting it was nearly midnight. Who in the world would be knocking on her door at that hour?

Something horrible must have happened. It could only be Sage or one of the Whitmans. It took a moment to get her frozen muscles to move, but finally she managed to get up and struggle toward the door.

She didn't want to open it, didn't want to find out who was out there this late at night. She loved her new place because it was away from the main hustle and bustle of Sterling, such as it was, but she was all alone in the woods. That thought normally didn't frighten her, but the only people who came calling this late at night were bearers of bad news.

She reached the door and listened but didn't hear any noise on the other side. "Who's there?" she asked, but she got only silence in response.

"I'm not opening the door unless you tell me who's there," she called a little louder.

There was a thump on the other side of the door that made her heart race. Someone was out there, and whoever it was didn't want her to know his or her identity. Slowly, trying not to make a single sound, she tiptoed over to her window and tried to work up the courage to peek outside. Easier thought than done, though.

When there were still no more sounds, fear filled her. And suddenly being in the middle of the woods wasn't quite as pleasant as it had been. Tiptoeing over to her phone, her heart raced as she dialed emergency services. Had she shut her bedroom window? She'd opened it earlier to let the cool spring air inside.

"Nine one one. What's your emergency?"

"Someone is at my door. They won't answer," she whispered into the phone.

"What's your address, ma'am?" Grace gave her address and the voice continued: "Please stay on the line. I'm dispatching the sheriff to your place."

The next ten minutes were the longest of Grace's life. She curled up in a corner of the kitchen, below the counters and away from the windows, and clutched her phone in a death grip as she waited for either the sheriff to arrive or the intruder to come through her door and end it all.

Fear. It was a tangible thing. Only moments before the knock had sounded on her door, she'd been tired, ready to drift into oblivion, and then that noise, the knowledge that someone who was up to no good was on the other side of her door, had made her adrenaline spike, shaking her to her foundations.

"It's just a prank," she mumbled to herself, although in her gut she knew she was lying to herself.

When a pounding sounded on her door, she nearly jumped out of her skin.

"Gracie, it's Sheriff Thompson. Open up."

Shivers racked her body as she got to her knees and then stood on wobbling legs. She hesitated at the door. "No one is there, Sheriff?" she called through it.

"You're safe now, Gracie. Open up."

The kindness in his tone made her suspicious, and her fear skyrocketed again. She undid the locks and threw open the door.

"I don't think you should stay here by yourself, Gracie" was the first thing the man said.

"It might have just been a prank, but I'm really glad you're here," she told him, her entire body shaking.

"You can hang up the phone now, darling."

Grace hadn't even realized she was still clutching the phone and pressing it against her ear.

"Oh. I . . . I'm sure it was nothing. I'm sure it was just my imagination," she told the sheriff, whom she'd known most of her life.

"It wasn't a prank, Gracie," he said, and he pointed at her door. She looked where he'd indicated and saw a note, written in big red letters, pinned to her door with a sharp hunting blade.

"What is this?" she gasped.

"It's a threat, and I don't want you here by yourself. You were real smart not to answer the door," Sheriff Thompson said.

Just then, a truck came racing around the corner of her drive, squealing to a stop only a foot from the bottom of her stairs. Cam jumped out, looking wild-eyed, wearing jeans with the top button undone . . . and no shirt.

"Grace!" He rushed up the steps, practically knocked the sheriff over, and pulled her into his arms. "Hawk heard the call. He dialed me right away," he said, holding her so tightly she couldn't breathe.

"I'm fine, Cam. I . . . I don't understand what's going on," she said as she fought back tears.

"This is too much, Grace. Too many things have been happening. I want you to come home with me now," he said, finally releasing her so he could look at her face.

"What do you mean, 'too many things'?"

"You're not unintelligent, Grace. Think about this. Someone was in your apartment, then there was a spill on the top of the outside steps right before you were about to walk down them. Your car was disabled, and you got lost in the snow," Cam said, and her heart thudded more and more wildly with each thing he listed. "And now this note. The person is letting you know they aren't playing. They want you afraid."

"Well, it's succeeded, Cam, because I am definitely scared."

"Gracie, you need to go with Cam," the sheriff said grimly. "You shouldn't stay here alone until we figure this out."

"But this is my home! They can't chase me from my home," she practically sobbed.

"It won't be forever. This is a small town with a lot of neighbors who are more like family," the man told her. "We'll figure this out and we won't let anyone hurt you, not ever."

"Please, Grace. Don't make me beg. Please just let me protect you," Cam said.

If he'd been demanding . . . if he'd insisted . . . if he'd been controlling, she would have faced her fears and told him to go away. But she was frightened, and he was being kind.

"This has to do with the case, doesn't it, Cam?"

"I don't know, Grace, but I think so. I think that whoever set you up wants to scare you or harm you so you can't talk."

"I'll pack a bag. I'm ready to do whatever it takes to stop this."

Cam sighed with relief before walking with her into the house. Sheriff Thompson waited until she was ready, and they all walked from the house together. Grace looked at the note one last time before the sheriff collected it for evidence.

I'M WATCHING YOU EVERYWHERE YOU GO!

32

Blind fury rushed through him during the ride back to his place, but Cam couldn't allow Grace to see that. She was frightened, and rightfully so. They could set up all the security measures they wanted, but some person had come to her home in the middle of the night and stuck a knife in her door.

The message was clear. He wanted to review the footage, but he didn't want her to know yet that it even existed. They were going to nail whoever was doing this to the damn wall. But for now, he had to keep it together.

She sat next to him on the bench seat of the truck, her arms around him, her head resting on his shoulder while he drove. He'd seen many sides to Grace Sinclair before, but this wasn't one of them. He'd never seen her in the grip of fear.

That only served to fuel his fury. As he pulled up to his house, the lights were burning, and several vehicles were in the yard. A small measure of his anger drained at the sight of his family.

"What's going on, Cam?" Grace asked as she looked up.

"I think there are a few people who want to make sure you're okay," he said as he turned off the motor.

"They shouldn't have come out. It's so late."

He took her chin and looked into her ashen face. "Grace, a lot more people love you than you realize. And if you think any of them would be able to sleep when something has happened to you, you're crazy," he told her before leaning down and caressing her lips.

The front door opened and his family filed out, waiting for Cam to bring Grace in. Of course, Sage was too impatient for any waiting. She rushed down the steps and pulled Grace from Cam's arms to hold her.

"I'm so glad you're okay! I didn't know someone was after you. I should have known. You told me strange things were happening, and I laughed it off. I'm such a fool!" she sobbed.

"I didn't know it, either, Sage. It's not your fault. Or mine. And it might not be as bad as it seems right now. Everything always seems so much worse in the middle of the night," Grace said, bringing Cam's rage back to the surface.

He managed to tamp it back down before Grace had a chance to see it.

"Well, you have all of us, and no one will get to you through this wall of muscle," Sage assured her as they reached the doorway.

Michael, Spence, Jackson, and Martin were all standing there, their faces solemn as they each took a turn giving Grace a hug.

"Alyssa stayed home with our daughter, but she said she'll be here first thing in the morning," Jackson assured her.

"You're all making way too much fuss," Grace told them. "I shouldn't have pulled you from your beds."

"We'd be furious with Cam if he hadn't let us know," Martin informed her. "The ladies are going to be mad enough I didn't call, but Bethel just isn't pleasant when she's woken up."

"We have some hot tea ready for you," Sage said, pushing the men aside and leading her friend into the living room.

Grace sat down and took the cup. Cam could see she was grateful to have something to hold on to so they wouldn't see her fingers shake. But it was too late. He'd already noticed, already knew how rattled she was.

"Really, I think it's a pathetic person trying to get a rise from me, which he did. But honestly, if he had wanted to harm me, he could have done it many times over."

That didn't seem to reassure anyone in the room. Cam looked at her and wondered if he was going to have to strangle her for scaring him so badly. He needed to punish someone.

"I'm going to go in the other room with my brothers while you sit with Sage," he told her, then bent down, kissing her firmly on the lips. Her wide eyes told him she wasn't expecting him to do that in front of his family. Well, too damn bad. She was his, and the sooner she accepted that, the better off they'd all be.

"Good. I want to visit with Sage."

Cam brought his brothers to his den. The first thing he did was pour a double shot of whiskey. When the soothing fire burned into his gut, he felt his nerves begin to calm.

"You all know what's been going on," he finally said.

"Bryson has already been called. We can go over the footage and see if we can identify this person," Jackson said as he followed suit and poured himself a drink.

"We need a plan of action. Because until this case is solved, Grace is in danger. Someone out there doesn't want to be caught, and the more I've been asking questions, the more the stakes have risen."

"Who have you been talking to lately?" Spence asked.

"Her parents."

The room went silent with that information. The brothers looked at one another, no one wanting to ask the obvious.

"Her parents certainly won't be getting any parentof-the-year awards, but they wouldn't do this to Grace, would they?" Michael finally asked.

"I don't think so," Cam replied, running a hand through his hair. "But someone in their circle is responsible. I just spoke to her father two nights ago, and I honestly don't think he knows anything about this, but I'm telling you that someone is talking to them, and that someone knows I'm closing in. And that person is getting desperate."

"And desperate people do foolish things," Jackson growled.

"Yes, yes, they do," Cam sighed. "Until this is solved, then, Grace doesn't leave our sight. She won't like that, but we can do it in a somewhat sneaky way."

"We're just going to have to figure out more creative ways to keep her company," Michael said, and grinned at Cam. "I'll babysit—no problem."

"Very cute, Michael," Cam said with a roll of his eyes. "But, yes, you'll get some babysitting time." He wasn't worried in the least that his youngest brother might hone in on his girl.

While Sage chatted with Grace, Cam and his brothers came up with a solid plan. If Grace figured it out, they would all be toast, but as of right now she wouldn't be alone for five minutes straight.

They just hoped she wouldn't figure out what they were doing.

33

"I have a job to do, Cam!"

A week had passed since someone had left that note on Grace's door, and she still wasn't any closer to finding answers. Cam had leads, and she was just going to have to allow him to do what he did best, although it wasn't easy for her to let go of the control she was so fond of having.

"I don't think it's a good idea for you to be at a very public party right now," Cam told her, pacing the room in front of her.

"I've had to put up with your babysitting me all week, and, yes, I know that's what your family has been doing. But now I'm done with it. I have a business to run, and in three days I'm throwing my client's rehearsal dinner. You can either keep your mouth shut and come with me, or you can stand down," Grace told him. "But make no mistake about it: I *am* going. Would *you* give up a case because someone had threatened *you*?"

Cam glared at her for several moments, but she

wasn't relenting on this one. He'd already insisted on being in the restaurant when she'd met with Kitty a few days earlier to finalize the plans for the party. And she was more than willing to compromise, because she knew he really did care about her safety.

She was not willing, however, to let him ruin her career. Planning events might not seem important to Cam, but she loved what she did, and it allowed her the freedom a nine-to-five job would never grant her.

"We still don't know who left the note, Grace, and we don't know how serious the person is about hurting you. I just traced some of the checks to a bank account yesterday. If the person is aware that we're closing in on them, they might get desperate, might want to eliminate you as a witness," he said, his voice calm as if trying to reason with her. That only irritated her more.

"I am cooperating fully with you, Cam. But I told you from the day I agreed to let you look into this case that I wasn't going to let it change my life, that I wasn't going to hide in some corner. You either accept that or don't. I really couldn't care less. I've compromised and I'm staying here at your place or at Sage's place when I have to get away from here, but I'm sick of being coddled."

"Is it really such a bad thing to have people care about you?"

Because he looked so confused, Grace felt a smidgen of sympathy for the man. Enough that she decided it was time they had a chat.

"Sit down, Cam."

"I don't know if I want to, not while you're using that tone." He continued pacing.

"You will either sit down and speak to me, or you can watch me pack my things up and go back to my house. I'm done with this."

"What do you mean you're done with this?" He stopped pacing, at least, and he turned, giving her his full attention.

"I'm done being overrun. I'm done with you and your brothers telling me exactly how to live my life. I'm done living in fear."

Maybe it was the fact that she was so calm, or maybe it was the seriousness of her tone, but her words seemed to penetrate his thick skull. He finally moved toward her and sat down, although he kept a distance of several feet between them.

"I'm not trying to run your life," he told her. "Nobody is."

"Yes, Cam, you are. I don't care if your intentions are honorable. The outcome is still the same."

"What outcome? Having you stay alive?" he snapped.

"No. Having me die a little more inside."

Cam was completely silent at her words. He sat there looking as if he wanted to reach out for her, but he was obviously unsure whether that would be a smart move.

"You're going to have to explain that, Grace."

"I told you most of my past, Cam, and about the relationships I've been in. Jimmy was the worst. I realize that now. Still I was stupid enough to then date Vince, who was just as bad, although he was smoother about his deceptions. Both of them took something from me, something I'll never be able to get back. But when they took that, I swore I would never put myself in a situation like that again. I would never allow anyone to tell me how to live my life. I'm too good for that. And even though I care about you, the way you treat me chips away at that feeling until I'm not sure if I care more or despise you more."

"I can't believe you would compare me to Jimmy or this Vince."

"That's what you're choosing to hear, Cam? Really? That's all you heard from everything I just said?" Frustration was making her voice squeak. She didn't want to show any form of weakness just then, not any at all. If she did, he would never listen to her.

"No. I heard what you said, but I'm nothing like either of those men. I honor, love, and respect the people I care about. I don't lie, cheat, or steal. So for you to compare me to them is a total insult to my character, Grace."

"And for you to not trust me enough to live my life safely is an insult to me. I can't be controlled. I don't know how many times or in how many ways I have to say this before you will understand that."

Tears threatened, but Grace would not give in to them.

Cam held her gaze, emotion burning in his eyes. She couldn't tell what he was feeling most— frustration, anger, sadness, confusion . . . or any number of other things. But if he didn't speak soon, maybe it was time for her to throw in the towel.

She started to rise, but Cam's hand shot out and he grabbed her arm.

"Please," he said quietly. "Just give me a minute."

Grace didn't resist when he pulled her down into his lap and wrapped her in his strong arms. Even though she didn't want to feel like she needed anyone, it was too hard to resist the warmth that flowed through her when Cam held her. It was everything she didn't want to feel, but that didn't erase the fact that it was true.

She realized he really was her hero. He just needed to learn how to trust her enough to save her- self sometimes.

"I know I come across as stern or controlling. I don't want you to think I don't trust you. It's just that I love you, Grace," he said, making her want to cry. "I don't expect you to say it back to me. I don't expect you to even believe me, not fully, but a part of you, a big part, knows what I'm saying is true. I love you and I don't think it makes me a monster to want to protect the woman I love."

Grace took a breath, and then another one. Her throat hurt from the effort it took not to reply to him, not to tell him what he meant to her. But she wasn't ready for that right now. She wasn't ready to fully trust him. When too much time elapsed, she decided to focus on the way she'd begun this conversation.

"If you care about me at all, you have to promise to start trusting me to take care of myself. You have to stop commanding me and instead be my partner."

She waited for his reply, waited to see what he would say next. It seemed like hours, but was probably only seconds.

"I *will* try. But can you also allow for mistakes?"

She wasn't expecting that at all. "What do you mean?" she asked, leaning back so she could see his eyes.

"I'll respect you, Grace, but I'm human. I'll make mistakes. Can you be understanding of that and give me more than one chance?"

"I'll give you everything if you give me a reason to."

That hadn't been what she'd been planning to say. The words had slipped from her tongue involuntarily. But when joy lit his eyes, she didn't regret saying them. He was trying to do right by her. She certainly could give him the same amount of effort.

"I'm going to make love to you right now, my beautiful Grace."

"Finally," she sighed.

Letting go, if only for a few moments, was liberating. As Cam kissed her, Grace gave him everything of herself in her response. His lips were unyielding as they captured hers, melting away the last of her resistance to this man she couldn't let go of.

They tugged at each other's clothing as their impatience to feel, to touch, to relearn each other's bodies ignited their passion. The warm air breezed across Grace's skin as Cam tossed her shirt away and then dragged off her pants, taking her panties with them.

Breaking their kiss only long enough to lift her into his arms, he rushed up the staircase and into his master suite, and set her down gently on his silk comforter.

"You're wearing too many clothes," she said as she sat back up and reached for his jeans, leaning in and running her lips across the flat plane of his stomach before undoing his zipper and reaching inside, feeling the full strength of his hardness.

Moans were wrung from his throat when she bent lower and kissed his erection, the fabric of his underwear the only barrier between his satin skin and her hungry mouth. "Mmm . . ." She couldn't get enough of this man.

"Grace, this isn't going to end like it did before," he warned her as she freed him from the confinement of his clothes and he scooted them down his legs and kicked them away.

She dropped from the bed, kneeling in front of him. "You're so beautiful, Cam," she sighed before sliding her tongue along his entire length, then drinking the moisture from the tip.

"Men aren't beautiful," he said as he dug his fingers in her hair.

"You are so wrong," she told him before closing her lips around his manhood. "Because there is so much about you that can only be described as beautiful," she said a few moments later.

"I'll be anything you want me to be," he said before a guttural groan tore from his throat.

"You like this, Cam?" she asked, leaning back to look at him while her hand moved up and down his throbbing arousal.

"Yes, baby, I like it."

"Good, because I like tasting you, touching you, stroking you," she said, and bent forward again to swirl her tongue around his tip.

"Enough!" He grabbed her arms and pulled her up, fire brewing in his eyes, danger in his features. "My turn."

When he pushed her back, she stumbled on the bed, and before she could say a word he was on top of her, his thickness caressing her folds while his mouth devoured hers.

They broke apart only long enough to take a breath, then their lips found each other's again. She ran her hands along his back, her nails scraping him as she tried to hold on.

"I want you inside me, Cam," she cried, lifting her hips to meet his. "Right now!"

"Yes, Grace, yes," he groaned.

He spread her thighs, and then with one deep thrust he was buried inside her. It had been too long, and that one thrust had her right on the edge of losing control.

"Not yet, Grace," he said between gritted teeth. "Let's do this together."

Then, hard and slowly so she could feel every inch of his penetration, he moved within her body. She shook in his arms as his lips ravished hers while his manhood consumed her.

The two of them climbed higher and higher, then his movements sped up, and it was too much for Grace. She clung tightly to him as her body released the exquisite tension. She squeezed him tightly as he continued to thrust in and out of her.

And a cry spilled from his lips as he rested against her and shook with the power of his orgasm. All the while, she was riding wave after wave of pleasure, sensations she had only ever felt with Cam, intensity that couldn't be explained. It was all good, it was all perfect, and it was only Cam.

When Cam finally rolled off her, then pulled her tightly into his arms, Grace didn't resist. Why should she even try to fight him? She was exactly where she wanted to be.

⚖️ 34

When Cam came down the stairs looking devastatingly handsome in his custom tuxedo, Grace's mouth not only dropped open, it also watered.

"You're a vision, Grace."

It took a moment for his words to process, and then she smiled. "I was going to say the same thing about you, Cam. Boy, do you clean up well."

"I wear a suit daily to work," he reminded her.

"Oh, a suit and a tux are two totally different things. You could stop traffic. And I shudder to think about the hearts you'll be stopping at this engagement party. Don't get any ideas."

"You're going to give me an inflated ego," he said as he approached and pulled her into his arms. "I hate to wrinkle your dress or screw up your makeup, but I have to taste these luscious red lips."

She got no more warning than that, and then he was kissing her with so much hunger, she was ready to call in sick and go back upstairs with him. When he pulled back, her body was flushed and her lips so red that they no longer needed lipstick.

"If you keep kissing me like that, you can wrinkle me anytime you like," she said huskily as she smoothed the front of her dress with her hand.

"It will be my pleasure, but a woman as beautiful as you look tonight needs to be shown off to the world. The future bride doesn't stand a chance of getting any attention as long as you're in the room."

"Mmm, Cam. Keep speaking to me like that and I might need to find a private corner at the party to show you just how happy your words make me."

"I'll find the location."

Her stomach quivered with arousal—even though he was saying it as a joke, she had no doubt that he would do just that if given the opportunity. Either way, Grace knew she would be well loved tonight. The sooner they went to the party, the sooner they could come back home. Now that she had been making love to Cam for three days in a row—three *solid* days, she joked to herself—she was afraid she'd never be able to stop. His lovemaking was addictive. *He* was addictive.

Grace practically floated to the car, and the ride to Billings was a damn sight more than pleasant, with Cam's fingers trailing across every surface of her body while his lips did wonderful things to her neck.

When the car stopped, Grace sighed in disappointment. There was now work to do, and she couldn't so easily drift off into fantasyland with Cam. She had to focus and be attentive to her bride-to-be.

"Drop the sulky look, Grace, or your client might think you don't like your job," Cam said with a laugh as he escorted her from the car.

"I normally love my job," she said with a mock glare. "But because of you, all I can think about right now is sex—sex in all sorts of places."

She felt a measure of satisfaction as his lips pressed together. For the next few hours he'd be focused on the unseemly thoughts and images dancing in her sex-mad brain, and his pants would stay far too tight.

"You go enjoy the open bar while I speak with the lovely bride-to-be," Grace said.

"Was that sarcasm I heard in your tone?" Cam whispered in her ear.

"Be a good boy and you'll be rewarded." Grace patted his cheek, then walked away, putting a little extra wiggle in her hips. She didn't even have to turn around and look to know his eyes were glued to her.

That was the power of a woman knowing she was wanted. Grace ignored any lingering doubts—she was determined to hang on to her happy thoughts. She wasn't sure what the future held, but who was? Life happened and things got in the way of the best of intentions.

If she simply chose to focus on the here and now, she would be much better off.

"Grace, I'm so glad you're here. You'll finally get to meet my James," Kitty said in her squeaky voice, a voice that was already grating on the remnants of Grace's nerves.

"I was beginning to think he was a myth," Grace told her with a forced smile.

"Oh, you're so silly. He's running late, so enjoy the party. After all, you're throwing it." Kitty threw back her head and laughed at her own stellar wit.

"Thank you, Kitty. Is there anything else you need right now?"

Kitty tilted her head as if she really had to think about that for a few moments. Grace wanted to grit her teeth. Of course there wasn't anything the spoiled heiress needed, because Grace was excellent at her job and she'd made sure the party was planned down to the last detail.

"I'm good for now. I'm going to go talk to my parents."

She didn't give Grace a chance to respond, just turned around and fluttered away. Why Kitty had insisted that Grace attend the party as a guest instead of just sitting in the background, running the event, Grace didn't know, but what her clients wanted, her clients got.

"Let me guess," Cam whispered in her ear, making her jump. "Your bride-to-be?"

"Yes, my bride-to-be," she said, wanting to kiss him when he handed her a glass of wine. "I will need about ten more of these to make it through the night. I've had some difficult clients before, but she has got to be the most spoiled one I've ever had to deal with."

"Weren't the two of you friends at one point?"

"No, just acquaintances," Grace said. "I only agreed to do this wedding because her parents are powerful figures in the community and if I make their princess happy, it will lead to other lucrative jobs."

"Why do this to yourself? Why not do something less stressful?" Cam asked as he led her to a corner of the room where they could talk more privately.

"Because I love planning parties and making someone's special day even more special. It's the career I've chosen."

"Then be choosier with your clients, Grace. You can afford not to take every person who walks through your doors."

"That would demonstrate a poor work ethic, Cam, and as it is, I live in Sterling, Montana, where there don't happen to be a lot of parties going on."

"My dad throws a few," he reminded her.

"And I love that I get to plan those from now on, but still, that's not enough. I need to stay busy or I'll go insane, especially with this embezzlement case up in the air."

"We will get to the bottom of this, Grace. I promise you."

"I have no doubt about it, Cam. You're a miracle worker, and at this moment that's exactly what I need. Now that I've decided to pull my head out of . . . the sand, I can see that I've been foolish to wait as long as I have. It's a good thing I have a dynamite attorney on my side."

"And a world-class lover," he said, leaning down and kissing her.

"Aren't you the one who kept wanting me to talk about the case endlessly?" she asked him. "And now you're trying to change the subject."

"I can't discuss a case with you while you're wearing that dress. There's a time for business and a time for pleasure," he said, kissing her briefly. "And tonight is most certainly a time for pleasure."

35

Although Cam would have liked nothing more than to hide away in the corner with Grace for the rest of the evening, he couldn't do that to her. This was her event, one that she had been working hard on, and he wanted to see her shine.

"If we don't sneak out from behind these strategically placed potted trees, I may have to find the nearest balcony," Cam told her after giving her what he promised himself would be the last kiss of the party.

"Now that you got me back here, though, I really like it," she said, making his knees a little weak.

Since she'd stopped fighting him during the last few days, they'd made love enough times to begin appeasing the ache he'd built up after not having her for years on end—but he still wanted her, still needed more. And when she was in seductress mode, his powers of resistance were minimal.

"I need alcohol," he growled, and pulled her away from the corner before he changed his mind.

"Stop," she said, and the panic in her tone made him do what she asked immediately.

"What's wrong, Grace?"

"My parents are here. Of course they're here, but I . . . I just don't want to see them," she said as she looked around her, searching for the nearest exit.

"Do you want to leave?"

"Yes," she said with a nod, then shook her head. "No. I'm not going to run from them, and I'm not going to be chased out of my own event."

"Good. Because you are strong and beautiful, and no one should ever chase you away from anything. You are so much better than either of your parents could ever be. Don't forget that, and don't let them alter how you feel. Sure, an engagement party for people you don't really like isn't an ideal way to spend an evening, but I've had worse dates."

Cam hid the smile he was feeling when Grace turned to glare at him. "Not the worst date? Definitely damned with faint praise," she growled. "Is my company not so pleasant this evening, Cam?"

"Hey! I know a loaded question when I hear one. Uh-oh . . ." Cam had made eye contact with her father. "We've been spotted."

Cam felt the tension vibrating through Grace's body, but he was impressed with how well she was holding herself together. She'd picked up her poise from years of living in a house with no affection, no genuine emotion. How sad that she'd had to put on an act for so very long.

"Grace, I was worried when I couldn't find you," Victoria said, and she air-kissed her daughter's cheek.

"It's not that big a party," Grace said with a smile in place.

"Don't act so modest, Grace. This is a beautiful party. You've done well," Donald said before he leaned in and actually let his lips make contact with her cheek.

"I'm not being modest. I've planned parties on a much larger scale than this one," she told her parents.

"That's not being very professional, Grace. I wouldn't speak about other clients while at an event for one who is paying you well now," Victoria said while patting her hair and looking around to make sure no one could overhear them.

Cam said nothing while this little exchange was taking place, but he noticed that Victoria Sinclair was dressed to the nines in a beaded blue gown that hugged her curves and flared below her hips. Diamonds hung around her neck and dripped from her ears—a shining statement of financial worth.

She was polished and composed and . . . fake. She was everything Grace wasn't, and not in a good way. Grace tried to hide who she truly was, but she couldn't. She was able to put up walls, but Cam had figured out ways to tear them back down.

Her father was beset by pride, but he was quiet and more difficult to read than his wife. The small talk between parents and daughter was awkward, impersonal, and loveless.

"You're being quite rude, Grace. Who is your date?" Victoria asked, and she focused entirely on Cam.

"You remember Camden Whitman, don't you?" Grace's arm tightened around his waist as if she were afraid to let him go and possibly hug her mother.

"Oh, Cam! It's been so long," Victoria gushed. "And you've grown into quite the handsome young man." She gripped his free arm and squeezed before leaning in for him to kiss her cheek.

Cam performed the obligatory gesture of socialites before leaning back and pulling Grace closer to him with one arm while sticking out the other and shaking Donald's hand.

"We've been away from Sterling for a long time now. I hope your father and brothers are well," Donald said.

"Yes, they're quite well." He didn't add anything more. Why should he? These people didn't really care. This was just meaningless chitchat to pass the time until they could get away from each other—civilization and its discontents.

Cam had attended many events like this one, and it never failed to make him appreciate where he'd been privileged enough to grow up. Sterling was a great community with honest people who had real emotions.

"How long have the two of you been seeing each other this time around?"

Before Cam could say anything, Grace answered.

"We aren't dating. Cam was just kind enough to accompany me this evening."

"Oh . . . with his arm wrapped around you, I just assumed . . ." Victoria let the sentence trail away.

"As you know, we've been friends for a very long time," Grace said.

Cam knew she didn't share personal information with her parents, but he still felt slightly annoyed that she'd denied they were a couple. Hell, they'd just been off in the corner making out. If they weren't a couple, he sure as heck didn't know how to describe what they were.

The need to make this woman care about him was almost consuming him, and that wasn't something Cam was happy about. Yes, he loved Grace. But she shouldn't make him forget anything and everything else other than her.

It scared him. And it made him want to retreat, especially while he was standing in front of her cold parents. No. He shouldn't be thinking that. If anything, Grace needed him now more than ever.

He wouldn't abandon her, not this time.

"I see that Olivia is motioning for us. You two have

a lovely evening." And just as quickly as Grace's parents had arrived, they took off.

"I'm sorry. They aren't the most pleasant of people to visit with," Grace told him as she pulled her arm from him.

He reached for her again, but she stepped back.

"Your parents have always cared above all for themselves," Cam said. "It's such a shame."

"Isn't it ridiculous that I even care?" She laughed but he couldn't miss the pain.

"No. Even if your parents turned out to be serial killers, you would still feel something toward them. No matter what they've been, they gave you life, and that makes you feel a certain . . . I don't know the right word . . . obligation, maybe, to love them."

"Yeah, something like that," she mumbled, but Cam knew he needed to change the subject.

Before he got the chance, Kitty approached. "I've been looking for you, but we keep getting stopped," the young woman said with her ever-present giggle.

"Is everything okay, Kitty?" Grace had turned back into event planner extraordinaire.

"Of course, silly. I want you to meet James."

The man stepped forward from behind a small crowd of people and both Cam and Grace froze in shock.

36

"It's been a long time, Grace."

Cam was locked there, for once in his life not knowing what to say. Grace managed to speak first.

"Jimmy?"

"What are you talking about, Grace? This is James Wells. He would never use a nickname like Jimmy. That's so hickish," Kitty said with a squeaky laugh.

"Darling, you don't need to defend me. I knew Cam when I worked for his father in my youth," he said, bending over and kissing Kitty's cheek. "I vaguely remember Grace from that time, too."

"Who are you?" Grace gasped.

"I'm not that poor little boy from back in the day, Grace. I got a great job at an art studio and worked my way up. That's where I met the love of my life, Kitty," he said, and hugged his fiancée tightly.

"Oh, pookie, you're so sweet."

Cam felt nausea roll into his throat. "You've done well for yourself in the last few years, *Jimmy*," he said. "Nice suit."

"Yes, I have. I'm not your whipping boy anymore, that's for sure," Jimmy snarled.

"It takes more than a suit, Jimmy," Cam said with just enough smugness to set the man off.

"James, don't let this man speak to you this way," Kitty said, her eyes rounded in shock, and she turned to Grace. "Why did you bring such an unpleasant man to my party?"

"I apologize for the misunderstanding, Kitty. There's . . . history between all of us," Grace said through gritted teeth.

"You have nothing to apologize for. Did your mother know you were planning the wedding of a man who once attacked you?" Cam said, fury echoing through every bone in his body.

"What?" Kitty gasped.

And that's when Grace lost it. This was all way too much for her to handle. She couldn't do this. No person could be expected to act professional in this situation. Not even with flashbulbs going off as cameras snapped the entire scene for the world to see.

"Do you practice that outraged gasp, Kitty? You never were much of an actress when we were younger," Grace snapped.

"How dare you!" Kitty's claws came out as fire lit in her eyes. "Don't forget who you're working for, little girl."

"Number one, I'm a year older than you, Kitty—"

"And a spinster, too!" Kitty shouted.

The entire room quieted as all eyes zeroed in on the four people in the center of the room. The sound of indistinct whispering filled the space as Cam wrapped his arm around Grace to protect her from these venomous people.

"You spoiled little bitch. I can't believe I let my horrid mother talk me into doing this wedding. I couldn't stand you from the first day we met, but you know what . . ." Grace paused as a waiter walked by. Grabbing two champagne flutes, she handed one to Cam and gave him a false smile before she turned to the rest of the room.

"I'd like to make a toast." Her raised voice caught the attention of the few who weren't aware of the battle royal that was under way.

"Grace, stop this right now." Victoria rushed to them and tried to pull her daughter away.

Cam sent Victoria a look that made her falter. "Grace has something to say. Let her be."

Victoria wisely took a step back.

"As I was saying. I would like to make a toast," Grace continued. "To the bride- and groom-to-be. They are obviously made for each other. May they tie the knot . . . around their throats."

With that, she clinked her glass against Cam's and then downed the champagne. Cam was shocked but also proud. Finally, Grace wasn't doing as her mother expected. Finally, she was freeing herself from the bonds they'd had her under her entire life.

"Each one of you has been nothing but a liar and a user in Grace's life. We're going to take our leave, and from now on you can stay the hell out of her way," Cam told her parents before downing his own glass and taking Grace's arm.

They turned to leave, and everything happened so quickly that Cam didn't have time to stop it. With a wild screech, Kitty ran after Grace, grabbing her hair and spinning her around.

"Don't you dare mock me at my own party and walk away," she yowled before her arm shot out and she slapped Grace in the face.

Cam again was frozen. He couldn't hit a woman, but he couldn't stand idly by while Kitty beat up Grace. But he didn't need to worry long.

"You pampered, spoiled little brat." Grace didn't bother with slapping. She made a fist and slugged Kitty in the nose, making the girl bleed all over her expensive white evening gown.

"Daddy!" the girl wailed as fat tears rolled down her cheeks.

"What has gotten into you, Grace?" Edwin Grier, Kitty's father, scooped Kitty into his arms while he scowled at Grace.

"Had I known I was planning the wedding of this scum of a man, I would never have agreed to this," Grace replied, fire in her eyes, but her voice calm. "He will use you and abuse you. Don't think for a minute that you're special."

"You're a liar," Kitty cried as she tucked herself against her father.

"I think it's best if you leave now, Grace," Edwin told her.

"Gladly."

With that, Grace turned and began marching toward the front door. Cam smiled at Jimmy—a promising smile, a look that assured the man he wasn't finished with him. He didn't move until he saw fear enter his eyes. Then he chased after Grace.

It was time for them to finish speaking about both of their pasts. They had no shot at a future while secrets still lay between them. Whether she wanted to or not, tonight they would be talking.

37

"Are you going to be silent the entire way back to Sterling?"

"I don't feel like talking right now."

Grace was still fuming, her adrenaline pumping, her nerves shot. When Kitty was gushing about her fiancé, James, she had never thought it could be the same person Grace had been stupid enough to have dated after he'd abused her.

Had she known what was happening, she would have had more time to prepare, more time to face the man she hated so much. But it was too late to kick herself now. The damage was done. Jimmy had managed to catch her off guard at a party with reporters present.

Grace's humiliation would be complete when her face was splashed across the society pages for being a bitter ex, and her career most likely had just gone down the drain. So much time put into something that was gone in one weak moment.

"Are you still in love with him?" Cam asked.

That broke Grace out of her reverie, and she turned to look at him. "How in the world could you ask me that?"

That's when she noticed that he seemed to be holding himself together by a very thin thread. She didn't understand why he was so upset. If anyone should be upset at this point, it was certainly her.

"No, I'm not in love with him. I've never been in love with him," she snapped, not in the mood to coddle Cam while she was feeling her own hurts.

"That's bullshit and you know it, Grace. You were with him when you were still supposed to be mine," he growled, his anger rising.

"What in the world are you talking about, Cam?"

Her anger drained in her confusion. She was also grateful for the privacy glass between them and the driver, although she wasn't so sure it was soundproof.

"I saw you with him. I came home my first vacation from school and I saw you with Jimmy Wells behind my father's barn, and he was kissing you."

Grace was silent as she processed his words. "I never cheated on you, Cam. I wouldn't have done that. I loved you," she said, trying to think of what he was talking about.

"Don't insult me by lying, Grace. I saw you!" he yelled.

"When?" Her voice was quiet. Maybe he didn't notice how quiet, but it was very, very quiet as she waited for his response.

"It was the beginning of summer after my first year of law school. We were supposed to get all summer together. I got home early and came searching for you. I found you—in the arms of another guy."

Grace's eyes flooded with tears, but she managed to push them back before she let them fall. What good was it to rehash this? Why were they doing this to each other?

"You told me you were staying there that summer to work," she said instead of asking all the questions she wanted to ask.

"After finding my girlfriend making out with another guy, I wanted to be as far from this farm as possible, so I went back and worked all summer near campus."

"Why didn't you say anything to me?" she asked.

"I was young and stupid—and ticked off," he said, his voice draining of anger. "Look, I told myself this didn't matter, that I wasn't going to dredge up the past, but I was just so angry . . ." He took a breath. "Seeing Jimmy just brought out the worst in me. I'm sorry."

"I didn't cheat on you. I didn't even entertain the idea of doing such a thing."

"Grace!" he shouted, then stopped. When he spoke again, he was more in control. "I saw you kissing him."

She had to think for a minute to remember that summer. Jimmy had kissed her. But it hadn't been a wanted kiss and she'd immediately pushed him away.

"I didn't date Jimmy until I knew you were gone, until you dumped me on the phone and then I heard rumors of all the girls you were dating. Then I only dated him because I was lonely . . ." Her voice trailed off. This hurt so much more than she wanted to admit, even to herself.

"No . . ." He stopped again. "The kiss . . ."

"If it was at the beginning of summer, he did kiss me, and I stopped him. I didn't want it," she told him. "But then you came back . . ."

"I was pissed and I wanted to prove something." Cam hung his head in shame.

They were both silent for several more minutes. Then Grace had to say something. "We had sex, and I thought everything was fixed and then you were supposed to come back in a couple of months for the dance. But I didn't hear from you again."

Cam didn't say anything for so long that she didn't know if he was going to answer. Her heart was breaking all over again as she remembered that painful time. She was so confused, so frightened, and she was all alone.

"I was saying good-bye to you in one way and thinking that I was getting what was owed to me in another. I was young, Grace. I was an idiot. I shouldn't have done that," he finally said.

"I guess we were both pretty foolish, weren't we?" she said, unable to keep the tears from her voice this time.

"I'm so sorry for hurting you."

They weren't looking at each other, and Grace was trying desperately not to fall apart, but when his hand reached across the space between them and grasped hers, she wasn't able to hold back the tears anymore.

They pulled up to Cam's house without saying another word. The driver opened the door and he helped her out. Her feet felt leaden as she walked up his steps and inside his house.

This night was ending so much less brilliantly than she'd planned. They'd started with smiles and were ending with tears. Why did life have to be so difficult? Why did there always have to be these roadblocks?

"I am sorry, Grace. I was hurting," Cam said, taking her hand again before she climbed up the stairs.

"Me, too, Cam. I guess we both made assumptions that we can't take back," she said, unable to make eye contact with him.

"Let's not leave it like this tonight. Let me take you to bed," he said, tugging on her hand, trying to pull her into his arms.

"I can't, Cam. Not tonight," she replied, not pulling back, knowing it would do her no good.

"Gracie, I care about you. We're good together."

"Please, Cam. I can't take any more tonight. Please just let me go."

"Do you mean forever, Grace?" he asked, his

hand tightening on hers. "Or do you mean just for tonight?"

She said nothing for several heartbeats. Could she let this man go? Or was he once again wedged so deeply within her soul that losing him would destroy her? She really didn't know.

"I don't know, Cam—I just don't know," she whispered.

"Okay. For tonight I'll give you space," he told her, and then released her fingers.

Grace climbed slowly up the stairs, knowing she couldn't turn around for fear that she'd go running back to him. But she desperately wanted him to run to her, to tell her he'd been a fool and that he would never hurt her again.

But even if he did that, she wouldn't believe him—not tonight, at least.

"I'm here when you're ready, Grace."

His words stopped her on the landing at the top of the stairs. She blinked and nearly turned back to him, but then she walked away, to the guest room. It was time to leave his house.

•

38

The world was lucky he was sitting behind his desk. Cam had been growling at anyone who got within three feet of him ever since Grace had moved out of his place and started refusing to take any of his calls.

Sure, she was staying with Spence and Sage, and he got nightly reports to the effect that she was safe and sound, but that didn't help his mood any— it didn't help his mood at all. Because what Cam wanted was Grace back in his home and back in his bed.

So they'd gotten into a fight. It wasn't something they couldn't fix—their wounds would heal—but the next day, when he'd woken up after only a couple of hours' sleep, she'd already left.

At first Cam had panicked, thinking that someone had managed to break into his house and stolen her away. But then he found the note, saying she was going to Sage's.

He called Spence, of course, to make sure that

she was, in fact, there. Knowing she was safe had helped, and that day he'd even been angry enough with her to think he was glad to be rid of her.

But then the week had dragged on and the more he missed her, the angrier he became with the rest of the world. When he wasn't thinking obsessively about her, he was thinking obsessively about her case. He needed to know how to help her and, more importantly, how to help *them*.

"Can I get you anything else before I go, Cam?"

"No. I'm fine." It was a wonder his legal assistant didn't march right out of his law offices after telling him where he could shove his bad mood.

But instead of yelling at him as he deserved, as he almost wanted, she just left him alone, like everyone else was doing.

And why? Because his thoughts were pinpointed on one woman—one dark-haired, exotic-eyed, beautiful, frustrating woman. Grace. It was always Grace, always had been Grace. She was his first love, and he had no doubt she would be his last.

But would she allow him to stay in her life? That was an entirely different matter. She was strong and independent, and the bottom line was that she just might not need him as much as he needed her.

"Cam, I have to talk to you."

Cam looked up to find Sage in his doorway. "Of course. Is everything okay with my brother?"

Concern flashed through him at the worried look

in Sage's eyes. She was normally a cool, collected woman. Right now, she didn't look so calm.

"Before I talk, I really need a drink—a stiff one."

She took off her jacket and sat down while Cam went to his liquor cabinet and poured them each a scotch. He had a feeling he would need it, to judge from the expression she was wearing. His body hummed with tension.

"Your brother is fine, Cam. I should have said that right away," she told him after taking a long swallow of her drink.

"Then this is about Grace." It wasn't a question. There were very few people who would cause Sage to look that way while talking with him.

"It's about Grace," she said, and her eyes filled with tears.

"You're going to have to explain to me what's going on," Cam told her, frustrated at all the preliminaries. Okay, she hadn't been in his office all that long, but it seemed like forever.

"You know she'll murder me if she knows I'm talking to you, right?"

"No, she won't, Sage. You're her best friend, and she trusts you. I'm the man who loves her, and she'll learn to trust me again."

"I know you love her, and that's why I've come to you with this."

"Then tell me, please."

Cam got up and grabbed the bottle of scotch again.

He had a feeling that they were going to need a lot more of it before this conversation was finished.

"You know about her relationship with Jimmy, right?" Sage downed her drink and pushed it toward him for a refill.

"Yes, Sage, I know about it, and I'd really rather not discuss that aspect of her life. Unless you know something to tie him to the embezzlement case—and I wouldn't be a bit surprised—I don't want to discuss that man."

"I don't know if he's involved, but I do know he raped her, shamed her, and then held something over her head for years. She finally walked away when she found him in bed with her mother, but I have a feeling he's the one behind these little acts of terror against her."

"Why? What could he possibly be holding over her?" This wasn't something Cam was expecting.

"This is so much harder than I thought. I don't want to betray my best friend. But she needs us."

"If you aren't going to tell me, then why in the hell did you come down here and throw out the bait?" Cam snapped, jumping from his chair and pacing his office.

"I'm trying to tell you," Sage countered.

"If I'm going to help her, then I need all the information."

"Jimmy was a monster—is *still* a monster. How do you think he managed to go from ranch hand to an important position in an exclusive art gallery? The man has skills, backwoods kind of skills, and he's dangerous."

"I know all of this, Sage."

Cam was losing his patience. He turned away and took in a long, deep breath as he tried to pull himself together. Sage needed to work up to telling him whatever it was she knew, and if he pushed her, she would clam up again.

"I'm sorry, Sage. I'm just worried about Grace."

"I'm worried about her, too," Sage said with a sigh. "We all abandoned her after high school. But it started with you, when you left and didn't come back that summer we graduated. You left for law school and she was devastated, but she had faith that it would all work out. While you were gone, she met Jimmy. Everyone knew she was your girl, and the hands warned the new kid on the ranch that Grace was a hands-off kind of gal. He ignored them. He pursued her. She didn't think anything of it at first—just that he was a nice guy and she was helping him."

"I was in law school, a good law school. Considering I was in foster care up until I was thirteen years old, that's a pretty damn good accomplishment. I didn't mean to abandon Grace. I was coming back for her. I was just busy . . ." Cam trailed off. He could spout that all day long, but he knew he'd left her, the calls starting to come in less and less, the visits rare. He'd left her because he figured she'd be waiting for him when he came back. He was twenty-two at the time, young and foolish.

"That doesn't matter. Grace turned her sadness into anger, and so she flirted a bit with Jimmy—not enough to cross a line, but enough to make herself feel wanted. Then Jimmy didn't appreciate the fact that she was playing with him."

When Sage's eyes filled with tears, Cam wanted to stop her, didn't want to hear what she was going to say, although he already knew. Grace hadn't admitted it that night a few months ago, but he knew what had happened.

"He raped her. She wasn't sure at first, because he had drugged her. And she didn't tell anyone, feeling ashamed and dirty. It was right after I left for college. He'd been priming her for an entire year, and then he did his filthy deed when she was all alone. We'd all left her, something I feel horrible about. She never told me, never told anyone. Then they moved away, and she figured she'd seen the last of him, but he showed up, and he had horrible images of her—horrible, Cam." Sage stopped to calm herself.

"What do you mean, 'horrible images'?" Cam asked.

"Once she was drugged, a friend showed up . . ."

Sage jumped from her seat at the sound of the wall breaking when Cam shoved his fist through it.

"What happened, Sage?" he thundered.

"There were pictures, lots of pictures of her with them, and the way they did it made her look like she was a willing participant," Sage whispered.

"Why didn't she go to the police? Why didn't she charge them with assault?"

"Her mother talked her out of it."

"What?" Cam stood rigid next to the window, the need to strangle someone so overwhelming that his fingers hurt. "Why? Why would she do that?"

"Because she convinced Grace that if she cried rape, they would turn it around on her, making the Sinclairs look bad. Mommy dearest couldn't allow that to happen," Sage said, scorn dripping from her tongue.

"Grace won't prosecute this bastard even with all of this. It's bullshit," Cam raved.

"And I think he's coming after her for more money, now that he knows she's back where it all began. I don't know if he's trying to get a nice fat sum of money in his account before his fiancée figures out exactly who he is, or if the well has run dry from his job—but I think he's trying to scare the crap out of her, make her weak, and then exploit her for all she's worth."

"Why wouldn't he just demand more money? This doesn't make sense," Cam said, anger still ripping through him, but trying to calm down so he could think.

"I don't know, Cam. I really don't know, but there's

too much coming at her right now, and I don't think she can handle anything else."

"So the threats have nothing to do with the embezzlement," Cam stated.

"I don't know. I don't know how any of this is happening to Grace. She doesn't deserve it," Sage said in a defeated tone.

"I'm going to solve this. I think it's time Jimmy and I have a little chat."

Cam couldn't hear anything further. He needed action. Yes, he was a man of the law, but at this moment the law couldn't help him. Although he had friends who could—no questions asked.

It was time to call them.

39

"Hi, Grace."

Her spine stiffened at the sound of his voice. Disgust and shame all at once filled her. "Why, Jimmy? Why are you back in my life? Why are you calling me?"

"Aren't you going to even ask how I got your number, darling?"

"I'm not your darling, Jimmy. I never have been, never will be," she snapped.

"You're just no fun at all, are you?" he mocked.

"Why don't you tell your fiancée—I know you stole my number from her—that you're a rapist and extortionist? I have nothing to say to you."

"I wouldn't hang up if I were you, Grace. I know that high-and-mighty tone. You think you're so much better than me—that you always have been. But you see, I've managed to pull myself out of that trailer park I grew up in. I've managed to make a name for myself—and find me a real respectable whore to marry, even. A very wealthy whore, at that," he said with a laugh.

"Then go back to your whore and leave me the hell alone," she snapped, her fingers itching to hang up, but she knew this wouldn't end until the filthy man said what he intended to say.

"I can't do that. You see, she's begun to grow suspicious that I'm not exactly who I say I am. She doesn't think I'm quite as wealthy as I've implied."

"So that's why you finally came out from hiding behind your future bride and let me see your face—you want money."

She fought to keep her voice even, to make it sound almost bored. What good would showing him emotion do her? None at all. It would give him power, and she was through with giving this man power over her.

"I need more money, darling. You know, not many people will want to hire an event planner who so willingly took slutty pictures when she was barely out of high school."

Grace was silent as she counted to ten and then twenty silently. She'd promised herself she would never again let this man manipulate her, and she wasn't going to do it this time.

"I'm not afraid of you anymore, Jimmy. You see, when I ran to my mother and told her I was raped, and she acted like it was my fault and made me go clean myself up before she was able to even look at me, I felt shamed and alone. I felt that way for years, until the day I walked into her bedroom and found her on top of you. Neither of you looked ashamed—you looked pretty damn hot for each other."

"What does that have to do with your pictures, sweetie?"

"I didn't pay you off because I was ashamed, Jimmy. I paid you off because my mother was ashamed. If you want to publish those pictures, you go right ahead and do that. But just remember that I know some pretty powerful people, and I figured something else out as the years went by . . ." She stopped, a smile creeping into her tone.

"And what is that?" The more she taunted him, the angrier he became. Good. She wanted him angry, because she was sure as hell pissed off.

"No one controls me. Try and use those pictures and I'll have you in jail for slander, extortion, and rape." She wasn't bowing down to him ever again.

He was silent as he tried to comprehend what she was saying. She waited.

"You can't do that," he finally spluttered.

"Oh, yes, I can, Jimmy, believe me. I don't know whether you still even have those pictures or whether you were smart enough to think of using them against me twice. But all the same, those pictures are evidence of what you did to me."

"No, they aren't, you stupid whore! They are consensual sex as far as the public will see it. I made damn sure of that. Your beautiful little face was posed just right—I placed your fat lips over my cock!"

"It's not that I have fat lips, Jimmy; it's that you have an incredibly small penis," she said.

"That's it. I'll show the world what you really are."

"You go ahead and do that. And then you'll see exactly what I'll do to you!"

The other end of the line was silent as Jimmy considered. She didn't care. Finally, she was able to tell this scum he held no power over her.

"No one will believe you. They never believe the woman," he spluttered.

"Oh, no, Jimmy, it's not a lie. It's the full-blown truth. And if you're the one breaking into my place, trying to scare me into doing whatever you want, though I don't know how you could think I could be scared of you, considering how pathetic you are, I suggest you stop. I won't stop until you're destroyed."

"You can't do a damn thing to me, you trashy rich bitch!" He was losing it more and more by the second.

"Oh, I can, Jimmy, because, unlike you, I have friends—very powerful friends who don't like to see me get hurt. You've broken the law, you've tried to scare me, and you are the one who will pay. You're not coming after me, you pathetic excuse for a man," she told him grimly. "I'm coming after you!"

"You won't get away with this! I guarantee you."

"I already have, Jimmy. If you so much as call me again, I will have you in jail so fast your head will still be spinning a week later. Stay the hell away from me, from my friends, from my town, from my life. Or pay the consequences."

Grace hung up the phone to the sound of Jimmy spluttering on the other end of the line. And as she sat back on her friend's couch, she smiled. A feeling of freedom filled her unlike anything she'd felt in a very long time.

Somehow she knew Jimmy would be too scared to retaliate against her. She could finally go home. So much had been happening to her in such a short period of time that she hadn't even had a chance to analyze how she felt.

Cam was back in her life, or had been until their last fight. Was she ready to give that up again? Was she ready to let go of the hurts of the past? Maybe it was time she did exactly that. First, she had to get a clear head, and she needed to be alone to do that.

But it seemed her troubles were over.

40

"Open the door, Grace!" There was no response, so he pounded with his fists even harder. "Open the damn door or I swear I'm going to break it down this time."

When the door came flying open, Cam nearly fell forward. He caught himself at the last minute and then found himself standing with Grace inside her house. They were both wearing scowls.

"I've told you all week that I need time to think, Cam—that I don't want to talk to you right now."

He hadn't seen her in nearly two weeks, because a week before she'd moved back to her house—and that had really irked him—she'd been avoiding him over at his brother's house. He was done with being avoided.

"You look stunning," he said, taking a step forward.

"Don't you dare sweet-talk me and expect to get not only into my house but into my pants as well."

"You're not wearing pants," he pointed out,

which only made the heat in her eyes go up another ten degrees.

"Get out right now, Cam, or I'm calling the sheriff."

"Good, call him. I need to talk to him about a case he's a witness for," Cam said smugly as he sat down on her couch and made himself at home. "You know the sheriff and my dad go fishing just about every Sunday when the weather permits."

"Yes, remind me of all the connections you have. I don't care. You're still trespassing."

She sat down across from him, folding her arms and glaring, letting him know in every possible way that he wasn't welcome in her place.

"That wasn't what I was doing at all, Grace. I was just reminiscing."

"I told you I needed time to figure things out, Cam. I'd appreciate it if you would give me that time." Some of the anger drained and he spotted the fatigue enveloping her.

"I'm sorry, Grace, but this couldn't wait any longer. I have a lead in your case."

The last of her anger vanished right before his eyes and she looked so vulnerable at that moment, he couldn't help but rise and move toward her.

"Don't, Cam," she said, but without any heat this time.

"You need to be held, even if it's just for a few moments," he told her, and pulled her from the overstuffed chair she'd sunk down into.

She fought him for only the briefest of moments before she allowed him to capture her in his embrace, and she rested her head on his chest.

"It's okay to not always be the strongest person in the room, Grace. You're strong, and that's admirable; but you're also a real person, and contrary to what you were taught, we all need others in our lives. We don't have to fight our battles alone, and we don't have to figure it all out by ourselves. Let me take some of your stress and pain on my shoulders. They're wide and strong and waiting to hold your burdens."

"You've always had the best lines, Cam." She sniffled.

"It might sound that way, but I love you, Grace. I mean what I say to you."

"You don't love me, Cam. You don't even know me anymore," she said, tears in her voice.

"I know everything I want and need to know about you."

"No. No, you don't. We were young and stupid when you left for college. We both made mistakes—mistakes that hurt people and that we can't take back."

"I know all about Jimmy, Grace. That wasn't on your shoulders. That was all him. Don't punish yourself for a crime against you. Your mother should go to prison for what she did to you."

Anger still filled him to even think of what Grace

had gone through—and, worst of all, he should have been there for her, shouldn't have assumed she was cheating on him, that she hadn't waited for him.

"We were both foolish when I left for college. I was selfish and wanted to see the world, thought I had everything in the palm of my hand. And you were just young and you trusted the wrong person. Can't we let go of the past and move forward? I still love you, just in case you didn't hear me. I still want to be with you. And though you might have a hard time admitting the truth, I can see it shining in your eyes whenever you let your guard down. I know you love me, too. I know you believe in us."

She was silent for several moments, so Cam stood there with her in his arms as he tried to show her by his touch how special she was to him. He never wanted to let her go. If he messed this up this time, he might not ever get over it.

"There are some things we can't take back from those days, some things we can't forget," she said, so much sadness weighing on her that it nearly ripped his heart open.

"Tell me, Grace. I'm sure we can figure this out," he assured her, pulling back so he could see her face.

"I need tea. Do you want tea?"

He could see she was trying desperately to hold herself together and that she was looking for an excuse to be alone for a moment. "Yes, tea would be nice." He gave her the chance to get away, but only for a few minutes.

When she came back in the room five minutes later carrying a tray with hot water, tea, and fixings, he was seated on the couch.

"You said there was a break in my case."

Her tone had changed from angry, and then sad, to neutral. She was holding it all in now. Cam wanted to fix that, but he knew she'd been controlled before, so he made himself let her work through it even though that wasn't easy for him.

"Yes. I have a plan on how to catch the person," he told her.

Finally, a spark of light entered her eyes. "Who is it, Cam?"

"I'm not going to say that right now. I want to get this person, and the only way to do so is by catching them off guard. I need them to trust me, to think I'm their friend."

"You don't trust me?" she asked, her voice deceptively calm.

"No." He didn't elaborate and her eyes narrowed once again.

"I've been taking care of myself for a very long time, Cam. I can handle this."

He paused for several long moments and then did something she would have never expected him to do.

"You're right, Grace. I'm sorry. I just want to protect you. But you need to know."

She waited and he said nothing further. "So . . ."

"It's Vince. He was incredibly good, but he's been siphoning money from his father's company and collecting money through this nonprofit in your name. He's watched you. He only takes money from the local bank when you're in the area, and then it immediately goes into an offshore account. He's covered his trail well, but we have him. He won't escape this now."

"Seriously?" she said after a few moments, completely thrown off by this. "I don't get it. I don't understand at all. I really thought it might be my mother. I was terrified it was her."

"I thought so, too, which is why it took me so long to find Vince. I wasn't looking in the right places. Axel made a big break in the case finding the company Vince's father owns in Chicago. After we got that information, it all came together."

"So does this mean it's over?" she asked, hopeful for the first time in a while.

"Not yet, but it won't be long now." He moved closer to her and put his arm around her. "I've missed you, Grace, really missed you."

"Cam, don't do this . . ." she begged.

"Just let me take care of you," he said, which stiffened her back.

"Of course: Cam to the rescue, because poor little Gracie can't take care of herself," she said.

"You're more than capable of taking care of yourself. I've seen you do it time and time again. But it's also okay to be taken care of once in a while."

"Maybe I am tired of doing it on my own, but it's not so easy to admit that," she finally said.

Cam's eyes softened and it was nearly her undoing.

"Grace, I'm going to pick you up in my arms and carry you to your room. Then I'm going to lay you down and crawl into bed next to you."

"No, Cam. I don't want that," she said, but she didn't mean it.

"All I'm going to do is hold you, Grace. Because I've missed you, and I need to hold you as much as you need to be held."

At those words, she stopped fighting him. So he lifted her up and carried her to bed, gently laying her down before stripping to his boxers and climbing in next to her, and then pulled her into the safety of his arms.

The two of them still had a winding road ahead of them, but Cam knew that if they didn't give up on one another, they could weather the storm and make it through anything, just as they'd made it through all the trials that had come before.

41

"I've thought about it, Cam, and you're right: I'm not going to let my fears keep me hiding in the dark anymore."

Cam stood in the doorway with a neutral expression on his face. Maybe he'd had enough. Maybe it was too late. She'd run from him one too many times, and maybe he was just finished, but she had to give this her all or she knew she'd be full of even more regrets than she already had. As it was, she had enough to last her a lifetime.

She'd paced in front of his door for nearly fifteen minutes before she worked up the nerve to ring the doorbell. This was it—this was do-or-die. If he turned her away, she would deserve it, but he'd told her he loved her . . .

She was prepared, though, for him to slam the door shut in her face.

When he said nothing after her heartfelt words, a closed door seemed inevitable.

"Are you sure you want my help, Grace? You've

asked for it before and then you've run from me as soon as I try to do what I think is right."

Grace couldn't tell what he was feeling or thinking from his tone. It wasn't exactly cold, but no one could call it warm, either. Fear made her want to turn and run yet again, but she'd convinced herself that she was done running, and certainly done hiding. She'd been through the pits of hell and back. She could get through this moment with the man she now knew she was fated to love until the end of time.

"You've been right all along, Cam. I was wrong—you were right. Does that make you feel any better? Does that make you want to help me?"

It hurt her a bit to admit that to this man. But she owed him the right to gloat, if only a little. She'd fought him so hard when all he'd been trying to do was help her.

"That's a start," he told her.

"And I'm sorry, Cam, truly sorry for my behavior."

She tried to open herself up, to let him look into her eyes and see that she was speaking the truth to him. If he could see the honesty in her actions, then maybe he wouldn't turn her away.

"That's a little better," he told her, but his voice was still cool.

"And I want your help. Please, will you help me?"

"All you had to do was ask."

Before she could say something else, his arm snaked out and he hauled her through the doorway and into his arms. He kicked the door shut behind him, pushed her up against it, and dropped his mouth onto hers, making her forget anything else she'd been prepared to say.

He pulled back, his body hard against hers as the fire leapt in his eyes. "I've held back with you, given you time, allowed you to continue running away when you should only run to me. I'm finished with all of that. I'm taking what I want now."

Grace didn't know what to say, but his tone, the barely controlled lust radiating from him— everything about him—made her tremble with need. Before she had even a chance to respond, the world turned upside down when he grabbed her and threw her over his shoulder.

Shock stopped her from protesting until he was halfway up the stairs, and then she cried out and began pounding her fists against the unyielding muscle of his back. "Stop this, Cam!"

But just as quickly as the ride had begun, she was dumped from his shoulder and landed sprawling on top of his bed with him looming over her. Before she had a chance to say anything more, he was tearing her clothes off.

Within seconds, she was lying naked before him, a canvas waiting for his artistic touch. She was panting, her breasts heaving, her entire body instantly ready.

"Cam . . ." She wasn't sure if she was trying to protest or begging him to strip and join her.

"Cry out my name, Grace. I plan on making you scream before this night is over."

She couldn't get a single word out as he stripped his own clothes off, and she held her breath as his magnificent erection came free, making her mouth water in anticipation.

"Are you ready for me, Grace?" he asked as he crawled up her body, the weight of his chest pressing against her breasts and the feeling of his solidness against her softness making her moan. "I've dreamt of you every single night since we were together last. I want to be inside you. I want to make you come over and over again, and I want to make sure you know that you're mine—only mine."

She barely managed to nod her head before his mouth covered hers. As he devoured her with his hot kiss, she clung to his shoulders and she arched her hips in invitation. She didn't want foreplay, didn't want sweet and slow.

She wanted fast, hot, and hard. She wanted this man to be out-of-his-mind crazy in lust for her, and only her. And right now she knew he was just as much hers as she was his.

Sliding a hand between their bodies, he cupped her breast, his fingers squeezing her peaked nipple and making moisture surge through her core. She pushed against him again.

"Please, Cam, please take me . . ." she moaned.

He captured her lip with his teeth, then soothed it with a swipe of his tongue, making her writhe beneath him. And then he didn't make her wait any longer.

After he positioned himself against her womanhood, she felt him push against her, and she pressed upward, encouraging him to enter her.

With a hunger he wasn't trying to hide, he drove inside her, burying his solidness deep and nearly sending her over the edge. Pleasure surged through her as she yielded to his command.

With each thrust he gave her, she climbed higher, screaming out his name as he gripped her backside and showed no mercy.

And with one more thrust, she was tumbling over the edge, soaring in ecstasy while her body convulsed around his manhood. With a cry tumbling from him, he slammed against her, their flesh slick, their cries of pleasure in perfect harmony.

When the last of her tremors died away, she felt the weight of him on top of her, and she didn't want him to move, didn't want this moment to ever end. It had been perfect—it was still perfect.

Sometime after her breathing came back under control, he spoke. "I needed that," he whispered as he slid off her. He immediately reached for her and pulled her against his side.

"I know what you mean," she sighed. "Why in the world did I ever fight against this?"

"I'm sorry I was cold when you first got here. It's been a strange month. I just . . . I don't want you to keep pulling away from me."

That admission warmed her heart. "I've messed up, Cam—a lot, where you're concerned. I let old hurts from the past influence what I did and said. I didn't look to find the full story, and I hurt you. I'm sorry, but I'm going to make it better."

"I don't want you taking all the blame on yourself, Grace. I have my own burdens to bear, and I know I share equal responsibility for the things that went wrong between us. But I want us to be partners now, to not hold anything back from each other," he said, lifting her chin and making her look into his eyes.

"I can't help but take on most of this. But I'm going to make it right—I'm going to fix this," she told him.

He was quiet for a moment, but he wouldn't release her eyes. "How do you plan on doing that?"

"I'm going to let you do what you do best and get the bad guy."

The surprise in his eyes delighted her. She didn't normally ask for help, but she knew she needed him for this, and she also knew she could count on him.

"It's about time you realized how much you need me." He stopped talking as he kissed her for a long moment before freeing her lips and looking at her with lust shining from his dark gaze. "I'll have all the necessary papers filed tomorrow."

Their talking stopped. And Grace didn't mind in the least—not while Cam was showing her exactly what she'd been missing each night she spent away from his bed.

42

Grace stretched her arms wide and smiled. The morning sun was shining, and it looked as if all of her problems were over. No one had left threatening notes at her place, the case against her had been dismissed, Jimmy and his fiancée were no longer together—Kitty had figured out he didn't have any money—Vince was well on his way to free room and board in a state prison, and she and Cam were nearly perfect.

Life was better than it had been in a very long time.

Jumping from bed, she showered and dressed warmly against the lingering crispness in the air, which was hanging on for dear life to the last moments of spring.

As she emerged from her home, she wondered what Cam was up to. He'd probably taken his morning jog already, and was currently getting ready to ride off to his offices to effect another dramatic rescue.

He was good at his job—excellent, in fact. If it weren't for him, she'd probably be either sitting in a jail cell or out on bail, waiting for a trial that could go either way. There was no way she would have found the evidence that linked Vince to the embezzlement. She very likely would have been convicted, and she'd have forever blamed her mother for setting her up.

Grace wasn't forgiving her mother for all the years of bitterness and envy Victoria had subjected her to, but she had finally begun to realize that there was always a story behind every action. Maybe someday Grace could talk to her mom, could ask her what her story was. It wouldn't be today, but she had a feeling she would eventually have that conversation.

She reached the spring-fed creek in about fifteen minutes and sat down. It had been another favorite place of hers on her ancestors' homestead. One of the things she loved best about the creek was the fact that it ran through her property and went all the way to the Whitmans'. If it had been just a little bit faster and wider, she could have taken an inner tube and floated down to his place.

Instead, he and Grace had walked alongside the stream in the height of summer, when the days were hot and they had too much time on their hands to kill. Those were the memories that had made growing up in Montana a blessing instead of a curse because of who she had been born to.

Cam had been a part of her life almost from her earliest memories. They had started out as friends, had then gone through a period where they couldn't stand each other—since boys were filthy creatures—and then they became friends again.

Grace really couldn't say when it had happened, but somewhere along that journey, she started seeing him as a young man—as a man she could love, and would love, forever and always. A smile fluttered over her lips as she realized that no matter how far or how fast she'd run, her love of Cam had always been with her.

They'd made mistakes as teenagers in too much of a hurry to grow up, but they'd made the mistakes together, and then they'd fallen away from each other. Yet, even through the challenges that life had thrown their way, one thing had stayed with Grace—and that was love.

She could deny it all she wanted, but she adored him. She adored the child he had been, the teenager who had accepted the gift of her innocence, and the man he was today.

He'd been telling her since she'd come home that he wanted to be with her, that he wasn't willing to let her go. They'd fought, they'd laughed, they'd loved. And Grace had a feeling they would do it for the rest of their lives.

It was also time to admit to herself what frightened her now more than anything else that had been happening in her life these past few months. She hadn't gone to the doctor, hadn't looked at the small changes in her body, hadn't wanted to face the truth, because she was terrified of the answer. Her hand fluttered to her still-flat stomach and tears filled her eyes.

She was pregnant.

Soon she would tell Cam. Fear would be with her, but she couldn't hide from her fears anymore. She had to face them, had to accept that some things in life couldn't be fixed by signing your name on the dotted line or pretending there wasn't a problem in the first place.

She had no doubt that Cam was a real man who wouldn't ever shirk his responsibilities. And she also had no doubt that he loved her.

They needed to talk. She walked back to the house and grabbed her purse and keys. She had so much to talk to him about, so much she needed to say. Anticipation made her drive a little too fast, but she made it into town safe and sound.

Seeing his vehicle parked at the law offices, she smiled. She ran inside, glad his secretary wasn't there yet. Maybe they'd make love first and then they could talk. Yes. That sounded like a brilliant idea.

She found him sitting at his desk. "Do you realize how unbelievably stunning you are?"

Cam looked up, a bright smile lighting his face up. "Isn't that my line?" he asked.

"I've missed you this last week," she said as she shut and locked his door, then began moving forward while unbuttoning her blouse.

"You have? I'm glad to hear that. It's been a busy

week for all of us." Even as he said this, he pushed his chair back and watched her prowl forward.

"Well, there's nothing to worry about anymore, Mr. Whitman . . ." She opened her blouse and modeled a sexy red bra that showed more than it hid.

"That's good, because all my worries just floated away," he said as she reached him and he pulled her into his lap.

"Kiss me, Cam, kiss me like you mean it," she demanded before winding her fingers through his hair and holding him there while she leaned into him, her lips resting lightly on his.

She didn't need to prod him any further. He wrapped his arms around her back, pulling her tightly against him and pushing upward, letting her feel his arousal press into her as she straddled his lap.

One hand reached around and cupped her breast through the lace of her bra, and she groaned into his mouth as she wiggled against him, needing to be closer, needing him inside her.

She was reaching for his belt buckle when the shrill sound of the phone ringing made them both jump. They ended the kiss and broke apart.

Grace laughed. "We're acting like we've just gotten caught necking in the basement," she said.

"Or like we just got interrupted before the good part."

"Every part is a good part. But you'd better answer. It might be a client who is in desperate need of saving," she told him before leaning forward and kissing his neck.

"I have voice mail," he groaned.

"Well . . ." She was so tempted to be irresponsible. But she stopped kissing his neck and lifted the receiver, putting it to his ear before she leaned over to his other side and ran her tongue along the side of his jaw.

"Camden Whitman." The greeting didn't sound friendly, which made Grace want to giggle again.

Any impulse to laugh died away when she felt his body stiffen—and not in a good way. Leaning back, she looked at his suddenly ashen face.

"I'm on my way." He hung up the phone and looked at her as if his world had just ended.

"What is it, Cam? Tell me!" she asked as she cupped his cheeks.

"It . . . it's my dad."

She'd never heard his voice so strained before. "Oh, no. What's wrong?" She almost didn't want to know.

"He's at the hospital. My brother thinks it might be a stroke . . ."

Grace knew she had to keep it together for Cam's sake. Swallowing her own fear, she climbed from his lap and held out a hand.

"I'll drive you. Let's go."

Cam slowly got to his feet, looking lost, looking like the young boy she remembered from so long ago. Everything else could wait. Right now she needed to be there for the man she loved.

43

Grace was grateful she knew the route to the hospital well enough to drive it with her eyes closed. Okay, maybe not quite that well.

Cam sat beside her, pale, his hands trembling. Her own hands were clenched tightly on the wheel to make sure he didn't see them shaking. The entire community loved Martin Whitman. If something were to happen to him, she couldn't imagine how the town would react. It would fall apart. He was the glue that held the place together.

"He's going to be okay, Cam. He's too strong and too stubborn to ever let anything happen to him."

"I know. I'll just feel better when I get inside and get more information."

When they finally arrived, they rushed from the car and into the emergency department, where they found Cam's brothers, their wives, and many other people from the community.

"Why aren't you in there with Dad?" Cam asked Spence, his voice shaking in panic.

"You know I can't work on him, Cam, and anyway, I'm a surgeon, not a neurologist," Spence reminded him. "They're keeping us updated. It does look like it was a stroke, but Eileen was with him, and they got him here fast."

"I want to go back there. Get me back there," Cam demanded.

"You have to calm down, brother," Jackson said. "It's bad enough that they're working on their boss's father. They don't need you in there shouting at them."

"He may be telling you to calm down, but those were the words I just said to him five minutes ago," Alyssa told him.

"We have a good staff here, Cam, and he got in here without any delay. He's going to be okay," Sage assured him, and she threw her arms around her brother-in-law.

"I know, Sage. I just need to see him. Did you see him?"

"Yes. I was in back working when Martin came in. I thought it best that I come out here," she told Camden. "He was already speaking better by the time he got here. They're getting him all hooked up and taking scans. The first hour after a stroke is critical, and Eileen got him here quickly."

Grace looked at Sage and then over at Eileen. Bethel was holding the poor woman as she sobbed quietly in a corner of the waiting room.

"What time did this happen?" Grace asked as two and two started coming together.

"I think about an hour ago now," Sage answered, and then her eyes widened as she looked at Grace.

Before anyone figured out what the two of them were thinking, the doctor came through the doors, and everyone turned to hear what he had to say.

"Thanks for your patience, Dr. Whitman. We have information about your father. Do you want to follow me into the back?"

"No, that's okay, Dr. Eiseman, everyone here is family, or family friends, and we all want to know what's happening," Spence replied.

"Okay. I'll explain this so everyone can understand," he told Spence before looking out at the rest of the group, who were standing by tensely.

"Martin had what we call a transient ischemic attack, TIA stroke for short, or what a lot of people call a ministroke. Some don't give these strokes the proper attention, but this is a warning, and you need to take it very seriously. A small clot traveled to his brain, and though we're still going through the scans, it looks like the episode isn't going to leave any lasting symptoms. We're very optimistic that there won't be any permanent brain damage."

"Then can we see him?"

"He's getting transferred now," Dr. Eiseman said, "but I want to repeat that TIAs are often a warning, letting us know we need to make some lifestyle changes so a major stroke doesn't follow."

"Is he still in danger?" Cam asked.

"We'll keep him overnight at the least, but I think the clot will dissolve fully. However, you should know that, after a TIA, one in three people go on to have a major stroke within a year. We need to get him on meds, and he needs to start doing some things differently."

"I'll make sure he follows through. I'm not losing my father," Spence said, the doctor in him never more evident.

"I know you will, Spence. Give the nurses about fifteen minutes to get him moved to his room, and then you can visit. If the people now filling this lobby are all here to see Martin, you know to take turns."

With that, Dr. Eiseman left them and a hush fell over the crowded lobby, which seemed to be growing more crowded by the minute as news about Martin spread through their small community.

Michael finally spoke up after maintaining his silence the entire time. "Does this mean he's going to be fine?" he asked.

"Yes, Michael, he should be fine," Spence assured his brother.

"I'm still not going to feel better until I can see him," Michael said.

The whole crowd nodded their heads in agreement. Fifteen minutes seemed to take forever, and then there was chaos when it came time to deciding who could go in first.

"Cam, why don't you and Grace take Eileen back there?" Spence said as he gave his brother a compassionate look.

Eileen objected. "You kids should go and visit him first," she said.

"I have a feeling he's going to want to see you," Spence told her before leaning down and kissing her cheek. "Go give him hell for scaring us so much."

Eileen attempted a smile but was unable to pull it off. Grace wrapped her arm around the woman and led her through the hallway to Martin's room. When they paused in the doorway at the sight of him, such a large, robust man looking so pale and tired with his eyes closed, it brought more tears to Grace's eyes.

"If he's sleeping, we shouldn't disturb him," Eileen said as fresh tears tracked down her face.

"Eileen? Is that you?" His voice was so hoarse, it broke Grace's heart. She stood back as Cam and Eileen moved forward.

"I'm here, darling. I'm here," Eileen whispered. She sat in the chair by the bed and reached out to take his hand.

He opened his eyes and gazed at Eileen with such a look of love that Grace could see the radiance from ten feet away. She felt like an intruder. Cam moved back by her and whispered in her ear.

"How did I miss this?"

"I don't know how any of us did, Cam."

"Now, don't you be crying for me, Eileen," Martin said. "I'll be just fine. I wouldn't leave you or my children. There's too much life still to be lived."

"Oh, Martin, I've never been so frightened. You're my life now, and I just . . . I can't lose you, my love."

She leaned forward and rested her head on his chest, and he lifted his free arm and wrapped it around her.

"I love you, too, Eileen, so much that my heart aches when you aren't around. Not everyone gets to find two soul mates in this lifetime, but I'm one of the lucky ones. You bring me joy and there's no way I would give that up to something as silly as an itty-bitty clot." His voice was stronger now, love coming through it loud and clear.

"Well, we're making some changes, Martin. I'm talking to your cook right away, and we're both going to eat healthier and drink less and get more exercise."

"I've been doing just fine with how I live, Eileen. This was just a little bitty thing, nothing to get so worked up about. I promise you that I'll still be swinging you around the dance floor when we're ninety."

"I'm going to make sure you keep that promise, Martin," she said, a smile finally filling her lips as she lifted her head and looked into his eyes.

"Then you will have to become my wife so you're with me every single day."

Eileen couldn't speak through her tears, but she nodded, and it was the most beautiful thing Grace had ever witnessed.

"Let's leave them alone," Cam whispered as he pulled Grace into the hallway.

"I thought you needed to talk to him," Grace said.

"I just needed to know he was okay, to see it with my own eyes. My dad has been alone for a very long time. He's found love again with an amazing woman. This stroke scared him enough, it looks like, to admit it to her—or maybe to us, I don't know, but I'm grateful. Let's go tell the rest of them to give the lovebirds a few more minutes."

"It's kind of funny, but I think your father and Eileen—the town's favorite grandparents—are going to have a wedding before I do," Grace said with a laugh.

"I wouldn't count on that," Cam muttered as they pushed through the waiting-room doors.

Grace's heart nearly stopped with his comment, but before she could ask him to clarify it, they were surrounded by people asking questions about Martin. Soon, Grace was pulled from Cam's hold, and the crowd between them kept growing wider.

When their gaze connected a few minutes later, she saw something shining in his eyes that gave her hope of finally getting her happy ending. Even though he hadn't asked her to love him forever yet, her own eyes answered him with a glowing yes.

"I need coffee. Can I get you any?" she asked Sage.

"I'll follow right behind you," Sage replied. "I want to chat with the nurse for a minute."

Grace walked from the room, the quiet a relief after the din of so many people talking at once. But a smile was on her lips. Although the day had taken a scary turn after starting out well, love was in the air right now and the possibilities seemed endless.

She decided to step outside and get a little fresh air. She'd meet Sage in a few minutes. She couldn't wait to tell all to her best friend—tell her she was going to marry the love of her life even if she had to drag him to the altar, which she didn't think she'd have to do, and then the two of them could gossip about Martin and Eileen.

Who would have ever imagined that—

"You stupid bitch. You've ruined everything for me. Now I'm going to ruin it all for you."

Grace froze at the sound of that voice—the voice she'd thought was gone from her life. But she'd already decided to face her fears, and she was through with running from people. Her body stiff, she turned and then the blood ran from her face.

"Yeah, you should be afraid, because today you're going to die—but not until I get something first!"

Before Grace could scream, run, fight, do anything, Jimmy's arm came up and he hit her in the head with the butt of the gun he'd just been pointing at her. Everything went black.

44

Grace's head was pounding and a buzzing was sounding in her ears as she tried to figure out where she was. She could tell even with her eyes still closed that it wasn't pitch-black, so either night hadn't fallen yet or she was in a lit room.

The last thing she remembered was Jimmy attacking her, then nothing. As much as she feared what she'd see when she opened her eyes, she had no choice. She had to try and figure out her surroundings.

Slowly, she cracked her eyes open, and the light and the movement of the car she found herself in sent more pain shooting through her head. Trying to move, she discovered that she was tied up in the backseat of what had to be Jimmy's vehicle, or one he'd stolen.

She looked toward the window, but that gave her no clue as to where she was. All she could see was a blur of green as Jimmy sped through what seemed to be a remote area. There were no billboard signs, nothing to show her any sort of location.

Trying to make as little movement as possible

now, she shifted on the seat, rubbing her hip against the back of the cheap vinyl to see whether her cell phone was still in her pocket. At that moment, it vibrated—she'd turned it off the ringer at the hospital—and she nearly sobbed with relief.

Her purse was nowhere to be found, and the fool must have assumed her phone was in there and gotten rid of it. As long as her phone was on her, she knew there was a chance she could call for help.

The car suddenly stopped, and Grace briefly considered shutting her eyes, pretending she was still knocked out. But the thought of not seeing what he was going to do next was too scary.

Holding her breath, she didn't have to wait long for Jimmy to exit the car and pull open the door to the backseat.

"Ah, you're awake. Good."

Grabbing her by the hair, he yanked her up into a sitting position, sending the pain in her head to a whole new level.

"What do you want, Jimmy?" she cried.

"You destroyed me, Grace. At first I was just going to shoot you in the head, end your life, and bring myself some sort of relief, but then I started to think about it as we were driving. And you see, my life is ruined because my source of money got cut off. I didn't want to have sex with your wrinkly old mom anymore, so she quit giving me my monthly payments. I wasn't thinking that was a problem, since I had a very wealthy fiancée. But then my fiancée figured out I didn't make as much as I'd claimed to make from the art gallery, so she left me—the shallow bitch."

"What does any of this have to do with me?"

"I want money, Grace. So if you don't want me to kill you, I need you to give me a nice, fat lump sum of cold, hard cash so I can start over somewhere else and keep living the life I've grown accustomed to. I can find me another rich whore to keep me nice and happy, and I'll be glad to walk away."

He pulled her from the car, toward an old trailer home sitting on an overgrown piece of land.

"Where are we?"

"Somewhere no one will be able to find you. This is my old friend's piece of ground, but he's not here anymore. I come here when I don't want to be found, when I need a week or two to do whatever I want."

A shudder passed through her at the thought of what he'd done at this place. She'd figured out very quickly that Jimmy was a thoroughly disgusting human being, but she was beginning to think she'd underestimated him—he gave new meaning to the word *twisted*.

"How do you expect me to get you any money while we're out in the middle of nowhere?" she asked as she tugged against the ties on her hands. If she could loosen them, he would eventually pass out and she could call for help.

"Once I have you all secure, I'll go and buy a computer with your credit card. And then you're going to transfer a nice, tidy sum into a bank account I've already set up. Before you can do anything about it, like putting your rich boyfriend on me, I'll be long gone."

He opened the squeaking door of the trailer and the stench that came out made her gag. She doubled over as she tried to breathe again.

"Dammit! I think something got in there and died," he snarled as he left the door open and walked away from it, pushing her so she fell to the ground, twisting her ankle.

Jimmy sat down next to her and then a whole new terror filled her at the look that came into his eyes. "It looks like we have a little time to kill . . ."

He moved closer to her and then yanked her over his lap.

"Don't do this, Jimmy. This isn't what you want," she said, trying to keep the fear and disgust from her voice.

"Haven't you figured it out, little girl? I can do whatever the hell I want to do." He stopped talking, but only because he had mashed his mouth against hers, thrusting his nasty tongue inside.

Gagging again, Grace fought him with all her strength, but it did her no good. Her hands were tied, her head was pounding, and her fear was growing by the second. He yanked the hem of her shirt as he pushed her to the ground, and her arms screamed in pain as he pushed down on her with his full weight and crushed them beneath her body.

"Please stop, Jimmy. I'll give you the money," she cried out when he released her mouth so he could pull at her shirt.

"I know you will, but since I don't have my whore lover or my sweet little fiancée anymore, I need someone to help with my needs."

"You don't have time for this, Jimmy. If you want to get money from me, you'll have to hurry. Cam will already be tracking me. We have plans for today," she told him. She kept her tone calm, her eyes on his, so he wouldn't think she was bluffing.

"He can't find you here," he said, but he seemed unsure.

"Yes, he can. They've known someone has been after me for a while now. They've been watching me, have placed security all around me. If you don't think he'll find me within a few hours, you're sadly mistaken."

The more she spoke, the stronger her words became. She needed to believe what she was saying, or there was no way she would get this monster to believe it.

Unsure, he stopped tugging against her clothes as he sat back, looking thoughtful. Grace twisted sideway and then sat up, her fingers tingling as blood rushed back to them. Tears were fighting to break free but she couldn't fall apart. If she did, she would lose everything.

"Just get the computer. Let me give you the money and then we can both be free."

"Free? I've been a slave my entire life. My entire life!" he screamed.

"I'm sorry, Jimmy. I know that must be hard," she said, trying her best to sound sympathetic.

"You don't know anything about it. You grew up rich. I had to fight for everything I ever wanted. I deserved so much more than you and your stuck-up parents. I had to bed your mom for years to earn money. At first it wasn't so bad, but she kept getting older . . ." His face was filled with disgust.

"You can get the money from me and never have to do anything you don't want to again," she told him.

"Shut up!" Reaching out, he slapped her hard enough that she tasted blood and felt her vision blur. She couldn't pass out again. She had to focus. "Just let me think."

Grace decided to be quiet as she pulled at her bonds. If she could get free, she'd grab the nearest thing to her and clobber this bastard, take his car and get away, call Cam, and get rescued. And Jimmy could spend the rest of his days as a kept man—in a state prison.

"People like you always think you're so much better than me. You think your money makes you someone special, that you can buy whoever and whatever you want. But you're wrong. Yeah, we all need money—it's what makes the world go round—but I'm smart, Grace, real smart, and I know I'm better than you."

"You're right, Jimmy. I know you're right." She'd say anything at all to get him to stop this. He stood up and grabbed his gun, and all the blood washed from her face, a tingling sensation taking its place. She was going to die. This would be how her story ended.

"I gotta get that money, Grace. I need it. But if I leave you here alone, you might get out of the binds, and you might run away," he said, pacing back and forth in front of her.

"I won't run away, Jimmy. I promise. I don't know where we are. I would get lost and then I'd never be found," she said.

"I know you, Grace. I know you," he said before turning back to her, his eyes wild as he pointed the gun straight at her. "I'm not gonna kill you, though, just shoot you in the leg so you can't run away. But don't move, okay? I'm not a real good shot, and I'd be awfully upset if I killed you before I got my money."

"Please don't do this, Jimmy. Please," she begged.

"I have to," he said before smiling. "But don't worry. I'm going to enjoy it." He cocked the gun and Grace finally allowed a tear to fall.

45

"Has anyone seen Grace? We were supposed to get coffee, but she's been gone for half an hour now."

Cam turned, immediately focusing on Sage. "What do you mean?" he asked as he glanced quickly around the hospital waiting room.

"I had to talk to the nurse, but Grace was going to meet me in the cafeteria for coffee," she said, and then concern filled her eyes. "She's safe, Cam, right? You solved the problems with her being harassed."

"Nothing has happened for a couple of weeks, but I don't like this," Cam said, and his brothers immediately tuned in to what was going on.

"Let's find her," Jackson said. "Something's wrong."

"Sage and I will check the back areas," Spence said.

"Hawk and I will check the south exits," Cam said.

"I'm going to talk to security and see if the cameras picked up anything," Jackson told them before moving in that direction.

"Everyone else, search the grounds. We all have

our cells. If you find anything, send out a group message," Bryson said.

Cam tried to hold in the panic that was threatening him, but when he and Hawk checked the doors and found no signs of Grace anywhere, he was consumed with worry.

When he found her purse behind the Dumpster near the parking lot, he went cold inside. She hadn't left this hospital willingly.

His phone rang as he picked up the purse, praying that her phone wasn't in it.

"She was assaulted by the south entrance by a man wearing black about thirty minutes ago, and the footage on the camera shows her being stuffed into the back of an older blue sedan," Jackson said.

"Why in the hell didn't they alert us?" Cam yelled into the phone.

"The guard was away from the monitor when it happened. I rewound the feed," Jackson growled.

"I have her purse. Get everyone out to the parking lot now!" Cam hung up and dumped out the contents of the purse, nearly sobbing with relief that her phone wasn't there. If it wasn't in there, then there was a chance it was on her.

Bryson arrived in less than a minute. "Is her phone on her?"

"I hope so," Cam said.

Bryson picked up his phone and dialed. "I need a

trace." There was a pause, then Bryson read out the number twice, and waited.

The rest of the group surrounded Bryson in silence, waiting for him to finish his call.

"We've got a location," he said after hanging up, "and a chopper is on its way here. We can only take three total."

"I'm coming," Cam told them.

"I didn't doubt it. Axel and I are coming with you."

The chopper landed and the three men climbed aboard. The next fifteen minutes were the longest ride of Camden's life. They had to land a far enough distance away from the location of the cell phone not to alert the assailant to their presence, but that meant they had to run a few miles across the terrain.

"She'd better be here," Cam said as they made their way toward their target.

"She will be," Axel said, his eyes focused and deadly.

That's when they heard Grace cry out, and all three of them picked up their pace. They came around the corner and what Cam saw made his blood run cold. Jimmy Wells was holding a gun and pointing it directly at Grace.

"I'm going to kill him," Cam snarled.

"Quiet. Don't let him know we're here. She's smart, Cam. She's holding it together. Let's get into position," Bryson said, and he and Axel moved in opposite directions, while it took everything inside Cam not to run forward. But he had to trust his friends who did this for a living.

"Hold still!" Jimmy yelled as Grace twisted on the ground.

"Don't do this, Jimmy. If you miss and kill me, you won't see one red cent," she yelled at him, finally getting to her feet.

Jimmy stalked forward, but she sidestepped him.

The crazed look in the man's eyes scared the hell out of Cam. He was going to shoot her. Cam couldn't wait any longer. He leapt from the bushes. "Jimmy!"

Moving much more quickly than Cam liked, Jimmy turned and faced him, then reached out and grabbed Grace, wrapping an arm around her and hiding behind her like the pathetic excuse for a man that he was.

"Don't come one step closer, or I swear I'll shoot her in the head and then shoot you next," Jimmy yelled.

"Let her go, Jimmy, and you just might live through this. We have you surrounded. Sure, you might get off a lucky shot before you're taken down, but I guarantee I'll survive it and then I'll make sure you get sent to the worst prison in this state for the rest of your miserable life."

"I'll kill you before you can ever do that!" Jimmy yelled.

"Then do it, Jimmy. Point the gun at me and fire," Cam taunted him. He needed to get that gun away from Grace's head. He had no doubt Axel and Bryson were in position, but there was no way they'd take a shot if there was any danger of hitting Grace.

"Go, Cam. Now. I don't want you getting hurt!"

"Shut up, Grace!" Jimmy yelled, his hand shaking, his finger still on the trigger.

"It's easy to take down a girl, Jimmy, real easy. Let's see how you do against a man," Cam shouted at him.

"I can take you anytime, you worthless office-working piece of crap. I'm the one who's always had to think on my feet. I didn't have a daddy to pay for me to be a lawyer," Jimmy said.

"You're talking a whole lot, Jimmy, but I don't see you coming after me," Cam replied, and moved closer.

"If you take one step closer, I swear I'm going to shoot her. I don't have anything to lose."

"Then I'll rip you apart limb by limb."

Cam watched the shift in Jimmy's eyes, watched the fury, and he finally got what he wanted. Jimmy pulled the gun away from Grace's head and he aimed it directly at Cam . . .

Three shots were fired.

46

Almost in slow motion, Grace watched Cam's body fly backward and blood start to spread out on his shirt. At the same time, Jimmy's body jerked behind her and she felt a splatter of moisture cover the side of her face.

He dropped behind her, and she ran forward as Cam fell to his knees. Footsteps signaled that people were running toward them, but she didn't pay any attention. All she cared about was getting to Cam.

She sank down in front of him and tried to reach out, tried to hold him, but her hands were still tied behind her back. A cry of frustration tore through her, and she didn't even recognize the sound.

Then she felt someone tugging on her hands, and she struggled against the person, fury spurring her on. She was going to rip Jimmy apart herself.

But suddenly Bryson was there before her, laying Cam back and putting pressure on the wound in his stomach. The ringing in her ears lessened as she finally realized someone was speaking.

"Stop fighting me, Grace. I almost have these ties undone."

She turned to find Axel behind her. She couldn't speak, couldn't thank him, couldn't even move as she focused on Cam. His eyes had rolled back in his head.

"Hang on, buddy, we're going to get you to the hospital," Bryson said as Axel freed Grace's hands and she was finally able to reach forward.

"Get here now!" she heard Axel say, and within minutes she heard the blades of a helicopter as it descended onto the field, right next to them.

"Jimmy is dead. Send the cops here. We need to get Cam and Grace to the hospital now!" Bryson yelled at the pilot, who ran out to assist them.

Bryson grabbed Cam, lifted him up gently, and placed him in the chopper, and then Grace felt herself being hauled through the air as Axel picked her up. She found herself sitting next to Cam, begging him to be okay.

Two gurneys were waiting when they landed on the hospital helipad. Grace was placed on one gurney, and she could do nothing when Cam was rushed away from her on the other.

She screamed, "I need to be with him! Let me off this. I'm fine. I need to be with him!" But no one was listening.

Suddenly, she became sleepy and had to fight to keep her eyes open, as something was dragging her down. "No. Please don't drug me, please," she sobbed. But it was too late.

Maybe minutes or hours passed. Grace didn't know. But she woke up crying Cam's name.

"It's okay, Grace. Everything is okay."

Trying to focus, Grace turned her head and found Sage beside her, and her best friend's eyes were red and swollen, her expression solemn.

"Cam? Where's Cam? Please tell me he's okay, Sage."

"He's fine, Grace. He woke up an hour ago and demanded to see you right away. The doctor gave him a sedative, but I'm afraid that if we don't get you in there, all hell will break loose," she said with a wobbly smile.

"Then take me to him."

Grace was still weak from the sedative, so Sage helped her into a wheelchair and began pushing her.

"The bullet hit Cam in the abdomen," Sage told her, "but it missed all vital organs. He's going to make a full recovery, but a sore one, and I have a feeling he's going to be a bear to be around while he's on bed rest."

The two of them approached a room that was almost rattling.

"I said to get her in here now or I will rip every one of these tubes out of me!"

"I guess he's okay," Grace said, a tiny smile flitting across her lips.

"Yep. That's pretty much what the entire hospital has been hearing for the past hour," Sage said.

And then she heard nothing else as she entered the doorway and her eyes met Cam's. He was flushed, his eyes sparking, and he was the most beautiful sight she'd ever seen in her life.

Sage wheeled her to the bed and she didn't even feel the tears rolling down her cheeks.

"You really scared me today, Camden Whitman."

He took her hand in his strong grasp, and his expression changed from anger to love in a heartbeat.

"That's my line," he told her, making a whole new set of tears fall.

"I've decided I'm not ever going to let you go again, Cam. I love you so much. When I thought I might lose you today, when I saw that blood . . ." She shuddered when she thought about it. And then she couldn't speak past the quiet sobs strangling her throat.

"You're taking my lines again, Grace," Cam said, lifting his hand to her cheek and wiping away her tears. "I thought for a brief moment that I might lose you forever, and I can't . . . no! I *won't* live in a world without you in it. Please, Grace, please, never again put me through the agony of not being with you. You complete me. You make me a better man. Through good and bad, through thick and thin, I want to be with you forever."

The room was silent. Cam's visitors sitting there

did not even dare to breathe for fear they'd be noticed and kicked out of the room. And then they'd miss this stirring scene.

"I love you so much, Cam. Yes, I want to be with you always. Can you forgive me for the mistakes I've made?"

His eyes rounded as he looked at her in shock. "We've both made decisions in life that have shaped us, taught us, and made us stronger. They aren't mistakes. They're all a part of who we are today. There's nothing to forgive, Grace. You're my reason for waking up each day, my reason to smile. I love you and I want to marry you and begin our family and our futures as one."

Carefully, Grace rose from the wheelchair and climbed in beside Cam, careful not to hit any of his IVs or put any pressure on his stomach. Settling her head in the crook of his arm, she had never felt so much peace and happiness.

"How soon can you get me to the judge?"

"Dad!" Cam said, a huge smile lighting up his face.

"As much as I want this wedding to happen, we aren't doing it from a hospital bed," Martin said with a laugh, his color already beginning to improve as he sat there in his wheelchair with Eileen right by his side.

"I guess I can give it a day or two," Grace said.

"Oh, you're going to give it more than that. We

have so much planning to do," Alyssa said, beaming from her place on Jackson's lap.

"Our family is almost complete," Martin said with a huge grin directed at his son Michael.

Suddenly, all eyes turned on him. When he realized what was going on, he shot up from his chair. "Don't look at me like that. I'm not even close to being ready to get married," he said, backing away. "Hell, I'm not even thirty yet!"

"The harder they fight, the quicker they fall," Martin said.

Michael made a quick exit from the room, and Grace beamed at her future husband. "Hmm, us girls will have to see who we can set Michael up with."

"You go ahead and do anything you want."

Grace leaned forward and got lost in Cam's kiss. Her life was only just beginning.